Sleeping with the enemy?

It was completely dark in the barn when Ellie opened her eyes. The temperature had dropped with night-fall, and she was shivering. But it wasn't the cold that had awakened her. Noah was up and moving around stealthily.

"What are you doing?" she challenged him.

"Nothing. Go back to sleep."

And then she understood what was happening. He was covering her with a blanket of hay—to keep her warm.

"You don't have to do that," she whispered.

"Sure I do. I don't keep you healthy, I don't find my son."

She had discovered him being considerate, and he was embarrassed about it. His concern was touching and at the same time disturbing. How could she go on regarding him as the enemy when he insisted on protecting her?

ABOUT THE AUTHOR

If setting has anything to do with it, Jean Barrett claims she has no reason not to be inspired. She and her husband live on Wisconsin's scenic Door Peninsula in an antique-filled country cottage overlooking Lake Michigan. A teacher for many years, she left the classroom to write full-time. She is the author of a number of romance novels.

Write to Jean at P.O. Box 623, Sister Bay, WI 54234.

Books by Jean Barrett

HARLEQUIN INTRIGUE
308—THE SHELTER OF HER ARMS
351—WHITE WEDDING
384—MAN OF THE MIDNIGHT SUN

Fugitive Father
Jean Barrett

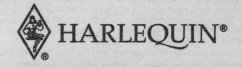

HARLEQUIN®

TORONTO • NEW YORK • LONDON
AMSTERDAM • PARIS • SYDNEY • HAMBURG
STOCKHOLM • ATHENS • TOKYO • MILAN • MADRID
PRAGUE • WARSAW • BUDAPEST • AUCKLAND

To my agent, Pattie Steele-Perkins,
who is always there for me.
Thanks, Pattie.

ISBN 0-373-22475-3

FUGITIVE FATHER

Copyright © 1998 by Jean Barrett

Printed in U.S.A.

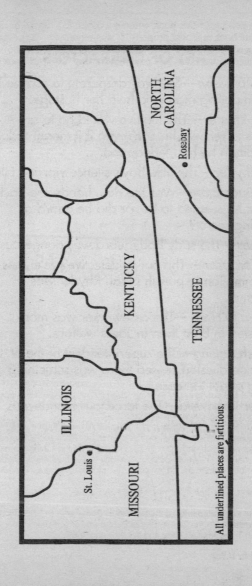

All underlined places are fictitious.

CAST OF CHARACTERS

Ellie Matheson—She was desperate to escape from the compelling man who held her hostage.

Noah Rhyder—The fugitive would go to any lengths to recover his son, even if it meant seducing the woman he had kidnapped.

Joel Rhyder—The little boy's silence worried Ellie.

Brett Buchanan—Was the rich, handsome bachelor all that he seemed to be, or did he guard a shocking secret?

Peaches—The surly bodyguard was dangerous.

Lew Ferguson—The police detective's relentless determination to punish Noah Rhyder was abnormal.

Sandra O'Hara—The caseworker was more interested in Brett than in Joel's welfare.

Hamish Bolling—The superintendent of the St. Louis homicide division sensed there was something wrong about the case.

Ginger Zukawski—The larcenous blonde was willing to cut a deal.

Chapter One

How do you tell a five-year-old child his father has been convicted of murder and is on his way to prison?

For the first time in the three years she'd been caring for temporary wards of the court in her home, Ellie Matheson regretted her role. Her foster training had prepared her to deal sympathetically with every variety of abuse and neglect, but this was different. *Vastly* different.

"Must be here somewheres. All I got to do is find it, and the treasure'll be mine."

With the phone still in her lap, Ellie watched young Joel Rhyder crawl along the floor, his fingers searching for the hidden catch that would release the secret panel in the wall beside the fireplace.

"Presto! I'm rich!"

His small hand had located the catch. The concealed door popped open, revealing in the deep recess behind it a pirate chest loaded with games and toys. Joel was as familiar with them as he was with the other imaginative attractions she had provided for her young charges in the crowded parlor—the puppet theater, the curving slide that descended from the second floor to the first, and the castle dollhouse occupying one corner. There was no area of Ellie's house that Joel hadn't explored. He had been with her all through the sensational trial.

He knows, she thought. He senses that phone call is going to drastically change his life, and he doesn't want to hear it. That's why he's playing so hard, why pretending is so important.

She couldn't postpone it. They were on their way. Difficult though it would be, she had to tell him.

"Joel."

"Huh?"

"Come on over here, sweetheart. I need to talk to you."

He hesitated, his reluctance evident in the way his hands clutched the lid of the chest. But he was too well-mannered to refuse her. "Okay."

He got slowly to his feet and crossed the parlor, planting his sturdy figure in front of the chair where she sat.

"There's been a final decision, Joel," she told him carefully, looking directly into his vulnerable face with its solemn, dark eyes. "That's what the phone call just now was all about. The judge awarded custody of you to your uncle. Remember how all those words were explained to you?"

He turned his head, eyeing the pair of artists' easels in the bay window. One of them was an adult size at which Ellie worked at every opportunity, the other a much smaller version for any youngster who wished to join her.

"Can we paint some pictures on the easels?"

"No, not today."

His attention wandered to the massive fern on its stand. "Let's give the fern a drink."

"We already did that this morning. We'd drown it if we gave it any more. You have to listen to me, Joel."

"What?"

"About what I just said," she appealed to him patiently. "Do you understand it?"

"I'm going to live with Uncle Brett."

His restless hand reached out and fingered the necklace she wore, stroking the clay-baked beads that were her own creation. She waited for him to ask about his father. Surely this time he would want to hear about him. Ellie didn't know how he felt about Noah Rhyder. From the start Joel had refused to discuss him, and she had wondered whether his silence was some form of self-protection.

"Joel?" she softly prompted him.

He went on playing with the strands of beads, refusing to meet her gaze. He was not going to ask about his father.

She couldn't do it, Ellie realized. She couldn't force the sensitive subject on him. The situation was too brutal, and she was a coward about it. Someone else, maybe his uncle or the caseworker, would have to tell him whatever might be necessary for him to know about his father. It wasn't her place to get involved in those kinds of explanations anyway. She was never supposed to offer anything but care and comfort.

He finally looked at her, and asked in a shy little voice, "Why can't I live with you?"

The earnest expression on his face tugged at her painfully. She had made the mistake of learning to care for him too much. "Because your Uncle Brett wants you to stay with him."

"You could come with me."

"Then I wouldn't be here for the other kids when they need me."

"There aren't any."

"Not now, but there probably will be when I get back from my vacation."

"Will you come and see me?"

She couldn't promise him that, not without Brett Buchanan's approval. "I'll try."

He was thoughtful for a few seconds. "Can I take Hobo with me?"

Hobo was one of the puppets from the cardboard theater. He'd become attached to the sad-faced tramp clown.

"I think Hobo would like that. We'll put him with your other things." Ellie got to her feet and moved toward the stairs. "You can help me pack them so you'll be ready when your uncle gets here. Then afterward you and Hobo can ride the slide down from the big bedroom."

"Hobo doesn't like the slide. It scares him."

"I didn't know that. I guess that's why he never uses it." The whimsical descent from the second floor delighted most of her charges, but Joel had avoided the slide during his stay with her. The result of a bad experience on a playground, perhaps.

Twenty minutes later, Ellie sat with the boy on the front porch swing while they waited for the arrival of Brett Buchanan. Joel's suitcase was beside him, Hobo in his lap. She observed him with concern as he absently played with the puppet. He was very quiet now. There was a forlorn look about him that made her long to put her arms around him and hold him close. She resisted that urge. It would only make his parting from her more difficult. All she could do was hope that his uncle had some kind of parenting instinct. Joel was going to need everything Brett could give him.

Seconds later a dark luxury sedan slid into her driveway and pulled up behind her aging van. Brett's driver and bodyguard was at the wheel, a surly, pugilist type who went by the unlikely name of Peaches. Brett was in the back seat of the sedan. He emerged, accompanied by a woman. Ellie felt Joel stiffen at the sight of his tall, broad-shouldered uncle. When she looked down, there was an anxious expression on his face.

"You like your Uncle Brett, don't you?" she murmured.

"Yes," he whispered.

"It's going to be all right, Joel," she assured him.

She took him by the hand and picked up his suitcase. Together they went down the porch steps to meet the arrivals in the driveway.

Brett Buchanan had all the charm and physical appeal of his murdered father, Howard, a state senator who'd been the victim of his son-in-law's rage. By all reports, Joel's mother, who'd died last year after a lingering illness, had shared her brother's blond good looks.

Brett was familiar to Ellie. He had been here twice before to visit his nephew. He'd petitioned the court from the start to have Joel with him. But Noah Rhyder's defense had strongly opposed that measure, so Joel had been placed with Ellie for the length of the trial.

However, the attractive redhead at Brett's side was a stranger. She came forward and introduced herself to Ellie. "I'm Sandra O'Hara from Family Services, Ms. Matheson."

She had a dazzling smile and a low, throaty voice. Ellie glanced with puzzlement at the credentials she displayed. "The other caseworker who was handling Joel..."

"Her load got too heavy, so Joel was assigned to me. There will be some follow-up down the road, but mostly I'm here to officiate the transfer of Joel to his uncle. It's just a formality." She turned brightly to the boy. "Your suitcase looks awfully heavy. Why don't I help you put it in the car?"

Ellie wasn't very good at hiding her emotions, particularly when they involved the children in her care. The concern on her face must have been evident as she watched Sandra O'Hara coax Joel in the direction of the car, because Brett turned to her with a soft, "He's going to be okay. I'll make sure of that."

She smiled at him gratefully. "I know you will."

"Starting right now, as a matter of fact. We're heading straight to Lambert from here and a flight to North Carolina. I've rented a place there in the mountains. A big place with all kinds of land around it and everything to keep a little boy occupied."

She knew he could afford it. The family had always been prominent here in St. Louis, and by all accounts Brett Buchanan was wealthy in his own right.

"I want to give Joel a fresh scene, somewhere far away from everything that's happened."

Ellie approved of his plan. "He needs a chance to recover and, as you say, away from all the unhappy associations here... Anyway, it sounds good."

She watched Sandra O'Hara trying to get friendly with Joel near the car, where the stoic Peaches remained at the wheel. He was shy with her, unresponsive. By contrast, the woman hadn't stopped smiling since her arrival, a perpetual smile that got on Ellie's nerves a little.

"You should know that Joel hasn't been told anything about the outcome of the trial," Ellie confided to Brett. "He hasn't asked at all about his father."

He nodded grimly. "Well, until he does..."

"I know, but sooner or later he will want an explanation. He's an intelligent, imaginative child, and it worries me that—" She broke off with a shake of her head. "I'm sorry. It's not my place to advise you on how to handle him."

"I don't mind. In fact," he said impulsively, "why don't you consider paying us a visit in North Carolina? You could help me with this adjustment period for Joel. You're good with him. I get the feeling kids find it easy to confide in you. Adults too, probably. I'm right, aren't I?"

Ellie laughed self-consciously. "Maybe. I have been accused of being a mother-earth type, whatever that means. I think it's because of my painting. People tend to get that sort of thing all mixed up with what they're convinced is the bohemian in you."

"Now there's an argument for North Carolina," he tempted her, his rich voice a complement to his elegant looks. "I can promise you all kinds of exceptional views to paint."

"I *am* going to paint mountain scenery, but in the opposite direction. I'm heading for the Ozarks first thing tomorrow morning."

She could afford to rent a cabin there for a week or so

now that she would be receiving the check for Joel's care. But she didn't mention that to Brett, maybe because she feared it would sound mercenary, as though she were profiting from the boy's tragedy. It was foolish of her, however, to feel any guilt. She needed the income from her foster work since she couldn't rely on what her art earned her. Not yet, anyway.

"Well, look, just in case you change your mind..." He produced a pen and a small notebook from an inside pocket. She watched him scrawl several lines across one of the pages, which he tore out of the book and extended toward her. "Here's the address for us in North Carolina. I'd like you to have it."

Ellie didn't have the heart to tell him that joining them in North Carolina was out of the question, and probably not a good idea in the first place. She accepted the offered sheet out of politeness, glancing at the address he had provided.

"Uh, one thing, though," he added. "I'd appreciate it if you'd keep that address strictly confidential. I'm sharing it with only a few essential people. There've been too many headlines already over this nightmare. I don't want the media bothering us out there."

"I understand," she promised him, knowing what he must be suffering over the loss of his father.

Sandra O'Hara interrupted their exchange. "The suitcase is on board. If you plan on dropping me back at my office before you make that flight..."

"Right." Brett moved toward the car.

Sandra paused beside Ellie, murmuring a low, "I couldn't help hearing what he was saying to you. Hon, the guy is gorgeous and a rich bachelor into the bargain. How could you have turned him down? I'd have jumped at an invitation like that."

Ellie didn't think the redhead deserved an answer. Her suggestion was inappropriate under the circumstances. Nor did she feel the woman would understand that men as smooth as Brett Buchanan didn't interest her in that way. Her ex-husband had cured her of that.

Excusing herself, Ellie went to say goodbye to Joel. He clung to her when she bent down to hug him. She could feel herself getting dangerously emotional.

"Take good care of Hobo," she instructed him softly.

Brett came to shake hands with her, leaving her with a last, tantalizing, "North Carolina in the fall—with the mountains a blaze of color. Think about it."

Seconds later, Joel waved to her from the back seat as the sedan pulled away with its four occupants. Ellie stood at the curb, waving back, until the car was out of sight.

Doing her best to accept the separation, she turned and started back toward the porch. The next-door neighbor, on her way to her evening shift at the hospital, called a friendly greeting from the open window of her compact.

"Have fun in the Ozarks, and don't worry about the newspapers and your mail. I'll take them in for you. See you when you get back."

Then the compact, too, vanished up the street, and the neighborhood was suddenly very quiet and empty. Ellie gazed at her narrow, old-fashioned house with its high peak that always seemed slightly lopsided. The home didn't qualify as a genuine Victorian. It was too late for that, more of a World War I vintage. But she had treated it like a painted lady, tinting the walls a blue-green, the trim and shutters raspberry, the accents ivory. Vibrant hues were vital to her, both in her work and in her environment. Her ex, David, used to complain all that color hurt his eyes. But Ellie had always loved the house, modest though it was.

At this moment, however, the place didn't look cheerful and welcoming. It looked lonely. It missed Joel.

And you, she told herself, *have to stop all of this. Good thing you're getting out of here for a bit. The Ozarks. First thing in the morning.* Which meant she had packing to do and a van to load before it got dark.

Ellie moved resolutely toward the house. It wasn't until she was back in the parlor that she realized she still had the page from Brett Buchanan's notebook in her hand. She glanced again at its contents. Then she laid the paper on the fireplace mantel and forgot about it. She wouldn't be needing the address in North Carolina.

WE'LL APPEAL THE VERDICT.

That's what his lawyer had promised him just before they led him away in cuffs following the judge's sentencing. The words were supposed to convey hope, but Noah knew better than that.

Appeals could drag on for months, years, he realized bitterly. And in the end nothing came of them, because without hard new evidence jury verdicts were seldom overturned. He would be locked away in a cell, and Joel would grow up without him. He could stand everything but that. The thought of losing his son drove him crazy.

The numbness that had muffled his response to his situation rapidly faded once he left the courtroom, like a drug wearing off to leave nothing but the raw pain. That and his outrage.

This was real. He was cuffed to a transport belt, wearing a bright orange coverall and seated in the back of a patrol car. There was a screen separating him from the two special deputies who were his escorts. He was on his way to a permanent facility. Boonville, someone had said. He was going to Boonville Prison, and there was nothing he could do about it.

His angry frustration must have been evident in the way his rangy figure went rigid on the seat. The burly prisoner who shared the caged rear of the car with him observed it with a raspy-voiced, "You got a kid you're leavin' behind, huh, Rhyder?"

Noah glanced at him. He had a face scarred by acne and a battered nose. He was Kenny DeMarco, a mobster with powerful connections, although those connections had obviously failed him since he, too, was on his way to Boonville. However, he didn't seem particularly worried about that.

"Yeah," Noah muttered.

"That's tough," Kenny said. "Shouldn't have to leave your kid behind. I like kids. No bull about 'em."

DeMarco was relaxed, almost nonchalant about the whole thing. He's probably been in Boonville before, Noah thought. He didn't want to talk about Joel with the mobster. He turned his head away, his hopelessness intensifying as he fixed his brooding gaze on the passing scene.

There wasn't much to see. They were traveling through an after-hours warehouse district, headed toward the interstate that would carry them out of the city. There was no other traffic in the area.

"This isn't the direct way," objected the young deputy from the passenger side of the front seat.

The senior deputy at the wheel responded with a brusque, "You ought to know the routine by now. We always vary the route. A precaution, remember?"

The patrol car moved on up the narrow street with the blank-faced warehouses looming close on either side, like the walls of a canyon.

The young deputy started to say, "This can't be ri—"

He was interrupted by a panel truck that raced out of a blind alley and stopped directly in front of them, blocking the street. Startled, Noah felt himself jerked forward on the seat as the patrol car slammed to a halt to avoid a collision.

"Back up," the young deputy said. "Get us out of here."

"Can't," the older officer said. "There's another vehicle now pulled up behind us."

"Hell, it's an ambush!" The young deputy reached toward the radio to call for assistance. That was when the officer at the wheel whipped out his service revolver and shot his companion through the head. The body slumped sideways against the door.

It all happened so swiftly, and with such casual horror, that Noah was too stunned to really understand the scene. It was only when the back doors of the patrol car were torn open, and grinning gunmen leaned in from both sides, that it all registered with him.

"You okay, Kenny?" one of them asked.

"I will be when I get out of this harness they got me in."

"Keys," the order was barked to the deputy at the wheel.

Seconds later the mobster had been freed of the cuffs and the transport belt. He nodded toward Noah. "Him, too."

"Damn it, Kenny, what are you doing? Guy's a witness. Shoot him, and let's get out of here."

"Shut up," DeMarco growled. "He's got a kid. Besides—" He snatched the revolver away from the deputy and began to wipe it clean of fingerprints. "Come on, get him out of that thing. I know what I'm doing."

When Noah's restraints had been removed, DeMarco shoved the .38 Special at him, holding it with his handkerchief-wrapped hand on the barrel.

"Here's how it works, Rhyder. You take the gun, and we let you go free."

"Why?"

"Because you killed that cop in the front seat. That's what this deputy here is gonna swear after they find him cuffed and gagged and with a convincing lump on his head. That's what *all* of us here are gonna swear if the worst happens and anybody gets caught. But the worst ain't gonna happen. Everybody's gonna be smart and disappear, right?"

"I don't like this," the deputy said nervously.

"Who asked you? You forgetting you were paid a bundle to cooperate? You made your decision, Rhyder?"

But Noah knew he had no choice. Not if he wanted to live. Not if he wanted to see Joel again. And for that he must be their scapegoat. His hand closed on the handle of the revolver.

"Get out of here, Rhyder. Lose yourself, and don't get recaptured unless you want to wind up in Boonville after all. Believe me, it ain't a nice place."

Noah ran, charging down the alley from which the panel truck had emerged. He didn't look back. He didn't permit himself to think about the young officer slumped in the front seat of the patrol car. He'd be finished if he thought about that deputy. He had to concentrate on other needs, like finding some way to get rid of this orange coverall that marked him as a fugitive.

But mostly he thought about where he was going. He knew the address. He hadn't seen Joel since his arrest, but his lawyer had informed him where and with whom his son had been placed. He had to get there before Brett Buchanan claimed him. No way was he going to let Buchanan have his kid. He and Joel would disappear together. And he wasn't going to consider the madness of his intentions. He was desperate.

Chapter Two

Ellie had turned on the TV, hoping to hear a weather report for her trip tomorrow. Busy with her packing, however, she somehow missed the forecast. She didn't bother switching off the set. It was a kind of company for her in the empty house as she moved from room to room, collecting her gear.

She was headed out the front door with another load for the van when she caught the familiar name on the latest newscast. *Noah Rhyder.*

She didn't go back into the parlor to listen. His name had been all over the news for months, and she was weary of hearing it. The trial was finished. Why couldn't the media forget about it, let those who'd been hurt by the tragedy try to recover and get on with their lives? But, of course, since he'd been sentenced this morning, ordered to prison, they were milking the story for its last morsel.

Ellie knew the segment would be just another rehash of the whole ugly thing. Noah Rhyder, a fallen architect who'd been threatening his father-in-law for weeks before the murder. Noah Rhyder, who had cold-bloodedly smashed in the skull of Senator Howard Buchanan in the family mansion in Ladue. She refused to hear it all again. She went on with her packing.

It was dusk by the time she had the van fully loaded.

She was probably taking too much with her. Aside from the fact that her art supplies alone took up a great deal of room, she had more clothes than she needed. Well, that's what vans were for.

The house felt cold when she got back inside. Late October and, with the sun down, the temperature had dropped. The TV was still on. She shut it off and moved to the thermostat, nudging up the dial. There should have been the reassuring rumble of the furnace kicking in. There was only silence.

Ellie made a face. The furnace was old and temperamental. She ought to be replacing it instead of spending precious funds on a week in the Ozarks. No, she needed this break. The furnace would have to wait for repairs until she got back. In the meantime, she was still cold.

There was wood already laid in the fireplace grate. Kneeling on the hearth, she got busy and kindled a fire. Flames were licking at the logs, sending out a comforting glow, when the doorbell sounded. Getting to her feet, she replaced the screen, flipped on the porch light, and pulled the front door back on its chain.

Ellie blinked at the sight of a uniformed policeman standing on her porch.

"Ms. Matheson?"

"Yes."

He held out his identification for her inspection, though she didn't doubt his legitimacy. She could glimpse through the gingerbread trim of the porch a patrol car parked at the curb, its light flashing.

"Is something wrong?"

"If I could speak to you for a minute, ma'am..."

His tone was grave. She didn't like it. "Just a second."

Closing the door, she released the chain, then opened up again, inviting him inside. He stepped into the parlor, a lanky, balding man who cast a glance around the room before he faced her with a thin smile.

"You been listening to any of the news reports this evening, Ms. Matheson?"

"I had the set on, but I... no, I haven't, actually."

"Uh-huh. Well, then you couldn't have heard about the escape."

"Esca— What are you talking about?" He was making her decidedly nervous.

"There was a hijacking of the vehicle transporting Noah Rhyder and another prisoner to the facility in Boonville. Both men got away."

She stared at him in shock. That was what the newscast had been about, not the trial. "How is that possible?"

"It's being investigated," he said evasively.

"But what has this got to do with—" She didn't finish. She suddenly understood why the police were visiting her. "You don't mean he would try to come here?"

"Ma'am, I don't like to alarm you, but you should understand that Rhyder is armed and dangerous. He killed one of the young deputies escorting him."

"Dear God," she whispered.

Until this moment, Ellie had reserved some shreds of sympathy for the man who was Joel's father. She'd wanted to think that, even though he had committed murder, there had to be something about him that was decent. Otherwise, how could he have produced a child like Joel? Now all she felt was disgust. Noah Rhyder had killed again, apparently without mercy. He deserved no one's sympathy.

"It's because of his son, isn't it?" she said. "That's what you're warning me about. You think he might try to come here to get Joel. Wasn't he told—"

"Yes, ma'am. He *was* informed that custody of his boy was granted to the uncle."

"Brett Buchanan already collected him." *And thank God for that,* she thought. *Thank God Joel is far away by now and safe.* "The child isn't here with me any longer."

"Maybe Rhyder realizes that, maybe he doesn't. Maybe

he isn't even thinking about trying to get to his kid. Probably all he's got on his mind is running. Look, he isn't going to make it. They never do. We'll have him back in cuffs in a few hours. Meantime, we just need you to be extra careful. I take it you haven't seen anything? Heard anything?''

She shook her head. "Nothing."

"You're going to be fine," he tried to reassure her. "Patrol cars will be cruising the neighborhood all night. We'll keep watching your house, and an officer will check on you again later. No way he's going to get anywhere near you, but if there's someone you'd like to stay with until—"

"No. I have some last-minute things here to take care of. I'm planning on leaving for the Ozarks early in the morning."

"Sounds like a good idea for you to be gone, just in case Rhyder should still be on the loose tomorrow. I take it that's what the loaded van in the drive is all about. I had a look through it before I came to the door to make sure it's okay, but you can't leave it out there unlocked all night."

"I wasn't planning to. I have a garage at the back, but I got sidetracked before I could put the van away." She explained about the furnace and her need to build a fire.

"Let's get it put inside right now," he urged.

Ellie got her keys from her purse and joined him back at the front door. She was ready to follow him out of the house when he stopped her.

"You have any doors or windows in here unlocked?"

"It's all tight," she assured him. "The neighborhood's always been safe, but when I started to care for children I made it a practice to lock up everything after sundown. That's why the front door was already on its chain."

"Good habit. Secure the door behind us now."

Full darkness had settled on the driveway. The officer had a large flashlight with him. When they reached the van, he directed its strong beam through the windows before permitting Ellie to slip behind the wheel. Then he walked along beside the van as she drove to the back, her finger hitting the opener to raise the garage door.

David had never shared Ellie's enchantment with the house. He had tolerated it, but only after a modern garage had been attached to the rear. She'd never liked the windowless structure, convinced it spoiled the original lines of the old house. In this situation, though, she appreciated its safety and convenience.

The shallow lot, however, made the garage too narrow. That's why it had been easier to load the van in the driveway and why she had to squeeze out of the car now before she went to the opening where the officer waited.

"Okay?" he asked, glancing around the interior of the garage.

"Yes."

"I'll check the outside before I leave. You see or hear anything you don't like after I'm gone, you go straight for the phone and report it to nine-one-one. Don't worry, Ms. Matheson. We'll catch him."

He moved away into the gloom as she punched the button to lower the door. Back inside the house, she could see the bobbing flashlight from the windows as he circled the house. Then he was gone, the patrol car pulling away into the night.

She was alone, and she thought about Noah Rhyder. He was somewhere out there in the blackness, probably miles away, but she couldn't shake her uneasiness. Couldn't stop glancing at the windows, expecting to see a livid face pressed to the glass. She wasn't satisfied until she went through every room in the house, lowering all the shades and turning on lights everywhere.

She was shivering when she got back to the parlor. Not nerves this time. She was cold again. The fire had burned low. There were two split lengths left in the basket. She added them to the grate. One of them was misshapen, requiring that it be perched precariously on the bars. The two logs caught and started to blaze, but they wouldn't last. She needed to bring in more wood from the stack at the front of the garage.

Her reluctance to go out there was foolish, she told herself as she passed through the dining room and the kitchen. The garage was perfectly secure. Hadn't she and the police officer made certain of that? She was spooking herself needlessly.

But once on the other side of the connecting door, she wasted no time in gathering the firewood. Her arms were loaded with split lengths when she heard it. The sound of the rear door on the van sliding back on its track. Ellie whipped around in alarmed disbelief as the tall fugitive, bearded and filthy, emerged from the shadowy depths of the van.

How was it possible? How could Noah Rhyder be here when the officer had checked the interior of the van? It must have happened while he was inside the house talking to her! Rhyder must have been out there watching and had seized that brief interval to enter the van and burrow down under all her things, recognizing it as an opportunity to get at her! All the time he'd been here, concealed and waiting!

He was no longer waiting. He was moving toward her, gun in hand. Her action was one of pure desperation. She released the logs from her arms. They went spilling onto the floor, rolling against his feet, tripping him up.

Tripping him up long enough for Ellie to escape. His curse bellowed behind her as she fled into the kitchen, slammed the door, turned the lock with fingers that trembled.

It was a flimsy lock. There had been no need for a stronger one when the garage was so solid. She knew the lock wouldn't hold. His body was already heaving powerfully against the door.

The phone! She could think of nothing in her mindless terror but reaching the phone! Calling for help!

She raced through the kitchen. Through the dining room. Her foot caught on the leg of a chair. She went down, sprawling on the braided rug. She could hear the door to the garage bursting open as she scrambled to her feet.

He caught her in the parlor just as she reached for the phone. Snatching her around, he pinned her against the wall, holding her there with a fistful of her long brown hair. She could feel the barrel of the revolver squeezed against her throat.

"Where is he?" he demanded, his voice like gravel. "Where's my kid?"

She was too frightened to answer him. Too aware of her hopeless situation. Even if she dared to cry out, there was no one to hear her. No one to help. The neighbor on one side was on her nursing shift at the hospital. The elderly man on the other side was frail and hard-of-hearing.

The hand wrapped around her hair tightened, making her flesh crawl when his knuckles came in contact with her scalp. *"Where?"* he growled, his hot breath lashing her skin as he shoved his face menacingly into hers.

"He isn't here," she managed to croak. "You can search the house if you don't believe me."

"Buchanan?"

"This afternoon. He collected Joel early this afternoon."

"And took him where?"

"I don't know. Back to the house in Ladue, I suppose."

There was a long moment of silence as their gazes collided, his dark, burning eyes searching hers for the truth. Ellie was suddenly, stunningly aware of a savage virility, an intensity that was dangerous but at the same time mesmerizing.

The spell was shattered by a noise from the fireplace. Alert for trouble, his head swiveled toward the sound. Ellie turned her own gaze. The precarious log had collapsed, one half of it rolling out of the grate to come resting up against the screen on the brick hearth.

The interruption reminded her of what she had momentarily forgotten. That Noah Rhyder had a gun to her throat, that he was a convicted murderer who had killed twice and wouldn't hesitate to kill again.

"Please," she whispered, "you're hurting me."

His mouth under the dark beard curled in a cynical little smile. "I'll do worse than that if you're lying to me." But the hand wound in her hair relaxed its hold, as if he were suddenly aware of the pain he was causing her. Surely, though, she was dreaming if she thought he was capable of any sympathy. In any case, he still kept the revolver trained on her.

Ellie had already made a decision. Whatever he threatened or did to her, she was never going to help this brute to get his hands on Joel. Whether he was his father or not, the thought of his getting to the boy sickened her. She would do whatever was necessary to prevent that.

There was another tense silence. She watched him warily. She could see by the fierce glow in those black eyes that he was attacking the problem of reaching his son.

The pronounced aroma of wood smoke shifted her attention to the fireplace again. The fallen log continued to smolder against the screen. Though most of its smoke was still drawn up the flue, wisps of it escaped into the room. But there was no danger from the fireplace. The only danger here was—

Oh, dear Lord!

She'd suddenly remembered. The fireplace mantel! The address Brett Buchanan had given her was there on the fireplace mantel where she had placed it earlier! That revealing scrap of paper was in plain sight, and if her intruder happened to—

"Okay," he abruptly decided, "we're going to make a phone call."

"I don't—"

"Just be quiet and listen to me. I'm going to dial the house in Ladue myself, just in case you try to reach a number I wouldn't like. Then you'll do the talking. Whoever answers, you tell them that Joel left something behind and could you run it over to him? We'll see if that's where my kid is. All right, come around here."

He gave her no chance to object. She found herself turned and pulled up against his hard length. He was so tightly pressed to her back that she felt seared by the heat of his body. There was something else, something she hadn't noticed before. A distinctly unpleasant odor. Not surprising. His clothing was smeared all over with a filth that didn't bear thinking about, probably in an effort to hide the blaze-orange coverall.

The warmth of his breath in her ear had her trembling again. "I'm going to be listening to every word of this exchange," he warned her softly, "so don't get any ideas."

The gun in his hand caressed her hip, reminding her of its grim presence.

"Now pick up the phone and hold it where I can reach it."

She obeyed him. His free hand reached around her, brushing like fire against the side of her breast as he punched in the number.

"Buchanan residence."

It was a woman's voice. She turned out to be the housekeeper. Ellie explained her call exactly as she had been instructed.

No, Joel wasn't there, the housekeeper informed her. No one was there except for her and another servant. Mr. Buchanan had taken the boy and gone away. She insisted she didn't know where or for how long. Possibly for many weeks. If Ellie wanted further information, she must contact Brett's lawyer.

Ellie was weak with relief when she finally lowered the

receiver, and Rhyder released her. She couldn't have borne another moment of his body hugged to hers, of his breath intimately mingling with her own as he'd leaned down to hear the conversation.

But he was far from through with her.

"Turn around," he commanded, "so I can see your face."

Sick with fear, she obeyed him.

"I'm going to ask you again. Where did Buchanan take my kid?"

"I've already told you—"

"I know what you told me, and I know what my lawyer told me. He said Buchanan visited your place while Joel was here, that the two of you were on friendly terms. How friendly, Ellie?"

"We discussed Joel's welfare, nothing else."

His gazed narrowed suspiciously. "Why do I keep feeling you're not giving me the truth? That the two of you were cozier than that? Maybe cozy enough to exchange confidences. With his looks and money, you wouldn't be the first woman to fall for Brett Buchanan. That what happened, Ellie? You fall for him?"

She kept thinking about the slip of paper on the mantel. She had to find some way to reach it and destroy that address.

"That's crazy, and if you don't let me do something about that log, we're going to be choking on the smoke in here."

The fallen log was her ally. The smoke from it had drifted across the room by now and was strong enough in the air that even he had to acknowledge it was a problem.

"Fix it then," he agreed. "Only don't touch the poker. Shove it back into the fireplace with your foot."

She nodded and slipped away from him, crossing the parlor on unsteady legs. He had the gun, and he was watching her every move. There was no way she could get rid of the address without his knowing it. But she was prepared to act and suffer the consequences.

"Hurry up," he ordered impatiently as she reached the fireplace and carefully removed the screen in order to prevent the log from rolling from the hearth onto the wooden floor.

Setting the screen to one side, she used her toe to nudge the log safely back against the grate while her hands rested casually on the mantel to support herself. Then, before he could stop her, her fingers flashed to the paper, snatched it from the mantel, and dropped it onto the hot grate.

There was a roar of realization behind her. Ellie flung herself out of his path, hitting a table as he launched himself toward the fireplace. By the time she had recovered and righted herself, he had managed to rescue the lower portion of the page, heedless of the heat into which he had thrust his hand.

The fluttering sheet had failed to land directly in the flames, had not been entirely consumed. She prayed that none of the address remained on that bottom half.

Before she could get away, he was on his feet and in front of her, his bulk squeezing her against the table.

"You little sneak! I ought to make you eat what's left of this!"

He waved the charred bit in her face. Ellie's heart sank. Though the rest had burned, nearly all of two words were still there, scorched but legible.

—orth Carolina

"North Carolina," he muttered, glancing at both sides of the scrap before crushing it into a ball and tossing it back into the fire. Still wielding the gun, he reached out with his free hand and seized her wrist. His fingers were like steel. "*Where* in North Carolina?"

"I don't know," she boldly lied, although she remembered the address clearly. "He only gave it to me as a kind

of courtesy. I didn't even look at it. I just stuck it up there
on the mantel and forgot about it until—''

She bit off the rest as his hand tightened forcefully on
her wrist.

''I don't think we're understanding each other, Ellie. I
mean to disappear. That's just what I'm going to do, only
not without my kid. Whatever it takes,'' he promised her
fiercely, ''I'll get him back. Nothing's going to prevent
that, and right now you're the only thing standing in my
way. So I'm going to ask you again. *Where* in North Carolina?''

Even though frightened by what he might do to her, she
shook her head, refusing to answer him.

''You stubborn—'' He stopped suddenly, his eyes
gleaming with understanding. ''You have the van out there
loaded with your things, all that stuff I was hiding under.
You're going somewhere. North Carolina. You're joining
Buchanan in North Carolina.''

''No,'' she insisted. Desperate to convince him that this
time she was telling the truth, she went on, ''I'm leaving
in the morning for a painting holiday in the Ozarks.''

The words were out of her mouth before she realized her
mistake. He smiled at her grimly.

''Looks like your plans are about to be spoiled.''

''You wouldn't—''

''Take you with me to North Carolina? I think so, Ellie.
Hell, it's just too convenient to pass up. Easy transportation
for me, a good place to hide. And, best of all, nobody to
ask questions about your absence. Vacation, remember?
Just the two of us alone together out on the road. And
maybe along the way, I'll persuade you to share that address.''

''You can't!''

''Sure I can. This tells me I can.'' He passed the gun
under her nose, then brought his face close to her own. ''I
guarantee you something, Ellie. Before I'm through with

you, you'll be begging to tell me exactly where Buchanan took my boy and why.''

She shuddered over the implication of his slow, soft promise.

"Let's go," he said, dragging at her arm.

She was horrified when she realized that he was pulling her, not toward the garage, but in the direction of the stairway. No one would know she was up there with him. No one could see in. The shades at all the windows were lowered. She had lowered them herself.

He jerked at her when she struggled furiously against his grip. "What is it now?" he demanded. Then he suddenly understood. "Oh, I get it. You can stop worrying, Ellie. I'm not interested in playing any games with you. I've got other business upstairs."

She gazed at him with uncertainty.

"Look," he said, "let's not make this any harder on each other. Just move."

He had released her arm, as if to prove she was in no serious danger from him as long as she obeyed him. She couldn't count on that, of course, but she could not go on physically resisting him, either. He was too strong for her. She would have to wait for an opportunity to—

"Come on," he urged.

He stayed close behind her as she preceded him up the stairs. He stopped her when they reached the top, taking a moment to check out the three bedrooms and single bathroom that opened off the tiny hallway.

"That one yours?" he asked, indicating the largest bedroom.

"Yes," she murmured.

"Inside." When she failed to move, he scowled at her. "What are you waiting for now?"

Hands clenched at her sides, Ellie entered the bedroom.

"Over there by the bed where I can keep an eye on you."

She gladly put space between them. But when she reached the four-poster and turned around to face him, her heart dropped like a stone. He had placed the revolver on a chair within easy reach, freeing his hands in order to remove his clothes.

Kicking off his shoes and lowering the zipper on the blackened coverall, he began to twist his way out of the garment, baring sleek muscle and a chest matted with dark hair.

Dear God, maybe he actually intended, after all, to—

"Don't just stand there. Strip off your own things."

He was out of the coverall by now and naked except for a pair of briefs that left little to the imagination. Clinging to the four-poster, she searched for a means to defend herself.

"What are you—" He stopped when he saw the expression on her face. "Didn't I tell you this isn't about that? I'm not a monster, Ellie, even if I look like one in this getup." He tossed the coverall to the floor. "We're going to find me a new outfit, that's all. Something that doesn't shout fugitive or stink of industrial gook. There was a vat of the stuff in an enclosure behind a warehouse. For all I know, I was helping myself to toxic waste." His mouth behind the dark beard split in a self-mocking grin. "Pretty ironic, huh?"

Ellie found nothing to smile about. "*I* didn't swim in a vat of industrial waste."

"No, not that bad," he agreed, eyeing her floral tunic top and matching leggings, "but bad enough. Hell, that thing screams 'artist on the run.' I want you wearing plain, dark clothes when we leave here. You must have something that isn't left-bank. Get busy."

The insufferable lout was insulting her life-style, her love and need for color.

"Unless," he added softly, "you want me to do it for you."

It was more than her hands that were clenched now. Her jaw was equally tight with frustration as she turned her back and began to undress. Her rigidness must have been obvious.

"Don't give yourself a stroke, Ellie. I'm not planning to watch."

But since she didn't trust him, she lost no time in clothing herself in navy slacks and a matching cotton sweater. She'd started to shiver, both from nerves and the coolness of the house. The warmth of the sweater was welcome, lending her a measure of courage when she turned around to face him again.

"And just what kind of outfit did you imagine I could provide for *you?* There isn't any man living in this house."

"No, but there was one, and not all that long ago either."

David. He knew about David and her divorce. He must have demanded every detail about her that his lawyer could supply, probably needing complete assurance that Joel was in good hands. That much, anyway, was in his favor.

"Guys have a way of leaving things behind, especially if they pull out in a hurry. Let's see if I'm right."

He was already at the closet she'd shared with David, flinging open the double doors, motioning with the hateful gun for her to find him something.

He was right. David had abandoned a pair of old jeans and a gray sweatshirt in a far corner of the closet. They were garments he'd worn when doing repairs around the house. He had intentionally left them behind with some snide comment about being through with old houses and their needs. Ellie had meant to throw them out, but it was one of those things she'd never gotten around to doing.

Noah Rhyder accepted the clothing from her, holding the jeans up against himself to test them for size. "They'll do. I'll have that, too."

He indicated a forgotten Cardinals baseball cap to one side of the closet shelf. Ellie handed him the cap, hoping he wouldn't delay getting into the jeans and the sweatshirt. The sight of him parading around in those briefs, his masculinity much too evident, was disarming.

But, to her dismay, he tossed the clothing onto the bed with a brusque, "Into the bathroom, Ellie."

What now? she wondered.

They crossed the hallway, entered the bathroom.

"Get into the tub," he instructed her.

She gazed at him, startled by his demand. "Why? What is this—"

"I've got my reasons, and you've had enough questions. Just do it."

She climbed apprehensively into the bathtub, willing herself to stop shaking. She hated for him to see how scared she was.

"Now sit."

Mystified and on her guard, she reluctantly lowered herself down into the tub. Giving her no explanation, he turned away to the sink.

Her toilet case, already packed with essentials, was there on the marble surround. Watching him as he rummaged through its contents, she understood his purpose. With her tucked down in the tub, leaving a comfortable distance between them, he could risk separating himself from the revolver. It was placed to one side of the sink while he helped himself to her scissors, safety razor, and shaving cream.

The transformation that followed amazed her. His black hair, which he wore on the long side, was snipped off until nothing remained but short spikes. Then he set to work on his beard, clipping away its heaviest growth with the scissors before reaching for the razor and cream.

His cleanly shaven face that emerged from the lather was no longer recognizable. It was a lean face on which no flesh had been wasted. A face whose craggy features she found strangely unsettling.

There was something else she could see in the mirror as he busied himself altering his appearance. Something she hadn't noticed before. On the sinewy hardness of his upper arm was a small tattoo of a sword wrapped in flames. She wondered if it was a souvenir of his youth. She knew from the coverage of his trial that he'd run with a tough crowd in his late teens and early twenties. There had been something about a motorcycle gang and several arrests, leaving him with a previous record when he was charged with murder. Though long ago and no more than misdemeanors, those priors hadn't helped his defense.

The tattoo reminded her that Noah Rhyder must be dangerous, a man not to be crossed. There was an intensity about him that was more than just desperation. He was...well, she didn't know. Maybe all twisted inside. He would have to be if he had killed twice, wouldn't he?

She needed to get away from him. But how? The gun. It was there on the sink, no longer within his grasp. Concentrating on his metamorphosis, he appeared to have momentarily forgotten its existence. What were her chances of getting her hands on that weapon?

"Don't even think about it," he warned her softly.

Hopeless. He must have been eyeing her in the mirror the whole time, sensing with a survivor's instinct the focus of her gaze. Her situation was as dismal as ever.

Noah went on watching her as he rinsed away the lather and toweled himself dry. Her anxiety was evident to him in the way she huddled in the tub, her shoulders all hunched up. She must be scared out of her mind. He was sorry about that. He hated having to play the part of the insensitive brute, to intimidate her like this. But what choice did he have when she was his only hope of recovering Joel? And forget trying to tell her the truth, because she'd never believe him.

But he didn't like the guilt he felt whenever he looked into her worried eyes. Unusual amber-colored eyes that bothered him on another level. A lot about Ellie Matheson was beginning to bother him, like that appealing mouth and her robust figure.

A woman like that could get to a man, start to make him regret he was anything but gentle with her. And he couldn't afford such a weakness, Noah told himself sharply, hardening himself against any further sympathy for her. Hell, she had lied to him, hadn't she? No, he couldn't trust her. Whatever her denial, there was still the chance that she and Brett Buchanan were more than just acquaintances, and he *knew* he didn't trust Buchanan. His former brother-in-law had been elsewhere when the old man was murdered. A solid alibi. But alibis could be bought when you had Brett Buchanan's kind of money.

So there it was. Noah had to force Ellie Matheson to accompany him. And not just because she was the key to Joel. He couldn't leave her behind to spill his destination to the cops. But traveling with her was going to be no picnic. He would have to anticipate her every move, not let himself be affected by—

Her hair. He could feel his gut tighten every time he looked at that long, long hair of hers. It was brown but not plain brown. In the right light, like now, it had fire in it. Damn distracting spilling down her back like that.

"Your hair," he said curtly.

"What about it?" she asked, flinching over the roughness in his tone. He had swung around from the sink. She could see a muscle twitching in his angular jaw as he stood there judging her hair.

"You're going to have to do something with it. It's too noticeable hanging loose that way, and I don't want either one of us attracting attention on the road. All right, out of the tub and back to the bedroom."

He was despicable, Ellie thought, grinding her teeth as she preceded him from the bathroom. Barking orders at her every other minute, and now he expected her to bind her hair. On the other hand, she decided when she reached the mirror in her bedroom, it could be worse. He could have come at her with the scissors.

She watched him in the glass as she dressed her hair in

a thick, single braid that descended down her back. To her relief, he was finally covering himself, pulling on the jeans and the sweatshirt. Her ex-husband had a very slender build. His jeans were tight on Rhyder. Good. She hoped he was uncomfortable in them.

He grunted something that she took to be approval for the braid when she turned away from the mirror. "You have a flashlight somewhere?" he asked.

She knew better this time than to express her puzzlement. "In the bedside drawer."

He helped himself to the flashlight, told her to collect their discarded clothing, and gestured her out into the hallway.

"This one of those old-fashioned laundry chutes down to the basement?" He indicated a metal hatch partway up the wall near the bathroom door.

"Yes." He was far too observant. Getting away from him was not going to be easy.

"Open it."

She lifted the trapdoor and held it while he directed the beam of the flashlight into the chute, satisfying himself that an empty laundry basket was in position at the bottom.

"Dump the coverall in there first."

She stuffed the soiled jail uniform into the chute.

"Now your things."

She followed the coverall with her tunic and leggings.

"That ought to do it," he said as she released the small door.

She had to admit that he was both resourceful and thorough. He had just effectively disposed of the telltale coverall, burying it under her own garments.

The expression on her face must have betrayed her, because he wore that warning look again. "I believe in covering my tracks, Ellie. You might remember that."

She didn't answer him. He started to wave her toward the stairway. That was when the front doorbell sounded.

Chapter Three

He dragged her with him, his long legs carrying both of them swiftly across the bedroom to a front window that overlooked the street. His eyes warned her to be silent, and she was too afraid of the gun in his hand to disobey him. She watched breathlessly as he stood to one side and carefully lifted the edge of the shade. Peering into the night, he muttered a savage curse.

Ellie glimpsed the flashing light of a patrol car at the curb before he dropped the shade. The police must be here to check on her again, just as that first officer had promised. Hope swelled inside her and then was rudely checked when Noah's grip tightened on her arm. His directions to her were terse and emphatic.

"We're gonna answer that door, Ellie, and you're going to satisfy the cop out there that you're just fine. You tell him you were on your way to bed, planning to catch a couple of hours of sleep before you hit the road. And you make clear they don't need to check on you again, because you've decided to be under way by midnight. You don't want to hang around the house with that fugitive still on the loose. Got it?"

She nodded mutely.

"You'd better make it good," he warned her, "if you want everyone to stay healthy."

The doorbell pealed again, insistently this time, as they descended to the parlor. With the revolver clutched in his hand, Noah flattened himself against the wall at the side of the front door where he could hear the exchange and watch her every move without being seen.

"Keep the door on its chain," he whispered. "And be convincing. *Real* convincing, Ellie."

She turned the porch light on, opened the door as far as the chain would permit.

"Just looking in on you again, Ms. Matheson, like we promised. Everything okay?"

He was younger than the officer who had called on her earlier. He had a boyish face that made him seem barely out of his teens. Ellie remembered the deputy that Noah had shot during his escape, remembered how she'd been told that he, too, had been young. She didn't dare to issue a warning through the crack, verbal or otherwise. Not with her captor standing right there with the raised revolver.

She assured the officer on the porch that she was fine, that she had neither seen nor heard anything suspicious. Then, in a flat voice, she briefly repeated Noah's instructions.

The officer didn't ask to come into the house. He accepted her explanation, leaving her with a cheerful, "You have a good trip, ma'am, and be careful on the road."

Ellie felt sick as she shut and locked the door behind him. She had just sent what might be her only opportunity for rescue on his way again in the patrol car.

"Douse the porch light, the ones in here, too," Noah hissed.

She obeyed him, plunging the parlor into a darkness that made her nervous even with the gleam of the lights from the front of the house and the glowing embers of the fire that had dwindled to almost nothing. He slid to the window, peered through a gap between the shade and the frame. She knew he was making sure the police cruiser had pulled away.

There was a tense, endless silence in the room after he drew back from the window. She watched him there in the shadows, waiting for his next move. He finally made up his mind.

"Get the rest of your things. We're leaving now."

He was worried by the arrival of the police at her door, fearing they might return to watch the house. She knew there would be no arguing with him.

He accompanied her back upstairs to collect her toilet case, followed her from room to room to make sure she turned off all the lights. Minutes later, after having checked her purse and handed it to her, he ordered her behind the wheel of the van. Then he joined her on the passenger side. She looked at him numbly as he slapped the Cards baseball cap on his head.

"There, all set. Just a happy husband off on vacation with his loving wife." He reached up and poked the garage door opener clipped to the visor. "Let's roll, Ellie."

She started the engine and backed out of the garage. There was no point in wasting her breath on any banal objection about how he couldn't possibly hope to get away with this. She could only pray he *wouldn't* get away with it, that they would be stopped before they ever left St. Louis and that he would be recaptured before he had hurt anyone else.

But there was no sign of a squad car as they traveled east through the city, no evidence of pursuit. No one in the other vehicles they passed displayed the slightest interest in her silent passenger, who was slouched low in the seat, the baseball cap pulled down over his forehead to minimize the risk of detection.

It wasn't until they crossed the Mississippi on the interstate bridge, and Ellie glimpsed in the rearview mirror the familiar Gateway Arch receding behind them, that despair settled on her in earnest. A despair triggered by the realization that she was his hostage. Forced to run with a fugitive whose intimate closeness she found absolutely daunting.

As if sensing her panic, he stirred beside her, mocking her with a low, lethal, "It's just you and me now, Ellie."

DETECTIVE LEW FERGUSON sat behind the wheel of his beat-up sedan, squinting through the smoke of his cigar as he watched the house in Webster Groves. There wasn't anything to see. The place was silent and dark, not a glimmer of light anywhere.

He'd rung the bell a few minutes ago, even tried the door. Nothing. Everything indicated it was locked and deserted. The radio reports he'd been monitoring all evening from the squad cars said Ellie Matheson was safe. Said Noah Rhyder had never come anywhere near her. Said Matheson was on her way to the Ozarks by now.

Yeah, and Lew wasn't buying it. He couldn't shake the feeling that something about this homely house of hers didn't smell right. That's why he went on sitting here in her driveway, smoking a bad cigar and wondering if he ought to risk breaking and entering. Tempting, real tempting, but they'd have his ass if he tried it. He wasn't supposed to be here at all. Wasn't supposed to come anywhere near this case again.

Lew couldn't accept that. The Buchanan murder had belonged to him, and Noah Rhyder had been his collar. He'd been hot as a firecracker on the case, and then they had taken it away from him. That smart-mouthed partner they'd saddled him with had brought misconduct charges against him, claiming he'd planted false evidence in his eagerness to get Rhyder. The review board had had no reason to dig into the past and had finally cleared him, but by then the case had gone to trial.

He should have left it at that, but Rhyder was an itch

he'd never gotten to scratch. And now…well, now the bastard was loose again, and Lew had another chance at him.

"You don't know it yet, Rhyder," he whispered into the darkness, "but I've got an old score to settle with you, and this time you don't get away from me."

He didn't care what it cost him in the department. His need to personally recover the fugitive was burning a hole in him. He *wanted* Rhyder.

"Whatever it takes," he promised himself.

Lew wasn't worried about his fellow officers beating him to Rhyder. If it happened, okay, but so far nobody was being smart about this manhunt. They weren't concentrating on the guy's major vulnerability. His kid. It was why Howard Buchanan had been murdered, not because the old man had caught his son-in-law cheating on the books. The prosecution had hammered away on that one. Lew knew better. He knew that Rhyder had wasted Buchanan because Grandpa was determined to get custody of the boy. And the kid was still his father's weakness, which brought it all back to Ellie Matheson.

Up until this afternoon, anyway, the boy had been with her in that house. Lew's connections had informed him that the uncle had the kid now, though nobody knew where he'd taken him. Lew wasn't certain how much Rhyder had been told, but one thing was for sure. He had to know the Matheson woman was a last link to his kid, so it figured he would have tried to get to her. Only he hadn't. Then why, Lew wondered, was he wasting his time sitting here?

He was stubbing out the cigar when a compact pulled into the driveway next door. A woman emerged wearing hospital scrubs. Probably a nurse returning from her shift. Lew was immediately interested. Neighbors saw things. Maybe this one had.

Heaving his bulky figure out of the car, he approached her, prominently displaying his ID so she wouldn't be alarmed by the presence of a stranger at this late hour.

"Detective Lew Ferguson, ma'am. I'm in charge of the Rhyder case," he lied.

She peered at his ID by the glow of the street light, saw that he was legitimate, and was ready to trust him. "Is that lunatic still on the loose? I heard about his escape at work."

"We'll get him back," he assured her confidently. "Thing is, I need to speak to your neighbor, Ms. Matheson. She was in charge of Rhyder's little boy and might be able to provide us with some useful information. Nobody at home, though. You have any idea where I could locate her?"

"Ellie? She was scheduled to leave first thing in the morning for a vacation in the Ozarks. We always watch each other's places when one of us is out of town." She glanced at the tall house. "If she didn't answer your ring, then she must have left already."

"That's probably just what she did do." Lew smiled, maintaining the casual pose that often got him results. "Only the place is as black as a coal mine. Guess she's not in the habit of burning a security light."

The neighbor frowned. "There should be a light showing. She always leaves one lamp on a timer. You think something could be wrong?"

"Naw, most likely forgot to set her timer. Still, the situation being what it is, it wouldn't hurt to check out the place. Just to be sure. I'm assuming you have a key."

The woman hesitated. "I guess Ellie wouldn't mind our doing that."

"Under the circumstances, she'd probably appreciate it."

"All right." She fished through her purse, producing a key. "It's for the side door. Ellie would have left the front door on its chain."

Lew followed her across the Matheson driveway. She unlocked the door and was just pushing it open when the phone in her car started to ring.

"It must be the hospital. There was a patient I was worried about. I told them to call me if there was any change."

"You go answer it," Lew told her. "I'll have a quick look-through on my own."

She looked uncertain for a second, then made up her mind. "There's a light switch just inside on the left."

The woman hurried toward the phone in her compact. Glad of her absence, Lew located the switch and entered the house. He found himself on a street-level landing where a stairway turned. The steps on the left mounted to the kitchen, those on the right descended to the basement.

Pausing for a second, he listened carefully. The place was silent, not a stir. He proceeded with caution, his police special in his hand. Moving from room to room, turning on lights as he went, Lew investigated the house from top to bottom. He'd been right to sense that something had happened here tonight. The house told him the whole story.

In the kitchen he found the busted back door. In the empty garage he saw the logs spilled on the floor. In the bathroom upstairs he found traces of dark hair in the sink. And down in the basement his eye caught the edge of a sleeve peeking out of a laundry basket. A sleeve whose dirt didn't entirely hide the blaze orange underneath.

Noah Rhyder had been here all right, must have managed to grab Ellie Matheson. So where were they now? But Lew knew the answer to that one, too. He could feel it in his gut. They had to be somewhere out there in her missing van. On their way to his kid, wherever that was. He'd stake his badge on it.

Procedure demanded that Lew return to his car and radio a report to headquarters. Have them get an APB out on the Matheson vehicle, along with a caution that Rhyder had probably altered his appearance. Yeah, that's what he was supposed to do. Only there was no satisfaction in that. He wasn't going to share Rhyder. He was going to bring him in on his own.

Lew would find some way around it all, some way to get the department to forgive him. If not…well, he was prepared for the consequences.

"Detective Ferguson, are you there?" It was the neighbor at the side door, sounding nervous as she called out to him.

He'd have to go up there and soothe her. Tell her that nothing was wrong and everything indicated Ellie Matheson had safely departed for the Ozarks. Then he would need to find out where Brett Buchanan had taken the kid. Lew knew someone who ought to be able to give him an address. With a little persuasion, that is.

ELLIE DIDN'T KNOW what time it was. The clock on the instrument panel no longer worked, and the interior of the van was too dim to read her watch. Nor was she about to ask her passenger. She preferred his silence, unnerving though it was. But it had to be well after midnight.

They were somewhere in Illinois, traveling southeast on the flat, monotonous interstate. Endless cornfields bordered the highway, the autumn harvest stripped from most of them. They looked as bleak in the headlights as Ellie felt. She wasn't sleepy, though. She supposed it was fear that kept her alert.

That alertness eventually paid off. When she finally began to wonder about the length of her unwanted companion's silence, she cast a furtive glance in his direction. His chin was down on his chest, his eyes closed. He had drifted off.

Her gaze cut back to the road. The traffic at this hour was very thin, but she couldn't afford to let excitement make her careless. Maintaining a steady speed, she checked on him again. No way to be certain of it, but he seemed to be more than just dozing. He looked like he was solidly asleep. The revolver was there on his lap, but his hand was no longer clutching it.

This was it! Her chance to get the gun away from him! But she couldn't just snatch it while they were under way. She would have to stop, try to ease it from his lap before he realized what was happening. A sign a few miles back indicated a rest area ahead. Perfect. There would be phones there, maybe other people. If she could just manage to pull off without rousing him...

She began to reduce the speed of the van in slow, easy stages, careful to avoid any sudden change that would disturb him. Her gaze was busy the whole time watching the highway, checking on her passenger, scanning the roadside for a signpost announcing the approach of the rest area. She must not miss it.

There! Just a half mile more to go!

Seconds later, she crawled along the exit lane, gently braking the van as she reached the parking area fronting the low brick building that housed the rest rooms. The van coasted to a stop under the tall security lights. Shifting into park, she eyed the man beside her. His eyes were still closed, his breathing slow and even.

There was no other vehicle in the parking lot. They were alone here. She was disappointed in that, but she could see a public phone on the wall near the entrance to the building. She gazed at it longingly, regretting that she had never equipped the van with a phone.

No choice about it. However alien and distasteful firearms were to her, she would have to relieve him of that gun. She could never hope to reach the public phone without it. If she tried to open her door, he would hear and be all over her. It was a miracle he was still asleep.

Straining against her seat belt, Ellie leaned toward him, willing her hands not to tremble as she slowly reached for the revolver in his lap.

Her fingers were almost in contact with the butt when, without warning, a pair of powerful hands seized her by the wrists. His enraged oath accompanied her startled cry, and in the next second they struggled furiously with each other.

Ellie went on resisting his painful grip, even though she knew it was useless to wrestle him for the gun. He was simply too strong for her. In the end, he flung her back and abruptly released her. By the time she recovered herself, she was staring into the muzzle of the revolver in his hand.

Their harsh breathing was the only sound inside the car. She lifted her gaze to his face. The light from outside was bright enough for her to read his expression, had there been one. He was simply looking at her. Looking at her with his dark, solemn eyes. Joel's eyes. How could this lout have fathered an angel like Joel? And how dare he have Joel's wonderful eyes? That's what got to her in the end. What made her wild with anger. Those damn mesmerizing eyes.

"Go on," she challenged him recklessly. "Shoot me. You might as well. Keeping me alive isn't going to do you any good. I'll never tell you where Joel is. *Never*. No matter what you do to me, you won't get it out of me, because you don't deserve a son like Joel."

"Shut up."

"I won't be quiet. I'm sick of your bullying me and sick of my being a quivering coward about it. So you might as well get it over with and kill me here and now. But before you squeeze that trigger, I'm going to have the satisfaction of telling you what a fool you are. Only a fool or a madman, and you're probably both, would think he had a chance of getting away. It's a wonder you've come this far. But it won't last. They'll capture you before you ever get close to Joel."

He leaned toward her, those black eyes pinning her with his fierce gaze. "You through?"

"No, I'm not finished. I haven't told you what a selfish animal you are. Because if you really loved Joel, if you were thinking of him instead of yourself, you wouldn't try to get him back. You wouldn't be planning to disappear with him. What kind of existence is that for a little boy? Forever on the run with a father who's a convicted killer.''

"Will you shut that mouth of yours?"

His face was so close to hers now that she could see the threatening fire in his eyes. Could almost smell the danger in him. But she was beyond caring about the risk to herself.

"When I'm good and ready, Noah Rhyder. When I'm damn good and ready."

What happened next was so sudden that Ellie had no chance to prevent it, much less anticipate it. In one second she had paused just long enough to seize a deep breath with which to go on blasting him. In that same instant he must have temporarily rid himself of the gun, because in the next second two hands trapped her startled face between them. Before she could issue a gasp, his mouth came crashing down on her parted lips.

God help her, he was kissing her! Kissing her deeply, his sinful tongue forcing a warm, wet entry into the recesses of her mouth which he plundered without mercy. Shocked by his assault, Ellie went limp, astonished at her own response to the kiss. It was mindless, intoxicating, and thoroughly disarming.

When he finally released her, she fell back against the seat, too stunned to voice the outrage his punishment deserved.

"Looks like I finally managed to silence that tongue of yours," he observed casually, retrieving the revolver from where he had stuck it in his belt. "Now, no more out of you. You do exactly what I tell you from now on, and I might just let you survive."

Ellie stared at him, too shaken to argue with him any further. That muscle was twitching in his jaw again, as it had back in her bathroom. It was like a warning flag, though she wasn't sure exactly what it signified. And maybe she didn't want to know.

Her mind was still in a turmoil from his kiss, unable to

forget the potency of it. Even now she could feel the slickness of his tongue, scent the virile odor of him, taste his warm breath mingling with hers. His mouth had captured hers with the force of a primitive brute, and she ought to be feeling nothing but disgust. Instead, she was experiencing all these treacherous responses that—

Oh, she had to get away from him! *She just had to.*

"What are you waiting for?" he said. "Get us back on the highway."

"I have to use the bathroom."

"You trying to pull another trick?"

"I'm sorry if nature is inconveniencing you, but it happens to be the truth." She wished it wasn't the case, but the tension of the situation had created an urgent need for her to relieve herself.

Noah glanced through the window, checking out the parking lot. It was still deserted except for their van. "All right, but make it quick."

He took charge of the keys as they left the van and headed toward the building.

Why? he wondered as he escorted her up the broad sidewalk to the glass doors. Why had he gone and done something crazy like that? There would have been other ways to stop her from telling him what he didn't want to hear. Instead, he had surrendered to temptation and kissed her. Gone and complicated what was already a mess.

He had to stop this. He had to keep his mind on his objective, not on Ellie Matheson's soft, fragrant flesh. Getting involved with her on any level was an invitation to carelessness. If she weren't an absolute necessity, he would turn her loose here and now. But as it was…well, he'd just have to watch himself with her from now on. Something told him that wasn't going to be so easy.

"Hold it," he said as they entered the open area between the two rest rooms.

She stopped beside him, following the direction of his interest in the snack machines ranged along an inner wall.

"Give me your purse," he said. "I'm starving. Wouldn't mind a soda either."

Ellie wasn't pleased by his command. "I not only get kidnapped, now I have to pay the expenses for it?"

"Yeah, well, I'm sorry but the state of Missouri didn't think I would need funds where I was going."

He took possession of her purse, found a supply of coins, and began to feed them into the machines.

"Will you hurry?"

"Relax, you'll get there."

Arming himself with the snacks and two cans of soda, which, along with the revolver and her purse, required an impressive bit of juggling, he jerked his head in the direction of the door marked "Women."

"All right, let's go in there and make you happy."

She was appalled when she realized he had no intention of letting her enter the rest room without him.

"This is ridiculous. Can't I be trusted to even go to the bathroom in private?"

"No, and unless you want an accident out here, you'll stop arguing about it."

Fuming, but too desperate to further oppose him, she smacked open the door of the women's room and headed for a stall. He was close behind her.

She rounded on him when she reached the stall. "I don't care what happens at this point. You are *not* coming in here with me."

"Guess that won't be necessary." She started to reach for her purse, but he held it away from her. "Uh, I don't think so, Ellie. Wouldn't want you giving in to temptation and scrawling some message on the wall in there."

She glared at him and entered the stall, slamming and locking the door behind her. Noah turned his back and leaned against the metal divider to wait for her.

He was busy stuffing the snacks and sodas into the pockets of his jeans when the roar of a heavy rig arriving in the parking lot outside alerted him. Trouble? He quickly squeezed the revolver into her purse where it would be concealed but still handy.

"We've got company," he warned her. "A truck on the lot. Just keep still in there, and no one gets hurt. The guy is probably interested in nothing but the men's room on the other side. All we have to do is stay put until he's gone. Understand?"

Before she could answer him, the door to the women's room burst open. Noah hadn't reckoned on female truckers. Both of the arrivals looked like they were built to take care of themselves. They were as surprised as he was.

"What the—"

The larger of the two eyed the purse he was hugging against himself. "All right, pervert, out!"

Noah thought fast. "Sorry, ladies. It's my wife. She's pregnant and, uh, not feeling so good. I was afraid to let her come in here on her own."

The trucker who had *Myrt* stitched on the pocket of her shirt ducked her head down to verify a pair of feet inside the stall. "Geez, I can relate to that."

Noah rapped his knuckles on the divider, calling out a concerned, "Sweetie, you gonna be okay?" There was a strangled sound from inside the stall. He smiled at the truckers. "She's gonna be okay."

"First pregnancy, huh?" Myrt asked sympathetically.

"I wish. We've got four at home. Twins. Two sets. But, hey, she wanted another one. Hurry up, dear. These ladies are waiting."

There was a loud flush. Seconds later Ellie emerged from the stall, her face as crimson as a sunset.

"Gee, hon," Myrt said, "you don't look so great."

"She'll be fine," Noah assured them. "I'll take care of her."

"I think you already have," the sarcastic one said, eyeing Ellie's waistline.

Sticking to her side like an overly solicitous husband, Noah went with Ellie to the sink where she washed and dried her hands. He was reminding her with his closeness that, unless she wanted a nasty scene, she was to do nothing to warn the truckers. Ellie remained wisely silent, but he knew she was incensed.

She waited until they were back outside to let him have it. Standing by the van, hugging herself against the sharp chill of the night, she tore into him.

"That was humiliating. Absolutely humiliating. Am I going to have to put up with this kind of thing every time I have to take care of a personal need?"

"Yeah, Ellie, you are." He put his face down close to her own, his voice turning hard. "I'm gonna be attached to you like a lamprey eel. All the way to North Carolina. No exceptions. You change your clothes, I'm going be right there to make sure that's all you're doing. You go to sleep, I'll be stretched out beside you. And if one of us winds up taking a shower, the other one is going be standing under the same spray."

He drew back, his voice softening. "It's going to be intimate, sweetheart. And you're not going to give me any trouble about it. When I tell you to move that shapely little tail of yours, you'll move it." He removed the gun from her purse, wagging it in front of her. "Otherwise..."

She stared at him, her eyes filled with loathing. But she said nothing, accepting her purse when he put it back in her hands.

He smiled at her. "Don't worry, Ellie. We'll get along just fine. Hell, we'll probably be real pals by the time we get to Carolina. Maybe eat off the same plate. What do you think?"

Chapter Four

Ellie was in that lethargic state halfway between sleep and wakefulness. Her only awareness was of a welcome warmth made possible by the blanket she shared with the solid body pressed close to her side. The air was cold outside their cocoon, so she was grateful for the heat her companion provided.

It was when she started to twist around, with a dreamy longing to snuggle against him tightly, that she felt the tug of the rope.

The sudden drag on her wrist was as effective as an alarm clock. Her eyes opened. She found herself fully awake and staring at a sleeping male profile chiseled out of rock. Memory rushed to the surface of her consciousness.

A picnic grove. They were parked behind a wall of shrubbery in a deserted picnic grove. Ellie remembered seeing the sign for it when he'd made her drive in here last night after she threatened to fall asleep at the wheel. The place was a small county park two miles off the interstate, somewhere in rural Kentucky.

He had found a length of clothesline she'd used to tie up her painting gear. He had made her sit beside him on the van's bench seat behind the bucket seats in front. Then he had lashed them together wrist to wrist, pulled the car blanket around both of them, and gone to sleep, confident she would be here in the morning. And she was, damn it.

Noah Rhyder had made good on his promise. He had bound her to him with the intimacy of an embrace, and it had made her frantic on more levels than she cared to examine. She must have spent a good half hour last night surreptitiously picking away at her restraint. But the knots he had used would have defeated a veteran sailor. Maddening, and he had never once permitted himself to be disturbed by her awkward efforts with her left hand. In the end, exhausted and regretting she wasn't ambidextrous, she had drifted off.

Now here she was, hours later, still roped to the man. The sun was just clearing the horizon. With the daylight to help her, what were her chances this time of freeing herself? His eyes were still closed. If she was very careful—

"Morning, sunshine."

Too late. He was already awake, his face turned now toward hers.

"You sleep okay?" he asked, his voice early-morning husky.

She gazed at him in a stony silence.

"*I* slept just fine," he said. "Dreamed about this alluring woman who refused to leave my side." His wide mouth parted in a drowsy grin. "I guess she wanted my body. Too bad I woke up before I got to the really interesting part. Oh, well…"

He yawned and stretched his long legs, his hand reaching down under the blanket to scratch his leg. It was his left hand, and it carried her attached right hand with it. Her fingers were rubbed slowly along his hard thigh. His action was deliberate and provocative. Every nerve ending in her body went on alert.

"Tell you what, Ellie. Why don't I catch a few more winks, see if I can get back into that dream. Then you can go on working at the knots. Maybe you'll get lucky."

She jerked at the rope, removing her fingers from contact with his searing flesh. "Will you stop playing games and just untie me?"

"What's your hurry?" He bent his strong, angular face close to her own. "Don't you like being cozy with me, Ellie? I think it's great."

His voice was a warm rumble that stroked her senses. His touch, as his free hand came up from the blanket and moved against her face, was even more seductive. The rough fingertips that stirred over her cheek generated a strange weakness at the bottom of her stomach.

"Turn me loose," she demanded.

"I'll do that, Ellie," he promised, his voice slow and deep, his mouth no more than a warm breath away from hers. "But first…"

"What?" she whispered fearfully.

His black eyes searched her face. Compelling eyes that at this moment had a surprising tenderness in them.

"Just tell me where Joel is, Ellie. That's all. Just give me the address."

His sensual softness had been nothing but a ploy, and she had almost fallen for it. She was angry with herself as much as him. She yanked fiercely at the thin rope binding them, not caring that the line bit into her wrist.

"You're dreaming again if you think I will."

"Who are you protecting, Ellie? My kid or your boyfriend, Brett Buchanan?"

He was taunting her again, probably hoping that if he pushed her hard enough she would explode on him emotionally and rashly reveal what he wanted to know. The man was cunning. She needed to be on her guard with him every moment.

"Fine," she said with as much indifference as she could muster. "You go on sitting here wasting time playing games with me. I'm not the one who's eager to get to North Carolina, so why should I care?"

"You don't care, huh? Then why are you squirming?"

"For the same reason I was squirming at the rest area last night. There's a facility out there, and I'd like to use it."

"All right," he agreed. "Potty break, and then we hit the road again."

He removed the rope from them with an infuriating ease, retrieved the gun and her purse containing the car keys from the front passenger seat where she had been unable to reach them, and motioned her out of the van.

Ellie obeyed him, shivering in an October wind that rattled the dry, rust-colored oak leaves overhead. The grove would be a pleasant place in summer with its tables scattered under the trees and a creek meandering through the meadows. Right now there was nothing inviting about it, which was exactly why Noah had decided it was a safe spot.

Nor would Ellie have recommended the plumbing. Except for an old-fashioned, outdoor pump, it was nonexistent. The best she could say about the solitary, rustic outhouse was that, after checking it out, he permitted her to use it in private.

He must have taken care of his own needs behind the closest tree, because when she emerged from the privy, the pump handle was squealing as he lifted water from the well. He'd already removed her toilet case from the van and helped himself to her spare toothbrush. There was no point in objecting.

Washing up under the icy stream that gushed from the spout was an experience Ellie didn't care to repeat. But she did feel less grubby once she'd splashed her face and cleaned her teeth. *He* was positively exuberant.

"Nothing like being a happy camper, huh, Ellie? Only one thing missing, and we're gonna take care of that at the nearest fast-food drive-up window."

But it wasn't breakfast that was on her mind once they

were back in the van and under way again. *Brett,* she thought. She had to see that he was warned of Noah Rhyder's intention to recover his son. Had to let him know that Noah, dangerous and eluding capture, was on his way to North Carolina. The police might have cautioned Brett already, but she couldn't count on that. They had no knowledge of the fugitive's destination and his current situation. She did.

There was only one way Ellie could alert Joel's guardian. She had to reach a phone, or at least pass a message to someone who would help her. But how could she manage such a thing when Noah was vigilant every second?

Wait. Hadn't he already taught her the answer to that one himself? He'd tried to weaken her defenses with his sensual tactics. She wasn't about to employ the same method on him in order to build a window of escape, but there were other ways to catch him off guard. Like pretending to care, to sympathize.

However, this was a long way from being the right moment for that. He was bound to be suspicious of anything too sudden or extreme. Her softening had to occur under believable circumstances, even appear to be reluctant. She needed to be patient. She needed to wait for the opportunity that would—

"Hey, stop dreaming and slow down. You're gonna miss the turnoff."

They were approaching the fast-food restaurant they had passed last night. Obeying his command, she eased the van into the lane for the drive-up window.

"All right, Ellie," he instructed her as they reached the speaker, "just our carryout order. No cute signals with it. Understand?"

She nodded as the server inside the building asked for their order.

"Same goes for the window," he added when the order

had been placed and they'd joined the line of cars inching toward the glass bay.

Another vehicle closed up behind them. Ellie glanced at it in the rearview mirror. The breath stuck in her throat. It was a highway patrol, a uniformed officer at the wheel. Her gaze slewed in the direction of her companion.

He, too, was aware of the car behind them. He was watching it in the outside mirror on his side.

"Don't turn around and look," he muttered to her. "You just stay put until we get to the window. Then I hand you the money. You pass it over, get the order, and take us out of here. All nice and easy, Ellie."

He was casual about it, but she could read the tension in him. He had her purse at his side. She knew that he had the gun somewhere down there, too.

The restaurant was very busy. It seemed to take forever to crawl up to the window, an eternity in which over and over she uttered a silent prayer for release.

But the trooper behind them apparently had no reason to be suspicious, and Ellie could think of no way to alert him. Not without risking lives, probably her own to begin with.

She was almost sick with anxiety by the time they reached the bay and received their order. All hope for rescue died as they pulled away from the restaurant, losing themselves in the traffic. There was no sign now of the highway patrol.

They were a mile down the road and nearing the access lane, which would put them back onto the interstate, when she had the satisfaction of spoiling Noah's relief.

"We have to fill up. We're practically running on fumes."

He swore angrily, slopping coffee on himself.

"It's your own fault," she accused him. "I told you when we left the picnic grove we needed gas, but all you could think about was breakfast."

Not trusting her, he leaned over to check the gauge for

himself. "All right, pull into that station up there. It's a brand you've got a credit card for."

He had missed nothing in her purse, Ellie thought sourly as she swung off the highway and rolled up to the pumps. Switching off the engine, she started to reach for her purse, but he held it away from her.

"Uh-uh . All you get is the credit card, and I keep the rest. Insurance, Ellie, remember?"

Taking possession of the keys, he slid from the van. She wasn't permitted to join him until he was on her side of the car.

"No need to go inside," he said, handing her the credit card. "Pay for it here at the pump. You handle the fill-up."

As usual, he was taking no chances. Making her do all the work while he watched. "Would you like me to wash the windows while I'm at it? Maybe check the oil and the tires?"

"Keep that up, Ellie, and I won't share any of the breakfast goodies with you. Gas," he ordered.

She was fitting the nozzle into the tank when another car whipped into the station, stopping near the building's front entrance. It was the same highway patrol car they had encountered back at the restaurant. With the possibility of rescue surging inside her again, she gazed at the vehicle with yearning, then slid a swift glance in Noah's direction.

He leaned against the hood of the van, looking relaxed and bored. She knew he was neither. He eyed the highway patrol car, then shot her a look of warning. He still had her purse. He was hugging it against his waist. She guessed that its bulk probably concealed the revolver in his hand.

It would be suicidal of her to cry out any appeal, but she kept casting hopeful glances in the direction of the trooper. He had emerged from his cruiser and was fitting coins into a newspaper machine. The officer was in no way interested in them.

"What's taking you so long?" Noah growled at her.

"The automatic lever keeps clicking off."

"Then feed it manually."

The trooper looked up from the newspaper he'd removed from the machine. His gaze shifted to the pump where the van was parked. He stood there for long seconds watching them. There was a slight frown on his face, an expression of sudden discovery. Had something in the newspaper aroused his suspicion? Tucking the newspaper under his arm, he sauntered toward them. Ellie stopped breathing.

The officer, looking like he meant business now, went straight for Noah. Noah didn't move from his negligent position against the hood, but she sensed how every muscle in him tightened and that he gripped her purse with a grim readiness. Her own hold on the gas nozzle was painful.

The trooper stopped in front of Noah. "You know, fellow," he said gruffly, "it's just an observation, but in this part of the world we don't let our ladies pump gas while we stand by and watch."

"Uh, sorry, officer. I've got a bad back. It just kills me if I try to bend forward."

The trooper grunted something, nodded at both of them, and then turned away, wishing them the familiar, "Have a good day," as he started back to the cruiser.

Ellie, unable to bear the loss of what might be her only chance for help, opened her mouth with the reckless intention of calling out to him. The words never formed. Noah was already at her side, nudging her with her purse. Reminding her of what would happen if she tried anything so foolish. She had no choice but to stand there and despondently watch the highway patrol pull away from the service station.

Minutes later the van was back on the interstate and speeding south. Noah munched on a cheese-and-egg concoction as he consulted a map he'd fished out of the glove compartment.

"That was too close for comfort," he said. "There's too

much traffic connected with the interstates, including cops. We're getting off. This exit down here. We'll take the back highways from then on. It'll mean a longer trip, but it ought to be a lot less risky.''

Ellie had no response.

"Hey, don't you want your Danish?" he asked her with an exasperating cheerfulness.

She shook her head. The prospect of prolonging their journey robbed her of what little appetite remained after the episode at the service station. Would this nightmare never end?

LEW WAS WAITING for her when she got home from the all-night joint down near the river where she waited tables. *And* hustled the customers, when she could get away with it.

Her apartment was in a crummy building in a section of St. Louis known as Dogtown. But then Ginger Zukawski had never been very particular, either about her habits or her men.

She was wearing a smile when Lew climbed from his car outside her building, but she wasn't pleased to see him.

"Hey, Detective Ferguson, I'm real hurt. You ain't run me in lately."

Her bleached hair looked harsh in the early morning light, and her makeup couldn't hide the bags that were beginning to form under her eyes. What did Peaches see in her? Lew wondered. Hell, his ex-partner had never had any taste in women, but he hadn't bothered to be serious about any of them either. Not until Ginger. She'd been in Peaches's blood ever since he left the force to take that job with Brett Buchanan.

"You worried about that, Ginger?" Lew asked, crushing his cigar underfoot on the sidewalk.

"I got no reason to be."

"We can keep it that way."

"All right, what do you want?"

"Nothing much. I just want to know where Peaches is."

She shrugged. "How should I know?"

"Because he tells you everything."

"Well, he didn't tell me that. All I know is he left town with his boss. Said he'd be away for a while, and he'd see me when he got back. Period."

"Come on, Ginger, let's have the address."

"Look, I don't have time for this, Ferguson." She glanced longingly at the door to her building. "It's been a long night, and I'm beat. I need some sleep."

"Keep on lying to me, and you'll get it in a lockup. I've got a couple of charges I could make stick. Like extortion, for instance. Or are you forgetting that last complaint I was willing to overlook?"

She glared at him. "Peaches ain't gonna appreciate you hassling me."

"The address, Ginger, and I'm out of here."

"I'm not supposed to tell. He said it was strictly confidential."

"Hey, I'm a friend. How's he gonna mind you sharing it with his friend? But if you go on holding out on me..."

"Okay, okay, you win. But I never told you. Understand?"

Nor did she tell him. Instead, she opened her purse and produced a slip of paper, showing it to him. North Carolina. Buchanan had taken the Rhyder kid to North Carolina. Lew copied the address in his notebook. Ginger was staring at him shrewdly when he returned the slip to her.

"This is about the guy that got away yesterday, isn't it? The kid's father, Noah Rhyder. You still got it in for him. Peaches told me how—"

"Be smart, Ginger, and shut your mouth."

"Hey, it's no skin off my nose. Can I go now?"

"Just as soon as I get your promise that we never had this little meeting."

"Suits me."

Lew watched her turn away with relief. When she'd vanished inside her building, he returned to his car and sat there behind the wheel, examining possibilities as he smoked another of his perpetual cigars.

Yeah, North Carolina. Had to be where Rhyder and the Matheson woman were headed. So, without involving the department, which he still had no intention of doing, what were his choices? He could try to hunt for Rhyder on the road, but on his own that would be about as smart as looking for a lost hubcap in rush hour. They could be anywhere out there.

He had a much better idea. He would fly to North Carolina, be waiting there to grab Rhyder when he showed. Lew's supervisor would stop him if he knew, but no reason why the old man should hear anything until it was all over. Then Lew would say that, being off duty for a couple of days, he'd flown east to visit his old buddy, Peaches, and just happened to be on the spot when Rhyder turned up.

The department would never be able to prove otherwise. And if they did, so what? Taking Noah Rhyder was worth any risk. He was excited about it, consumed with the need to personally send the bastard to Boonville where he belonged. Or maybe, if Rhyder gave him any serious trouble, straight to hell.

WITH HER SITUATION as fearful as it was, nature should have been the last thing on Ellie's mind. But it was impossible not to be captivated by the rural landscape rolling past the windows of the van.

They were in Tennessee now and headed east again, pursuing the long, winding highway that Noah had selected from the map, which unlike the interstate was almost empty of traffic. She could drive and still admire the countryside with its October hues of russet and gold.

It was all out there to be savored by her eager artist's

eyes. A haze on the wooded ridges. Beef cattle browsing in stony pastures. Yellowing bracken on the steep banks of the roadside and in the ditches thickets of sumac so violently red that no palette could compete with them.

But Ellie longed to try. Wanted to be out there with her paints and brushes, putting on canvas a tangle of muscadine sprawling over a weathered fence while a turkey vulture circled in a mellow sky. Instead, she was trapped here with—

"So, Ellie, what kind of painting is it you do?"

Uncanny. Had he read her mind? Impossible. He had probably made the connection because of the scenery, just as she had. Even a lout like him couldn't be immune to its appeal on a morning like this. Well, fine. He could enjoy it in silence. She had no intention of making friendly conversation with a man who was holding her at gunpoint. Of discussing a subject that was sacrosanct to her just because he was bored. Or, worse, because he was making another effort to soften her.

But her refusal to respond didn't stop him. He was arrogant enough to ask and answer his own questions and be fascinated with his dialogue while he did it.

"With all that gear back there, it ought to be impressive. So what medium are we talking about? Oils, watercolor? Maybe both, huh? Watch the truck, Ellie."

He didn't have to tell her. She had already slowed for the pickup that pulled out in front of them from a farm lane. There was a yellow dog in the back.

Noah lounged on the seat and continued his discourse. "But that's not the interesting question here. The interesting question is, are you traditional or modern when you slap on whatever paint it is you use? Bet I know. You know how I know? Your house back in St. Louis. Says it all, Ellie. Sweet and sentimental. And that's how you'd treat that creek out there."

They were in a deep hollow, crossing a stream thickly bordered by willows.

"If you were to paint that creek, Ellie, you'd faithfully put in every leaf and rock. Maybe add a cute little puppy on the bank."

She said nothing, but her hands tightened on the wheel.

"You don't mind my observations, do you? I mean, it's not like I don't know something about it. I am a trained architect, after all. And a damn good one at that," he boasted. "Art and architecture. Yeah, it's all the same. Just line and color when you come down to it."

They passed a field of sorghum, a hedgerow, and then another field where wild turkeys were fattening themselves on fallen grain.

"Yep, you're into traditional art for sure." He nodded, smiled, then said, "I hate traditional art. Know why I hate it, Ellie?"

She was smoking mad by now, but she held her silence.

"It's because of the clients I had. Well, some of them. I'd give them contemporary buildings. That's what they asked for. Contemporary buildings with lines that were pure and clean. And you know what they went and did? Garbaged up the walls with all this junk. Calendar art. Look out for the pickup. He's making a left. What is it with these people? They don't have turn signals?"

Ellie slowed again for the truck. Her jaw was aching from the effort of keeping her mouth shut.

"These walls," he continued. "These walls I designed cried out for modern art. Simple paintings with bold splashes of color. But they ruined them with covered bridges and lighthouses and quaint farms."

You know what he's doing, don't you? Deliberately provoking you. Trying to take advantage of you again. He can't wait for you to lose your temper. Don't fall for it. Hold your tongue.

"Nothing emotional about a covered bridge. I mean, hey,

it's a covered bridge. But an abstract painting…you can always find new things in it, new feelings, right?''

You will be quiet. You will say nothing.

"You know the way I figure it? If you want a nice little picture, go out and buy a camera. Why are we stopping? I didn't tell you to stop."

She brought the van to a halt on the shoulder of the road, lifted the gear into park, and swung around in her seat to face him. She was livid.

"You've barked orders at me since last night. You've held a gun on me. You've tied me up. And I took it. I took it all, because I had no choice. But what I will not take, *refuse* to take, is another word of this rubbish about a subject that's sacred to me."

"It's just an opinion, Ellie."

"It's not an opinion, it's an indictment from a smug idiot who knows nothing about it. Because if you did know anything about traditional art, you'd respect it, like all forms of honest expression should be respected. You'd realize that traditional art is something most people can relate to since they can easily recognize its forms, which is not a bad thing even if certain snobs keep trying to tell us it is. You'd understand that the best of it demands talent and technique that can't be disguised, and when it's sincere it deserves to be celebrated."

"Oh."

"That's it? That's all you have to say?"

"Uh, yeah, that's about it. What about you, Ellie? You finished?"

"Yes. No. If you don't like the way I'm driving, then you take the wheel."

"Can't. No license."

She didn't care if he had the revolver. She'd didn't care if he shot her. She wanted to smack him. Instead, she shoved the gear into drive and pulled back onto the highway.

He was silent now as the van gathered speed. She didn't trust that silence. She waited until they were a mile or so down the road, and then she sneaked a glance at him. He was wearing a complacent little smile. Its meaning was as plain as if he had leaned over and whispered to her, "Gotcha."

He had done it again, managed to turn her own emotions against her. Why? Because on some perverse level it satisfied him to keep her in a turmoil? Or was it a kind of weapon to control her?

Either way, she had made another mistake. She had passionately defended her beloved art and in the process revealed more about herself than she'd intended. Would he use that against her?

She didn't know. He was an enigma. Except for one thing. She was beginning to understand that, whatever his origins, Noah Rhyder was not the uninformed ape he pretended to be. He couldn't have been a successful architect otherwise. She should have remembered that.

If Ellie had any doubt about this, he dispelled it a moment later.

"The painting over your bed," he said, his tone entirely sober this time. "The winter scene with birches and a stone wall."

"You noticed it?" Considering the events back at her house, she was amazed he would have paid the slightest attention to that picture, or any other on her walls.

"I noticed it. Yours?"

"Yes."

"Tell me about it."

"I don't think so."

He ignored her objection. "The light on the snow. I liked the way you caught the light on the snow."

His simple approval both warmed and confounded her. That winter landscape was one of her favorites, but David had been indifferent to it. Now the man who was her kidnapper was telling her he appreciated it, was offering her the kind of understanding her ex-husband had never demonstrated.

"So you don't hate traditional art, after all."

"Maybe not. How did you manage the light?"

"Sometimes you don't manage it. You just get lucky, and it happens."

What was she doing? She had no business discussing her art with Noah Rhyder, surrendering to his praise. It was dangerous. *He* was dangerous.

Ellie concentrated on the road. That was the wisest thing to do. The *safest* thing. But Tennessee was a big state. It was a long, long road, and surviving it was a challenge growing more treacherous by the hour.

Chapter Five

"I'm hungry."

How could he be thinking of food again, Ellie wondered, after that enormous breakfast he had put away back on the interstate, including the Danish she had refused?

"It isn't noon yet," she pointed out. It was the first thing she'd said to him since their exchange about her art more than an hour ago. He had respected her silence this time, maybe because he preferred it himself.

"I don't care. I still want lunch." He consulted the map spread across his knees. "There's a town coming up. Ridley. We'll see what's cooking there."

She didn't argue with him. Any one of their necessary stops offered her the potential opportunity to escape or to communicate her need for help.

But Noah, exercising his usual caution, ordered her into another fast-food restaurant when they arrived in Ridley moments later. Once again he kept contact to a minimum by choosing the drive-up window. This time there was no police cruiser in sight. No one was interested in them. They were just another vehicle passing through.

Noah surprised her when they pulled away from the restaurant with their order.

"We've been sitting in this damn car for too many hours. This time let's go find somewhere outside to eat."

She was afraid to agree with him, fearing he would find it suspicious and change his mind.

Ridley was an old-fashioned country town in a wooded river valley. The main street was also the highway. There was a sign on its edge that directed travelers to a town park out along the side of the river.

"Let's try there," he said.

People, she thought eagerly. There was the likelihood of other people occupying the park. The chance to pass a message.

But Ellie was disappointed when they reached the place. It was a weekday, and no one was around. They were the only car in the lot.

"Perfect," Noah said as they emerged from the parked van.

For you, maybe, she thought sourly as she watched him pocket the keys. He had one of her sweaters tied around his middle. It concealed the revolver stuck inside his waistband.

The park was long and narrow, bordering the shallow stream that was more of a creek than a river. She had no choice but to accompany him as he struck out along the path that followed the waters burbling over a rocky bed.

The van was well behind them before Noah found a deserted spot that satisfied him. They settled at a picnic table within sight of a small, Victorian-style gazebo.

"Now, Ellie, isn't this nice?" he asked as he unpacked the sandwiches, fries, and sodas from the bag.

Under other circumstances she might have agreed. The morning chill had lifted. There was a drowsy, autumn warmth in the air. Leaves drifted down from the tulip poplars and the hickory trees while the midday sun poked through the clouds, spangling the river with golden lights. It was a lovely, lazy setting for a meal—if she hadn't been sharing it with an escaped killer. She ate in silence.

Noah gazed at her across the table, thinking how despondent she looked as she bit into her ham-and-cheese sandwich. He was responsible for that look, and for a moment he was seized by a spasm of guilt. Then he hardened himself against any dangerous sympathy. He told himself he couldn't afford to be soft with her, knowing she wouldn't hesitate to turn him over to the cops at the first opportunity. Told himself he had yet to be convinced she wasn't involved with Brett Buchanan, and Buchanan had his kid.

But he couldn't stop looking at her. She had found a scarf in her bag and tied it around her neck. A boldly patterned thing, bright as a butterfly. He'd wondered at first if the scarf was a gesture of defiance because he'd ordered her to remove her eye-catching outfit last night. He had since decided that the scarf was not a conscious opposition. It simply relieved the drabness of her navy slacks and sweater, and Ellie needed vibrant colors. They were as essential to her as air and water. He already understood that much about her. Against his better judgment, he let her keep the scarf on.

There were other things Noah noticed. Couldn't keep himself from noticing. There was a small white scar on one side of her chin. He wondered how she'd gotten it. He found the scar appealing. He also liked the faint laugh lines at the corners of her amber eyes. They made him wonder how old she was. Somewhere in her early thirties, he guessed. Probably six or seven years younger than himself.

Damn it, what was he doing? If he didn't watch himself, he'd be wondering what fascinating little details he could discover under those slacks and the sweater. With the mess he was in, he had no business being interested in her as anything more than a means to an end.

They had finished their lunch. He attacked the discarded wrappings with an angry resolve, crushing them into a ball which he tossed into a nearby refuse container.

"Ellie."

She looked up, wearing a puzzled frown. "What?"

"It's raining."

She had been so preoccupied she hadn't noticed how the clouds had thickened while they ate. He watched her hold out her hand, palm up, to verify the first drops that were falling.

"Let's get back to the car," he said.

But it began to rain in earnest as they left the table. The van was too far away. They would be drenched before they could reach it.

"The gazebo," he decided. "We'll take cover there until it lets up."

They ran to the structure, gaining its shelter just seconds before the rain escalated into a downpour. There was a small bench in the center just wide enough for two people, providing they squeezed close together. Noah could see how reluctant she was to share the bench with him. But the gazebo was so tiny that its single seat offered the only protection against a soaking. She had no choice.

"What did I promise you last night?" he asked when they were settled side by side. "At the rest area, remember?"

She didn't answer him. She tried to move away, except there was nowhere to move.

"Told you we'd be cozy, real cozy. Looks like that's just what we are, Ellie. At least until the rain lets up."

He was teasing her, but it wasn't so funny. The heat of her body intimately pressed against his was starting to arouse him, giving him crazy ideas about the two of them. Hell, he could still taste her from that reckless kiss last night, and right now he wanted a lot more than her mouth. He could swear she wasn't totally unaffected either.

This wasn't smart, he thought. He had to find a way to defuse the sexual tension between them while they waited out this rain, or they'd both be in serious trouble. Maybe if he talked to her, tried to relax her a little on the subject of Noah Rhyder...

Why? he asked himself. What difference did it make what she thought about him? But it did matter, he decided. For one thing, he was getting damn tired of watching her every second, forever worrying about what she might try next. And for another...well, keeping her in line by having her think the worst about him was just something he no longer wanted to do, although he was afraid to look too closely at that one. The point was, if she started to trust him a little, maybe she wouldn't be so eager to see him back in handcuffs.

Yeah, and you're gonna win the lottery, Rhyder, and live happily ever after. That's right after you prove your innocence to the state of Missouri.

All right, so he was a fool to think he could convince her that he wasn't a monster, but how else was he going to get Joel's address out of her? *Nothing ventured, Noah...*

"You think I'm pretty bad, don't you, Ellie? A cold-blooded killer keeping you alive only because I need that address."

She wished he would stop trying to be friendly. It only made everything harder. She also wished he didn't have that voice as he leaned toward her, warm and deep and disarmingly rough around the edges. It was unsettling enough to have his hard body hugged against hers on this scrap of a bench.

"I don't want to hear this," she told him sharply.

"Why? You afraid a little doubt might slip past your conviction that I'm guilty as sin? Maybe even a little sympathy? They say that happens between kidnappers and their victims. That what you're guarding against, Ellie?"

She was about to surge to her feet, move away to the edge of the gazebo, endure a soaking. Anything to avoid listening to him. Then it struck her. She'd been so unnerved by the threat of a seductive trap that she had failed to recognize the opportunity she'd been waiting for. The chance to soften his vigilance by pretending to care, and he was giving it to her himself.

Don't overplay it, Ellie. The man is no fool.

"Go on then," she urged him, pretending to be immune to his challenge. "This ought to be good. A talented man like you, an architect and all, should be very inventive when it comes to the fiction of just how pure he really is."

"Okay, so I'm no saint. I've got some things in my past I'm not happy about. But murder? Uh-uh. I sure as hell didn't shoot that deputy when I got away."

He told her the story of what happened and how his escape occurred without his direct involvement. She had to admit it was a persuasive explanation, but she wasn't falling for it.

"I see," she said dryly. "And this bad cop, the one who shot his partner, did he also kill Senator Buchanan?"

"That one is a bit more complicated."

"I just bet it is."

He was quiet for a moment while he marshaled his thoughts. Or, rather, she told herself, his lies. The rain continued to fall without interruption, beating with a hollow sound on the roof of the gazebo.

"How much do you know about my ex-father-in-law?" he asked her suddenly.

Ellie shrugged. "Only what I've read or heard on the newscasts. That he was old St. Louis money and that no one seemed to have any complaint about his record in office."

"Yeah, Howard was a smart politician and, publicly, a pussycat. Privately, he was a ruthless bastard."

"Naturally, you would think that."

"I had a good reason for my opinion of him. He didn't want Jennifer to marry me. Loathed the idea of me as a son-in-law. I wasn't good enough for his daughter."

"You and how many millions of other sons-in-law, except they don't go around murdering their fathers-in-law because of it.''

"Oh, I wasn't worried about his disapproval. In fact, Howard was pretty decent after Joel was born. By then I'd earned my stripes as an architect, so I was *almost* respectable. In fact, he was a major investor in the project I was designing and building. We were recycling an old brewery into upscale shops and apartments.''

Ellie remembered the references to that project during the trial. She detected the note of pride beneath his bitterness when Noah spoke of it now.

"It was a big undertaking involving a lot of funds. I didn't want Howard's money in it. I didn't want to be obligated to him, but Jennifer pleaded for it. I think she figured it was a way of bonding me to her family. I should have refused. I didn't. She was already sick at the time, and I wanted to please her.''

He paused. There was silence in the gazebo except for the sound of the rain slashing against the trelliswork. He's remembering his wife, Ellie thought. She was disturbed by that. She didn't want to have to regard him on that kind of level. It made him too human, too vulnerable.

"It was okay while Jennifer was alive," he continued. "There was no trouble on the project, but after she died it all fell apart. Howard wanted custody of Joel, and although there was no way I was going to allow that to happen, he was ready to do anything to get him. Including sabotaging the project.''

"For what purpose?''

"To help build his case against me as an unfit father.''

"They said you were dipping into the funds. That your father-in-law discovered it and was ready to bring charges. There was all that evidence at the trial.''

"Yeah, from an accountant who was paid by Howard to cook the books and make it look like I was the one who was cheating. The guy would have been in serious trouble if he'd told the truth at the trial. I guess he figured perjury was safer.''

Ellie stirred restlessly on the bench. "You're not making a very good defense for yourself. Everything you've told me so far adds up to a motive for murder.''

"It gets worse.''

"Yes, I know. You were alone in the house with Howard Buchanan the afternoon he was murdered.''

"I was there,'' he admitted. "I went to get Joel. He was spending a couple of days with his grandfather while I met with the auditors to try to sort out the accounts. Joel was gone. Howard told me the housekeeper had taken him to the zoo. My kid is crazy about animals.''

"He loves the tigers," Ellie murmured.

"And the bears.''

They exchanged smiles, briefly sharing this innocent knowledge about his son. And then she quickly looked away, watching the rain on the river.

Noah went on. "By then I was pretty sure what Howard was up to, and all I could think about was getting my son away from that barn of a house in Ladue and never taking him back there if I could help it. That's when Howard told me he had no intention of letting me keep Joel.''

"He admitted how he was ruining you? Or I should say how you *claim* he was.''

"In so many words, yes. We had a pretty rough scene, just the two of us in that elegant library of his.''

"And you struck him.''

"I was angry, damn angry. And I was scared of losing my kid. Yeah, I hit him, but Howard Buchanan was alive and healthy when I stormed out of that house.''

"They said you were running away.''

"They were wrong. All I did was drive around the city for a while to cool off, and then I went looking for Joel. Only, before I could find him, the cops found me.''

"Your fingerprints were on the fireplace poker that killed him."

"*Thumb*print, Ellie. Nothing else. The murderer wiped off the poker after he used it, but that much got left behind."

"Either way, your hand was on the poker."

"Howard asked me to stir the fire while he took a call. We were still being polite to each other at that point, so I obliged him. And, no, I didn't hit him with the poker afterward. Not my style, Ellie. I used this." His fingers closed into a fist, which he swung past her nose. "I never touched the poker again after I stirred the fire. When I walked out of that place, it was leaning against the hearth where I'd left it."

This was altogether different from listening to the reports on the ten o'clock news, she thought. There was a reality here, an earnestness in the way he told his story that made her uneasy. All of it had to be lies. She knew that. Then why she was afraid of hearing any more?

"All right, you didn't kill him," she said impatiently. "Some phantom murderer appeared on the scene afterward and smashed in his skull. Who?"

"How do I know? Maybe Brett Buchanan. There was no love lost between father and son. They were too much alike, including the women they chased."

"Brett was in Chicago at the time on a business trip. That was established."

"Right, solid alibi, no motive. *I* had all the motives, didn't I? The prosecution even made it look like I believed I'd be able to get my hands on the wealth my son inherits from his grandfather. The jury loved that one."

"Why do you bother to tell me all this?" she asked him, her voice deliberately emotional, as if to suggest she was torn by indecision, no longer unquestioningly convinced of his guilt.

"You know why. It's because of Joel. Because I need

to get him away from Brett Buchanan. That's why I'm on the run and why I intend to disappear with my son. I don't trust him with Buchanan.''

"That's crazy.''

"Maybe. But what if it *is* possible that Brett murdered his father, or paid to have him killed? What if it's dangerous for Joel to be in Brett's custody?'' He leaned toward her, his voice as low and seductive as the serpent's in Eden. "Think about it, Ellie. That's all I'm asking you to do. Just think about it…''

She faced stiffly forward, refusing to look at him. She could feel him gazing at her, watching her closely. She made sure her face registered uncertainty, that her expression would satisfy him she was actually considering the possibility of his innocence.

And the awful thing, the *frightening* thing about her performance, was her knowledge that it wasn't entirely a pretense. Her scheme to relax his guard had backfired on her. She found herself shaken by the concept that maybe, just maybe…

No! Common sense told her he had to be responsible for the deaths of both Howard Buchanan and that young deputy. Anything else was too far-fetched, nothing but a cunning temptation he'd concocted because he would do or say anything to trick Joel's address out of her.

"Rain's stopped, Ellie. We can go now.''

She was relieved. They left the bench, started back toward the van. Both of them were silent now. She regretted the scene she had slyly encouraged in the gazebo, but it did have one result in her favor.

There were public rest rooms next to the parking lot. When she indicated her need to stop there before they resumed their journey, not only did he permit her to go alone into the women's side but this time he let her take her purse with her. He was actually beginning to trust her!

Once he'd checked out the rest room to make certain it

was empty, she hurried inside, leaving him safely behind on the sidewalk. She wasted no time in locking herself into a stall, opening her purse, and searching excitedly through its contents. She would scrawl a plea for help, a message she'd leave where it was bound to be discovered. Maybe she'd even have time for a second note she could hide in her clothing. That way it would be ready to pass to someone, anyone, should the opportunity ever occur.

Where? Where was her pen? She never failed to keep one or two of them in her purse, along with a couple of pencils. And there were always bits of paper. She raked frantically through the assortment. Gone. Even her lipstick had been removed. Nothing to write with or write it on, unless you counted several tissues.

Damn him. He had managed at some point to empty her bag of anything she might use to contact help. No wonder he had trusted her to keep it. There was nothing here that would do her any good. Disgusted, she started to close the purse. That was when her attention was captured by the packets of sugar which had accumulated on the bottom. Her fingers sifted through them. She was seized by an inspiration.

OFFICER JUDY BELUCCI presented herself in the cluttered office to which she had been summoned.

"Sir?"

Superintendent Hamish Bolling waved her to a chair in front of his desk and went on studying one of the crime lab reports that were routinely submitted to him. Judy slid into the chair and waited for him to shift his attention in her direction.

She had a lot of respect for Ham Bolling. He was a thirty-year veteran of the St. Louis police force, a bull of a man with grizzled hair and glasses that were forever sliding down his nose. Like most of his officers, Judy regarded him as tough but scrupulously fair.

However, she was puzzled by Bolling's action in connection with the manhunt for Noah Rhyder. The homicide division Bolling commanded was not responsible for recovering the fugitive, but he had asked her to be an unofficial liaison between him and the team that was in charge of the search. He hadn't bothered to explain the request.

Superintendent Bolling finally shoved the report to one side and looked at her over his glasses. "All right, Belucci, what's the latest from the other side?"

"Not much, sir. Kenny DeMarco is back in custody and not talking." Bolling nodded impatiently. He obviously already knew the mobster had been recaptured. "But Rhyder is still out there somewhere. They think now he can't be alone, that someone must be hiding him, only nothing has turned up so far."

"His kid?"

"In the East and safe with his guardian. It isn't likely Rhyder will get anywhere near him, even if he tries."

She watched the superintendent poke at his slipping glasses. He was silent, thoughtful for a moment, then he made up his mind.

"Tell you what, Belucci. Let's get Lew Ferguson in on this, see what he has to say."

She was surprised. "Sir," she reminded him, "you removed Detective Ferguson from the case before it ever went to trial."

"I know, but the review board was satisfied the spot of blood on Rhyder's shirt cuff wasn't planted evidence." He shrugged. "And who knows. Maybe it could have happened when Rhyder punched Senator Buchanan in the nose and not when he finished him off with the poker. With all the other evidence, it ended up not mattering. The point is, Lew seemed to have gathered a lot of information about Rhyder. With his knowledge, maybe he has some insights that could be useful in locating the fugitive. Something we could pass on to the team."

"Detective Ferguson is off duty for a couple of days, sir."

"Call him. Have him come in."

Judy got to her feet. She didn't like Lew Ferguson, maybe because he was too much of a loner, but it wasn't her place to say so. There was something, though, that she did feel entitled to ask before she returned to her desk.

"Sir, you never explained when you gave me this assignment just why you're so interested in the fugitive. Our division was finished with Noah Rhyder when he was sentenced. Is there something about the case that doesn't satisfy you?"

He shook his head. "No, I'm convinced we got the right man. To tell you the truth, I'm not sure what's got me itching. Let's hope Lew can scratch it for me."

But that wasn't going to happen anytime soon, Judy realized an hour later when Bolling called her back into his office from her desk in the bull pen.

"Sir, I'm unable to reach Detective Ferguson. He doesn't respond to his pager or answer his phone. I did speak to his landlady. She saw him leave the building with a suitcase, but she has no idea where he was going."

Judy watched Ham Bolling frown with displeasure. An officer's personal life was his own business, but the superintendent expected his people to maintain some channel of contact with the department, whether on or off duty. Lew Ferguson had apparently chosen to ignore that rule.

"All right, Belucci, let's have it."

"Sir?"

"There's something else on your mind."

She had to hand it to him. He had uncanny perception. "It's just that I ran into Phil Gates on my way to communications."

"Lew's last partner. With narcotics now."

"Yes. I asked him about Detective Ferguson, thinking maybe he knew how to reach him. He didn't, but he did share something about Ferguson and the Buchanan case that he said no one wanted to hear at the time.''

"Go on."

"He said Ferguson had this intense need to prove Noah Rhyder was guilty. That it was more than just a good detective determined to get the murderer. *Personal.* That was the word Phil used to describe it. He said Detective Ferguson was too personal about it."

This time Bolling didn't bother adjusting his glasses. He removed them altogether. "Maybe I've got more here than just an itch that needs scratching. I think Lew and I need to have a real discussion. Keep trying, Belucci. I want him located."

Chapter Six

The sealed sugar packets were the kind that fast-food restaurants supplied with containers of coffee. Whenever Ellie, who hated waste, was given more of the packets than she needed, she tucked them away with the intention of one day making use of them. She rarely did. Instead, weeks or months later, while cleaning out her purse or glove compartment, she would discover the forgotten collection, stale by now, and throw it away.

Sitting there in the rest-room stall, Ellie blessed both her thriftiness and her failure to sanitize her purse in the last six months. She counted the packets which had settled to the bottom of the bag. There were fourteen of them. Was that enough?

How much sugar did it take to foul up a carburetor? She had no idea. She wasn't even sure that sugar poured into a gas tank would have any effect at all on a car. Maybe it was just an automotive myth.

On the other hand, short of doing nothing, and that had become unthinkable, what else was left for her to try? Noah was guarding her too carefully to permit her to escape or to contact help without risking lives, including her own. But if she could secretly sabotage the van, stop him cold in his tracks...

All right, so a dead engine wouldn't prevent him from

reaching North Carolina. It would, however, force him to seek repairs or another method of transportation. Either way, it meant contact with other people. A situation in which he might be identified or where she could safely signal her need. If nothing else, it would delay him, and time was his enemy.

Anything was possible, providing, of course, she could manage this little trick without his knowledge. But if he'd left the packets in her purse, it couldn't have occurred to him that—

"What's taking you so long in there?" he called, startling her with the sound of his knuckles thumping on the rest-room door.

"I'll just be a minute," she shouted back.

The sugar! She couldn't leave it in the packets like this. It would have to be loose, ready to dump into the tank. How could she contain it until then and at the same time conceal it in a way that would appear innocent? There was nothing available but the tissues.

Working with a feverish haste, Ellie slit the packets and dumped their contents into layers of tissue. All the while she feared that at any second he would lose patience, burst into the rest room, and discover what she was doing.

"Hey!" he called again.

"Coming, I'm coming."

Slipping the tissue-wrapped sugar into her purse, and covering the bulge with a couple of crumpled tissues, she flushed the empty packets and left the stall.

Noah gazed at her suspiciously when she joined him on the sidewalk outside. "What were you up to in there all this time?"

"Chiseling an SOS with my nail file. Look if you don't believe me."

"Think I won't?"

Taking her by the hand, he drew her back inside the rest room where he rapidly checked both stalls. Ellie held her breath, praying she'd left no telltale grains of sugar behind and that he wouldn't demand to search her purse again.

Satisfied, and without mentioning her purse, he ushered her out to the van. They had lost considerable time here in the park, and he was in a hurry to get them back on the highway. He wasn't going to be pleased by the necessity of another stop. Too bad.

She waited until they'd regained Ridley's main street to tell him. "We're low on gas."

"Again?" he grumbled.

"It was early this morning when I last filled up. Since then we've crossed Kentucky and a good chunk of Tennessee. How far do you think this van can go on a tank of gas?"

"All right, pull into the next station, and make sure that like the last one, it has a credit card facility at the pumps."

They reached the edge of town before she found what he ordered. Once again he appropriated the keys after she turned off the engine.

"Okay, Ellie, you know the drill."

She did. It was what she had been counting on. Thankfully, he let her keep her purse when she climbed from the van, regarding it as harmless now. He still had her sweater tied around his waist to conceal the gun in his belt. He didn't need her purse anymore for that.

Repeating his caution of this morning, he mounted guard at the hood of the van while she handled the fill-up. Now comes the fun part, she thought. Executing a bit of legerdemain on a man who had the eyes of a worried panther, which meant she had to get the sugar into the gas tank without his catching her doing it. But Ellie had foreseen this part and planned for it.

While waiting for the tank to automatically fill, she opened her purse and removed her credit card from her wallet. He would approve of her having the card out and ready, anything to lessen their time at the station. It made a reason to leave her purse conveniently open, hanging by its strap from her shoulder.

Seconds later, the snap of the shutoff indicated the tank was filled. Her finger quickly depressed the lever as she removed the nozzle, allowing gas to trickle down the side of the van. Muttering over the "accident," she reached inside her purse.

"What are you doing?" he demanded when she produced the wad of tissues.

"Just mopping up a bit of spilled gas. Well, it's your own fault. You make me nervous watching my every move."

He grunted something, but he remained at the hood while she dealt with the spill. His watchful gaze even flicked away long enough, when another car pulled into the station, to permit her to swiftly tip the contents of the tissues into the tank. When he looked back, she was securing the cap.

Her tension was almost unbearable by the time they left the station. But she had done it! She had sneaked the sugar into the tank! How long before it worked? *If* it worked.

Lord , she hoped it produced results, provided her some avenue of escape. Her need to get away from him was growing more urgent with every hour she spent in his potent company. She hated the emotions he stirred in her. They confused her, especially after the park, creating doubts she didn't want.

It was afternoon when they finally put Ridley behind them. She disliked leaving the town where service stations were readily available. A dead van out on the open road would definitely complicate things, and she had sort of hoped that before then... But so far there were no signs of trouble. Anyway, she couldn't expect to order a breakdown in an ideal location.

They were on the highway now. Ellie kept waiting for some sound or sensation that would tell her the engine was failing. There was nothing, not a stutter or a falter.

"What are you listening for?" he challenged her.

Had her anticipation been that obvious? She was going to have to be more careful. But since he was already questioning her concern, she decided not to hide it.

"I thought maybe the motor was running a bit rough."

"Sounds fine to me."

That was the problem. It didn't sound anything but normal. The minutes passed, and it went on performing smoothly. It must have been better than a half hour since the sugar had gone into the tank. Why hadn't the carburetor suffered by now?

Face it, Ellie. It was a wasted effort.

Her disappointment was considerable.

Another twenty minutes went by. They were in rugged country now, heavily wooded ridges and deep hollows with the farms few and widely scattered. And that's where it happened. The van was climbing a long hill when it started to miss and chug. At the top the engine gave out. Ellie coasted onto the gravel shoulder.

There was a brief silence. Noah ended it with a healthy curse, followed by an exasperated, "Don't say it, Ellie. I'd hate to hear how I should have listened to you."

"You should have listened to me."

He glowered at her. She was able to conceal her satisfaction, mostly because the sugar couldn't have picked a worse spot to finally work its magic. There were no other cars on this stretch of the highway and not a dwelling in sight. She hadn't planned on stranding them in the wilderness.

"Maybe you can fix it."

"I'm an architect, Ellie, not a mechanic."

"Well, all I know how to do under a hood is check the oil."

"Then let me suggest something."

"Like what?"

"Try starting it again."

"Oh."

She turned the key, and the engine came back to life. But it was plain that it was still ailing and that they couldn't depend on it to take them the rest of the way to North Carolina.

"Hold on," he said, producing the map as they continued to sit by the side of the road with the engine trembling and threatening to expire again.

She watched him as he opened the map and consulted it.

"Yeah, here it is." He held the map toward her, showing her what he intended. "We just passed it back down the hill where it joins the highway. A county road." He traced the line on the map. "See, it's only a few miles along here to a town called Homer. Bound to be a mechanic there."

"You're an optimist. This engine is sick. We'll get stuck out there along a back road."

"So we hike to Homer and a tow truck, and along the way you get to scout locations for your next masterpiece. It's the nearest town, Ellie."

She was getting exactly what she'd schemed for. Why was she beginning to regret it?

"I don't suppose we have a choice," she agreed.

She turned the van around with care. It protested the effort but kept breathing. This time gravity was on their side. They rolled down the hill without a problem.

"Coming up on the left, Ellie."

His constant directions were irritating and unnecessary. She could plainly see for herself the sign that marked the turning for Homer. When she braked and swung the wheel, the van stalled again. She coaxed it back to life, pumping furiously to feed it sufficient gas.

"You're going to flood it," he warned.

She glared at him, fought a rising panic, and managed to ease the vehicle through the turning. They proceeded along the narrow county road, dipping, then laboring over another rise.

"Careful," he cautioned. "There's a sharp bend coming up. Are you watching the gas? This thing is spitting again."

"If you think you can do any better, then you take the wheel," she snapped at him. "Otherwise, just close your mouth and let me drive."

He was silent. They continued another mile along the winding road. The van was coughing in earnest now.

"Don't think we're gonna make Homer, after all," he decided, scanning the roadside. "Hey, a mailbox ahead. Looks like the entrance to a farm on the other side. We're in business, Ellie. They've got to have a phone."

She wasn't so sure about that. The rusted rural mailbox was leaning at a drunken angle, and the mouth of the driveway just beyond it looked fit for nothing but horses. But she couldn't argue their need for immediate assistance. The van was barely clinging to life.

Slowing, she turned into the lane. They jounced over ruts and grassy humps, crawled about fifty yards, and arrived at a stand of overgrown lilacs. The van wheezed to a halt, uttering a final death rattle before subsiding into an ominous silence. Ellie knew, even as she tried to start it again, that it was hopeless. The vehicle was going nowhere this time.

"Guess nobody's at home," Noah said, indicating what was left of the house just beyond the lilacs.

It must have burned years ago, she thought in disappointment. All that remained was a chimney and a stone foundation.

"Aha, they relocated. See it?"

She did. Farther along the lane, perhaps a quarter of a mile distant across fields and meadows, were a house and a barn. The farm, which looked intact, was nestled against a hillside.

"Maybe we'll get to use that telephone, after all. Come on, Ellie."

She grabbed her purse, joining him as he climbed from the van. The track curved away to the left and then doubled back again just below a gentle slope. A footpath, or what was left of one, offered a shortcut through the yard of the ruined homestead. Direct route or not, it was choked with waist-high weeds and brambles. Noah started to wade through them without pause, looking back when she didn't immediately follow.

"What are you waiting for?"

"If it's all the same to you, I'll stick to the driveway."

He stopped and turned around. "You forgetting the rule, Ellie? Where I go, you go." He began to back away along the path, as if demonstrating its innocence. "Some location painter. Worried about a few thistles."

"I don't suffer for my art. At least not that way." She turned her head to glance longingly at the lane, indicating her preference for it. "Why should I when—"

She broke off in bewilderment as she looked back. She was talking to empty air. There was no one there on the path. He was gone, not a sign of him.

"Hey, where are you?"

No answer. This was crazy. Short of being snatched by aliens, how could he just vanish into nowhere? She hesitated, struggling with an urge to turn and flee in the direction of Homer. No, she couldn't do that. Not without knowing what happened to him.

Moving forward, she cautiously followed his course through the weeds. The thread of the path carried her straight to the explanation for his disappearance. In fact, she almost stumbled into it herself.

A well. He had backed into an old, stone-lined well. It had probably once been equipped with a hand pump on a wooden platform, but the pump had been removed when the well went dry. Since then the platform had rotted away, leaving the abandoned well wide open.

Ellie knelt on the crumbling, ground-level lip and peered into the depths, fearing what she would find. The well, hand-dug, was several feet in diameter and perhaps twenty feet to the bottom. The walls were still intact and so was the figure gazing up at her from below.

"Wondered when you'd decide to get here."

"Are you hurt?"

"No, I came down like an arrow, never touched the sides, and landed in about two feet of muck. It was as good as a net, but it stinks like hell."

If he had broken his neck, her concerns, as well as those of the state of Missouri, would have been solved. But she was glad he hadn't, though she refused to question her relief.

"People who own this land ought to be shot for leaving a thing like this wide open," he complained.

"Maybe they thought no one would be dumb enough to fall into it. Can you get out?"

"Does it look like I can? We'll need the rope from the van. You'll have to tie several lengths of it together, or it won't reach. Hope there's a tree up there for you to wrap your end around."

"And you're sure you aren't injured?"

"Told you I wasn't. What are you waiting for?" She didn't answer him. "Ellie?"

"Yes?"

"You're not going to help me out of here, are you?"

She smiled down at him where he stood in the gloom. "Don't be silly. I wouldn't just leave you down there. But you're going to have to be patient. It may take me a while to get back here with the local sheriff and his deputies."

Noah gazed up at her where her beguiling face was framed against the circle of light. He thought she'd softened back in the park where he had shared his story with her.

He thought maybe she had begun to believe him, trust him a little. He was wrong. And he was angry.

"Why, you little—"

She drew back, her head disappearing from view. Her voice floated down to him, sweetly taunting. "I hope there are some frogs down there to keep you company. *Sympathetic* ones."

Then she was gone.

ELLIE GAZED in discouragement at the farmhouse. She would find no telephone here, or any friendly occupants to help her. Now that she was at close range, she could see the place was little more than a shell with a roof that was beginning to collapse. The barn was in better shape, but like the house it must have been deserted for years.

Now what? she wondered. Homer, of course. She had no other choice. She had to hike to the town and hope that, along the way, she could either signal a passing car or find a farm that *was* inhabited. Not that she was counting on either one. This was lonely hill country.

Homer was still a good distance away, and the afternoon was lengthening. She needed to get moving. Instead, she stood there, looking back up the long slope. She was reluctant to return to the county road by retracing her path to the useless van. It would mean passing close by the well.

Ellie was trying not to think of Noah and how she had left him down there. Trying not to feel guilt over her action. Why should she when he was a killer, a fugitive who had kidnapped her? When, ever since St. Louis, she had been praying for escape and the chance to turn him in?

No, she wouldn't go near that well again. If she did, she might surrender to temptation, make the effort to haul him out. Was there another route? She thought there might be.

The track didn't end here at the farmhouse. She could see that it passed the weathered barn before curving to the right along the breast of the hill. She remembered noticing, just before they'd turned into the driveway, that ahead of them the county road swooped down to the left.

Ellie thought it was very likely the lane behind the barn joined the county road after that loop, possibly lessening the distance to Homer. There was every indication it was the primary entrance to the property, because the drive ahead of her was in better condition than the one behind her, as though it had been maintained for regular use.

It made sense, and she decided to go with it.

Crossing a ditch behind the barn, where water spilled away from a spring-fed pool, she struck off up the dirt track that clung to a man-made terrace on the side of the hill.

An artist who favored the pastoral couldn't have asked for a better scene, with the farm down in the hollow and the woods on her left a riot of autumn colors. Ellie cared about none of it at this moment.

She cared even less when the track rounded the hill and plunged into the woods, putting the farm out of sight behind her. It was a dense woods, thick with tangled growth. With the sky still overcast and the afternoon already waning, shortened by the season, the light was anything but cheerful. She refused to think of being caught out here after sundown. There was still plenty of time to reach Homer before nightfall.

But Ellie was less confident about that as the minutes passed and she failed to reach the paved road. How far had she come? Difficult to tell with the track dipping and winding every which way through the forest.

Her certainty that she was following the farm's driveway ebbed rapidly as she moved on without result. This couldn't be right. The distance was too great, the lane too rough and narrow now. She didn't know why it had been cut through the woods, maybe just to fell and haul timber. Whatever the reason, she had made a mistake in choosing it. What now?

There was a fork just ahead. When she reached it, she

stopped. She had a decision to make. The left branch was the main track, but it twisted off in the wrong direction, looking like a tunnel that would vanish into the heart of the forest. The other branch, though no better than a footpath, offered more hope. For one thing, it sliced straight through the trees in what had to be the right direction for the county road. Even better, she could see clear daylight in the distance, an indication that the path emerged from the forest.

There was a third choice. She could play it safe and return to the farm and that other connection to the county road. But Ellie was reluctant to do that, not because of the time she would lose or the necessity of passing the well. Going back would mean dealing with all that forest again, and she wanted to leave the woods.

It was suddenly too quiet in here, the shadows too thick now. She didn't like it. Sensible or not, she wanted the quickest way out. The path promised that.

Seconds later, hurrying along the trail, she had the uneasy feeling she was no longer alone. The silence was even deeper than before, but she couldn't shake the impression of someone, or something, behind her. Was she being stalked?

Pausing, she listened. Nothing. And then she heard it. A rustling off in the underbrush. She wasn't imagining it! There *was* something out there watching her!

Whatever it was, Ellie wasn't interested in identifying it. All she cared about now was getting to that opening at the end of the path. Her mouth dry with fear, she rushed toward the light, only to face another disappointment when she arrived at its source.

This wasn't the end of the woods. It was a clearing, what they called a heath bald in the eastern mountains. It was carpeted with mountain laurel that would dazzle the eyes when it bloomed in the spring. Just now the stuff was nothing but a frustration as she squeezed through its snarled, shiny growth, the tough branches whipping her legs and snagging her clothes.

A root caught her by the ankle, throwing her to the ground. The earth was still wet from this morning's rain. Her hands and knees were plastered with mud when she picked herself up and moved on, determined to gain the other side of the clearing where the path continued through the trees.

She was winded and weary when she reached the place. She didn't care what was after her. She had to rest. There was a stump, and she perched on it, clutching her purse. Alert for trouble, she looked, listened. No sign of anything, no menacing sound. She heaved a sigh that was part relief, part despair.

No point in denying it. She was lost, no longer able to tell north from south. How could she have been such a fool to get herself caught in here? And how was she going to get out? If she wandered around much longer, it would be dark. The thought of spending the night in these woods, alone with whatever lurked out there in the trees, made her shudder.

There was something else, something she could no longer block from her mind. Noah. He would be trapped in the well until morning. Whatever he had done, she couldn't stand the thought of him in that deep hole all night. He must already be imagining the worst, suffering the certainty that she had left him there to die.

She had to find a way out of here. She had to get back to him, even if it meant retracing her route.

Ellie was on her feet, ready to pursue the path, when she heard it again. A body stirring in the underbrush not far away. It wasn't any small animal like a squirrel either. This was something much larger, something that grunted. The hairs stood up on the back of her neck.

She no longer considered going back through the laurel

thicket. She thought about nothing but running in the opposite direction, which was exactly what she did.

Crunching over fallen nuts and drifts of leaves, she fled through the trees. Whatever was behind her was not staying behind her. It was coming after her. She could hear it crashing through a mass of dogwood and wild grapevines.

What had happened to the path? It had somehow disappeared. *Forget about it. Just keep moving.*

Seconds later she could have shouted with joy when the woods thinned at last. Not that she had breath left in her for anything more than racing through the last of the white oaks and the shortleaf pines.

She was out at last! And there below her was the derelict farm. She had circled back to where she had started. All this time she had been going nowhere. It didn't matter, not when the farm offered safety.

Nothing left to negotiate but a steep pasture. If she could reach that barn, somehow barricade herself inside...

Too late! The thing pursuing her was directly behind her now, snorting like a pig. Ellie stopped and whipped around in terror to confront her enemy.

It *was* a pig. And not a friendly farm animal either. She had heard about the wild razorback hogs that roamed the remote country in Tennessee. They were large, savage creatures, and they didn't like their territory invaded. This one apparently regarded Ellie as a serious trespasser.

He wasn't charging. Not yet. He had come to a halt when she turned. He stood there a few yards away, taking her measure. He had the meanest-looking eyes of any beast she'd ever encountered. Trying not to arouse him, she kept very still, which was nearly an impossibility since she was trembling in every limb.

The seconds passed, and they felt like eons. The hog pawed the ground, suddenly worried by something behind her. She didn't dare turn her head to learn what. A moment later a familiar voice spoke softly at her back.

"Keep it easy, Ellie. We don't want to make bacon here unless we have to."

She didn't question his silent arrival, didn't wonder how he had managed to get out of the well. She didn't think about anything but how glad she was to see him as he moved cautiously to her side. He had the revolver in his hand. The hog eyed him nervously.

Noah raised the gun. "If you get tough, pig, I get tough right back. What's it gonna be?"

The animal was undecided.

"I figure," he whispered to her, as if he were convinced the hog would actually understand him if it overheard, "that he's like these street gangs I once had an acquaintance with. You get caught on their turf, you'd better be prepared to bluff your way out of it. Unless, of course, you run like hell."

"I tried that. It didn't work. I hope you know what you're doing."

"I don't, but he doesn't realize that." Noah raised his voice, waving the gun. "Come on, pig, make up your mind. Either you back off, or you get a taste of this."

The hog lifted its head with disdain, pivoted sharply, and trotted back into the woods. Ellie resisted the temptation to hug Noah with relief as he stuck the gun back into his waistband.

"Let's get out of here," he urged, "before he decides to come back."

She had no argument with that. They scrambled down the open hillside, not stopping until they were within reach of the barn. He turned then to regard her, grinning over the mud on her hands and knees and the snag in her sweater.

"Looks like you had a rough time of it in the wilderness, Rembrandt. Lost your way, did you?"

"At least *my* mud doesn't smell."

"Yeah, well, you try staying daisy-fresh climbing out of a hole in the ground."

"But you did manage it."

"Eventually. There were enough crevices between the stones to dig into, providing a person was mad enough to stick with it. And I was. Not very nice of you to leave me down there, Ellie."

"Are you still mad?"

"I'll let you know. After we've cleaned up. Looks like the sink is over here."

She offered no objection, following him as he led the way to the spring-fed pool. The water bubbling over a rocky ledge was shockingly cold, but it looked pure enough to drink. Ellie was so thirsty that she risked it, using her hands to cup water into her mouth. They spent the next several minutes silently ridding themselves of the worst of the mud.

She looked up when she was finished, knowing she could no longer avoid an expression of her gratitude. "Thank you for saving me from Porky," she said briefly.

He nodded an acknowledgment, making no further reference to her desertion of him in the well. Nor did she offer any apology. The situation was already getting too friendly. How was she going to betray him after he'd rescued her like that?

Of course, he rescued you, she told herself sharply. He needs you to find Joel. Just remember that.

What a mess. She was back to where she had started, his prisoner again. Only this time the circumstances were worse. It was already dusk, they had no transportation out of here, and the sky was threatening another downpour.

He must have read her concern, because he offered a nonchalant solution. "Looks like we spend the night in the barn there, Ellie."

She didn't relish the prospect of another intimate night alone with him. But she had no better suggestion. Besides, even if it had been possible to go on to Homer, she was too weary at this point to attempt it.

"I guess we don't have a choice about it," she agreed, glancing in the direction of the house with its sagging roof. "At least the barn doesn't look like it would come down on top of us."

"Funny thing about appearances," he observed. "Back at the van we would have sworn that house was all in one piece. It just goes to show things aren't always what they seem. People either, huh?"

If he was referring to himself, she wasn't prepared to discuss the subject again. Turning her back on him, she started for the barn. He came after her, catching up with her as she climbed the earthen ramp and ventured through the yawning doorway.

The twilight had deepened, leaving the lofty interior heavy with shadows. There was the smell of dust and moldy decay in the stillness.

"Think we're gonna find our bed up there," he said, indicating a loft that revealed in the gloom a quantity of abandoned hay. "You prepared to spend a night in the hay with me, Ellie?"

He might have been joking, but she eyed the loft with uncertainty. "Maybe it's better if we go back to the van."

"Sure, we could do that. Wouldn't hurt us to get wet."

He nodded toward the open doorway. She had been too busy worrying about bedding down in the hay with Noah Rhyder to notice rain was falling. The kind of hard, steady rain that had settled in for the night. They would be soaked if they tried to reach the van now.

"You win," she said.

He motioned her toward the ladder, staying close behind her as she scaled it. The last of the daylight, stealing between the gaps that were everywhere in the walls of the building, permitted them to find their way around the loft. There were also chinks in the roof through which the rain dripped.

They managed to find a dry corner where they lowered

Fugitive Father

themselves on a mound of hay. There was a silence between them as they sat side by side, knees drawn up. Ellie was aware of the awkwardness of the moment and feared its result. She was relieved when he spoke, even if the subject was a painful one.

"Don't suppose you gathered any nuts when you were out there in the woods?"

"You *would* remind me of how hungry I am."

"Nothing we can do about it until we get to Homer."

Silence again. No other sound but the rain beating on the roof. The tension was between them again. She dealt with it by extracting a comb from her purse. Her braid had suffered on her flight, with escaped strands poking in every direction. She unfastened what was left of it.

When she became aware of him gazing at her intently in the murky light, she stopped combing her long, loose hair. There was an expression on his face that made her insides flutter and her fingers tighten on the comb.

"Relax," he growled suddenly. "I'm too tired from that well to play house with you. Or barn either."

She could sense a harsh determination in him when he stretched out on the hay, his back deliberately turned to her. There was no mention tonight of binding their wrists together, even if the rope had been available. They both knew she wasn't going anywhere.

She listened to the sound of the rain. Seconds later she could also hear the sound of his deep, even breathing. He was asleep. Realizing that she was equally exhausted, she couldn't prevent herself from burrowing down in the hay and drifting off.

It was completely dark in the barn when, sometime later, she opened her eyes. The temperature had dropped with nightfall, and she was shivering. But it wasn't the cold that had awakened her. Noah was up and moving around in a stealthy manner.

"What are you doing?" she challenged him as she felt a mysterious activity around her body.

"Nothing. Go back to sleep."

And then she understood what was happening. He was covering her with a blanket of hay to keep her warm.

"You don't have to do that," she whispered.

"Sure I do. I don't keep you healthy, I don't find Joel."

She had discovered him being considerate, and he was embarrassed about it. His concern was touching and at the same time disturbing. How could she go on regarding him as the enemy when he insisted on protecting her? This had to stop! She couldn't go on being susceptible to him, either physically or emotionally. She had to detach herself, and then somehow...

But it would have to wait. Now that he had heaped the hay over and around her, she was no longer cold. She was nothing but sleepy.

Much later, when she stirred again, she was vaguely conscious that the rain had stopped. There was the call of a whippoorwill somewhere out in the night. It was a comforting sound. Equally reassuring was the presence of the man settled close beside her, but she was much too drowsy to go into that.

The next time she came awake it was daybreak, with fingers of pale light stealing through the cracks of the barn. Curled on her side, she was aware of Noah next to her in the hay. He was on his back and snoring softly. The revolver was out of his waistband, probably because it had been uncomfortable trying to sleep with it there. It was down at his side now between them, his fingers clasped around the butt.

No longer in a vulnerable fog, alert now, Ellie realized what she had to do.

Chapter Seven

She didn't stand a chance of getting the revolver away from him. If she tried to snatch it from his hand, he would be awake in a flash. She had made that mistake before and didn't care to repeat it. And, face it, even if she had it in her possession, she had no idea how to use it. Nor did she *want* to use it.

What Ellie did mean to do, if she could manage it, was to render the weapon useless by removing the bullets. She had been terrified of the thing ever since he had invaded her house back in St. Louis, scared that if he didn't deliberately shoot her, or someone else, he might accidentally discharge the thing in a tight moment, which could be just as bad.

Considering her fear and hatred of guns, what she intended was probably very foolish, but she was prepared to risk it. Anything to disarm him. Once she had the bullets, she could easily dispose of them, and with care and luck he would never know that she'd emptied the chambers. Not unless he tried to use the gun anyway.

She checked on him. Still sleeping. Either she acted now, or she'd lose her chance. Quietly, slowly, she slid along his length until her eyes were level with the revolver. It had a swing-out cylinder whose chambers contained the ammunition. That much she could see and understand. The question was, how did you release the cylinder? Must be that little thingamabob there. Nothing else made sense.

All right, she knew what she had to do. The trick was to open the cylinder without disturbing him, an operation that would require steady care. Why not? She was an artist capable of light, delicate brushwork. How different could this be?

Making sure his eyes were still closed, ordering her fingers not to shake, she steadied the weapon by its barrel with one hand. With the other hand, she applied pressure against the sliding lever without shifting the gun. She caught her breath. What if she made a mistake? What if she fired the thing?

There was a soft click. The revolver was angled in such a way in his grasp that the cylinder popped open without a protest. Even better, Noah never stirred. Neither the sound nor the slight movement had been sufficient to wake him. Now all she had to do was ease the bullets out of the chambers. Where were they? She couldn't see them.

Squinting, she peered into the swing-out cylinder, searching for the ammunition. There was a very good reason why she couldn't locate the bullets. They weren't there. All six chambers were empty.

"Interesting area for your head to be, Ellie," came his deep, lazy voice from above her. "Some guys might define the position as damn arousing. Even be prepared to accommodate you."

He was awake. For all she knew, he'd been awake the whole time and silently laughing at her. Her gaze lifted accusingly.

"It isn't loaded."

"It could be. Wouldn't take much effort on your part." He grinned down at her lasciviously.

She shoved herself back from the vicinity of his hip, glaring up at him. "Damn it, you know I'm talking about the gun."

"Oh, that." He carelessly tossed the revolver into the hay on his other side. "No, hasn't been loaded since St. Louis. I took out the ammo first thing after I got the piece. Hell, Ellie, guns are dangerous. I'm surprised at you. You think I would have been carrying around a loaded revolver stuck in my waistband? I could have shot off something vital to me."

He hadn't wanted to hurt anyone, including himself. This was what he was telling her in his flip way. She should have appreciated that, at least been relieved by it. But all she could feel was smoldering anger.

"Let me get this straight. You've terrorized me with that thing, kidnapped me, held me hostage, threatened me at every turn, and the whole time it was empty. Does that about cover it?"

"Well, yeah."

"I see. And now that I know, you don't seriously imagine you're going to go on controlling me."

She hadn't meant her challenge as an invitation for a demonstration, but that's how he chose to regard it. Scooting down in the hay, he put his face on a level with hers. "I don't think I need a gun anymore," he confided, his voice suddenly low and husky. "I think maybe I've got something better."

There was nothing about that battered face, so close now that his strong nose almost touched hers, she should have found appealing. Bits of hay clung to his chopped-off hair. He hadn't shaved since the night before last, leaving his lean jaw shadowed by a stubble of beard. The dark eyes forcefully holding hers gleamed with arrogant confidence. She ought to have considered all of it distasteful, been outraged by him. Not mesmerized by his raw, searing gaze. Not breathlessly aware of the heat of his body squeezed intimately toward hers.

"We both know I'm right, don't we, Ellie?"

There was a mellow, smoky quality in his voice now. It

was seductive. Seductive and alarming. She strove to combat it.

"Do we?"

"I think so." He lifted his big hand and touched her hair. His fingers were long and surprisingly sensitive. "I like your hair swinging loose like this. It's got fire in it. Sends off sparks like those amber eyes."

"Then maybe you'd better back off before you get burned." What was she doing telling him something like that? And why didn't she just remove herself from the situation? There was no gun or rope involved this time. Nothing to hold her down here. Nothing but his bold mouth moving toward hers.

"Not a chance, Ellie," he promised her with a whisper roughened by desire. "Not a chance."

It was there again on the side of his jaw. That muscle she had noticed twice before, twitching like the steady beat of a pulse. She found it strangely provocative. But before she could question it, his mouth had angled across hers.

His kiss was slow at first, almost languid as his hand continued to stroke her hair. Then he deepened their joining, his fingers telegraphing his need by winding themselves into her hair, tightening against her scalp while his lips tightened against her mouth. She, too, experienced the urgency of that kiss, her mouth welcoming his probing tongue.

Where was her resistance? Why was she permitting this wanton assault? Even worse, she was participating in his kiss. A connection that left her weak and confused and fatally susceptible.

He indicated as much when his mouth finally lifted from hers. "See, Ellie, much better than bullets."

Struggling to quell her rioting senses, she managed to croak a dry, "I don't think something like this would have helped if that pig had decided to charge us last night."

"Then I would have had to wrestle him into submission. Maybe something along *these* lines."

Before she could object, he seized her by her wrists and rolled her onto her back. When she tried to free herself, he covered her with his powerful length, his body pinning her down in the hay as he continued to hold her by her upraised arms.

"Let go of me," she demanded.

"Just trying to show you, Ellie."

She made the mistake of twisting her hips in an effort to throw him off. All she succeeded in doing was having her own body betray her. Her nipples tightened into rigid buds when his chest pressed against her breasts.

"Soft, Ellie," he murmured. "You are so damn soft."

His mouth lowered to hers, claiming her with another lingering kiss that involved his stroking tongue, his warm breath mingling with hers, and the musky aroma of him in her nostrils. Tremors coursed through her as he prolonged the kiss, savoring her lips with gentle little nibbles. His hands had released her wrists and were busy skimming the sides of her breasts. How was she supposed to withstand him when he was so blatantly, aggressively male? When her treacherous body yearned for his?

This was madness. He was a killer, a fugitive. She wasn't supposed to want him. It was wrong, wickedly wrong.

There was a complacent glint in his eyes when his mouth parted from hers. "Told you I didn't need the gun. Could be I've even made you forget all about Brett Buchanan. Have I, Ellie?"

Sanity returned to her in an angry rush. She heaved against him violently. "Let me up," she insisted. *"Now."*

He regarded her for a moment in silence, then complied, levering himself away from her. Ellie scrambled to her feet, putting distance between them before she trusted herself to turn and face him again. He was standing now, watching her.

"Unless you want to add rape to all the other charges against you," she informed him swiftly, "don't ever try anything like that again."

"Funny. How did I go and get the idea that force didn't have much to do with it?"

She was shaking by now, determined to deny his effect on her. "You think I wouldn't turn you in now, don't you? Well, you're wrong, because the first chance I get..."

NOAH DIDN'T DOUBT her promise, nor his need to prevent any opportunity to hand him over to the cops. She'd been waiting to do just that since St. Louis, and it looked like their little tussle in the hay changed nothing.

At the moment, however, he had no reason to deal with this threat. They had the country road to themselves as they tramped toward Homer. A few cars passed them, but none of them were interested in stopping. He didn't blame them. At this point in the journey, he and Ellie were looking pretty unsavory. The night spent in the barn certainly hadn't helped.

If there were inhabited houses along the route, they were located well off the road. Noah wasn't willing to invest any further time in investigating them. That left the necessity of this long hike.

Under other circumstances, it would have been a pleasant walk. The weather today was agreeable with clear skies and a warm autumn sun. There were mockingbirds in the cottonwood trees and the residue of last night's rain sparkling on the kudzu vines that sprawled over the banks on both sides of the road.

Yeah, even though he was on the run and worried sick about Joel, he might have enjoyed it. If he hadn't been so hungry his insides were howling. And *if* his companion had been willing to offer him more than a hostile silence as she trudged beside him.

Ellie had barely spoken to him since they'd left the barn.

Well, fine, let her fume. He had his own anger to deal with.
Anger with her because she was convinced his kisses had
been nothing more than an exercise in domination. And
anger with himself for having played that little game with
her in the loft. It was a temptation he should have resisted.

Then, to make matters worse, he had gone and taunted
her about Buchanan. Just like some damn jealous lover.
What the hell was wrong with him anyway?

But Noah had an uneasy feeling that he knew *exactly*
what was wrong with him. He was falling for her. Well, it
figured, didn't it? He had a positive genius for lousy timing.
It was the reason why he was in this mess, because if he
hadn't gone to the Buchanan mansion that afternoon…

Forget it. It had happened, and he couldn't go back and
change it. But he could still prevent a serious involvement
where Ellie Matheson was concerned. There was no future
in it, nothing but the certainty of hurting both of them. So,
no more episodes in haylofts.

He slid a glance in her direction. She had bound her hair
in the braid again. Good. She was much less alluring that
way. Yeah, sure she was. Who was he kidding? She could
shave her head and he would still want her. Given half the
chance, he'd take her right here in the ditch.

Wasn't going to be easy keeping his promise not to touch
her again, was it? In fact, he knew it was going to cost him
a massive effort in self-restraint, and even then…

IT SEEMED TO ELLIE that most of the towns in this part of
Tennessee were situated in valleys, and Homer was no exception when they finally reached it. It was a sleepy-
looking, seen-better-days community strung out along a
curving ravine. They could view most of it from the heights
at the edge of the road where Noah stopped her before they
descended the last stretch.

"You get a choice before we go down there, Ellie," he
instructed her sternly. "Either you swear to behave your-

self, or—'' From his back pocket he produced the hateful length of clothesline he had retrieved from the van and waved it under her nose. ''—I tie and gag you and leave you parked behind the bushes over there until the van's repaired.''

The hike had been longer than they'd anticipated. She was too hot and exhausted to argue with him. She gave him the promise he demanded, though surely he must realize she had no intention of keeping it. But she would have to be careful about a contact with anyone in Homer. Noah had the revolver concealed again under the sweater wrapped around his waist. Its empty chambers might no longer be empty. He could have kept the bullets after removing them and reloaded the gun while she'd used the privy before leaving the farm.

It was in this cautious state that Ellie accompanied him down the steep hill. They passed the first houses at the edge of town and arrived at an intersection that offered them what they sought.

Ray's Gas and Repairs looked more like a graveyard for dead automobiles than a service station. But, judging from the size of Homer, it could be their only choice. Noah was prepared to risk it. *Why not?* she thought sourly. *It isn't his van.* Ellie had long since regretted her clever little strategy with the sugar in the gas tank. None of it had turned out as she'd planned, and at this point she was feeling positively bleak about the whole thing.

A bell tinkled above the door as they entered the ramshackle station. The interior was cluttered with junk, most of it looking like it hadn't seen a dustrag in years. There was no one in evidence, but from an open hatch in the back wall came the clang of metal against metal.

''Be with you in a minute,'' someone yelled from that same direction.

The bell must have been heard, which Ellie thought was

rather remarkable considering a TV had been left blaring on the counter.

"You keep quiet and let me handle it," Noah warned her as they waited for the mechanic to appear.

She eyed him in silence as he tugged at the brim of the Cards baseball cap. He'd put it on again during their walk, probably not to protect his head from the sun but in another effort to avoid recognition. Pretty unlikely in this place, she decided.

Seconds later Ellie had a reason to change her mind about that. She was busy sneaking looks for a telephone. The possibility of making a call was remote, but she didn't want to miss any opportunity. And that included somehow alerting the mechanic to her situation. She wasn't at all interested in the noisy television set. Not until the newscaster turned to a startling update on Noah Rhyder's escape.

"St. Louis police, suspicious about the murder of a deputy transporting the two prisoners, disclosed this morning that, after lengthy questioning, the surviving deputy confessed to killing his partner. He had been hired to stage the getaway of mobster Kenny DeMarco. DeMarco is now back in custody. Fellow prisoner, Noah Rhyder, though not involved in the scheme, is still at large." A picture of Noah with his beard and longer hair flashed on the screen. "And now a report on farm prices here in—"

A hand reached around from the hatch and switched off the TV.

"What can I do ya, folks?"

The mechanic had a drawl you could slice and a cheerful, freckled face. Leaning over the hatch, he wiped his grease-stained hands on a rag as he waited to help them.

Ellie was too stunned by what she'd heard on the newscast to offer him more than a glance. Her gaze fastened on Noah. His face was impassive. Whatever he felt about the report, or her reaction to it, he was careful not to let it show as he approached the hatch.

"Got a problem with our van, Ray."

The exchange that followed barely registered with Ellie. Noah explained their predicament. The mechanic listened, made sympathetic sounds that involved his tongue against his teeth, and promised to take his tow truck and haul their van into town. Yes, he could work on it right away. No, it wasn't necessary for them to accompany him. He had a helper out back who'd ride along. Breakfast? Well, sure, he could recommend a place just down the road here. The Sweetwater Café. Best grits in town. Time they ambled over there and ambled back he'd have the van here at the shop.

Ellie, still shaken by the newscast, made no attempt to communicate with the mechanic. Her mind was in a turmoil, able to think of nothing but Noah's innocence in the slaying of the young deputy. He had tried to tell her he wasn't guilty, and she had refused to listen. Then if he hadn't killed the deputy, was there a possibility— No, the murder of Howard Buchanan was an entirely separate issue. But the truth was, she no longer knew what to believe.

Her uncertainty remained with her on their short walk to the café. No one in the place indicated a particular interest in them. If they had seen the newscast, they weren't connecting the fugitive back in Missouri with the man and woman who strolled into their local café. She had hoped he *would* be identified somewhere on their journey. But then why should he be recognized when he had altered his appearance and, until now anyway, had avoided all direct contact with people? Besides, though he might be major news back home, they were a long way now from St. Louis. Ellie was silent as they were seated at a corner table at the back. She knew she ought to be making an effort to escape Noah's eternal vigilance, to contact the police. There were people here. Any one of them could help her. What was she waiting for?

She eyed her companion after their orders had been

taken. He had to be nervous about their presence in a public place. It involved all kinds of risk, including her threat to expose him. But if he was worried, he didn't show it.

"Don't you have anything to say?" she asked him in an undertone.

"Yeah, I should have ordered the waffles instead of the pancakes."

"You know I'm talking about the newscast."

He maintained his casual expression. "What's to say?"

"That you're relieved you've been cleared of that deputy's murder, for one thing."

"Okay, it matters. Now if you want to watch me get really ecstatic, it'll take the state of Missouri vindicating me in the death of Howard Buchanan. But we know that's not going to happen, don't we?" He leaned toward her across the table. "How about you, Ellie? You ready to believe in my innocence? Ready to swear you won't holler for the cops the minute I turn my back on you? Ready to share Joel's address with me?"

She could promise him none of those things, and both of them knew it.

She was still struggling with doubt and indecision when they returned to the service station. Ray had the van in the stall and was about to investigate its problem. Noah permitted her to remove a fresh outfit from her luggage before the mechanic went under the hood, trusting her to change in the dingy rest room with its stained fixtures.

Ellie felt less grubby once she'd washed up and put on clean slacks and a tunic top. By the time she emerged, Ray had located the trouble. She was afraid to hear it, knowing that Noah would never let her near another rest room when he learned about the sugar. Were there earthquakes in Tennessee?

"It's just what I figured it might be when you described the way she was behaving," the mechanic reported. "You got an ignition problem."

Ellie stared at him in disbelief. Her knowledge of cars was practically nonexistent, but she understood enough to realize that sugar in a gas tank could have no connection with a faulty ignition system. Could it?

"Are you sure?" she challenged the mechanic. "I mean, couldn't it be the carburetor gummed up or, say, the fuel pump? Something like that."

"Not a chance. It's ignition for sure."

Ironic. It had never been the sugar at all but something entirely unrelated. Her furtive effort had been a waste and a mistake, because the van would have quit without it. Now she had just gone and made another mistake. She had opened her mouth without thinking. She could feel Noah gazing at her suspiciously. It looked like that earthquake might occur after all.

"So," the mechanic asked, completely unaware of the sudden tension in his garage, "you want me to go ahead with the repair? Take a couple of hours."

"You do that, Ray," Noah assured him. "And maybe we'll take a little stroll around town while we wait for it. See the sights."

Before Ellie could object, he seized her by the hand and dragged her outside where they couldn't be overhead. When they reached the area of the pumps, he dropped her hand and turned to confront her with a pair of stormy eyes.

"All right, confession time. What did you do to the van?"

"I don't know what you're talking about."

"Like hell. You've got guilt written all over your face in big fat letters."

He was right. She could still feel the flush on her face that must have betrayed her the moment Ray explained the problem.

"We're not moving from here until you tell me," Noah warned her.

Why not? she thought. What was he going to do to her?

Lifting her chin in an attitude of defiance, she described in malicious detail her sneak attack on the van back in Ridley. When she was through, he smiled at her. It was not a pleasant smile.

"Real resourceful of you, Ellie. But did you actually think that a few measly packets of sugar in a full tank of gas would stop an engine?"

"If you're such an expert, why didn't you identify our problem to begin with? And since the sugar made no difference in the end, you don't have a reason to be angry about it."

"Oh, yeah, I do, because you tried to sabotage my transportation. I ought to break your neck for that. No, I've got a better idea. Hey, Ray," he shouted toward the raised door of the stall.

The mechanic's freckled face appeared in the opening. "You want some directions for that stroll?"

"Just one. Is there any place in town where we can shop for clothes?"

"There's Danielle's Boutique, which is a real hoot because everybody knows Danielle is Hazel Stoddard from over Iola way."

"It's for me, Ray."

"In that case, try Better Buy Discount. Down the end of Main Street. Just follow the road."

The mechanic ducked back into the stall. Noah turned to her. "Time I had something to wear besides your ex-husband's castoffs. Homer is gonna be real content with you, Ellie. Before we leave here, what with the repairs and some new outfits for me, that credit card of yours ought to get a real workout."

THE VAN WAS HAPPY, purring with new life as they regained the main highway and headed east again. Ellie's companion was also satisfied, his temper soothed by a shopping bag stuffed with purchases from Better Buy Discount.

She was the only one who was less than pleased. Noah's new wardrobe had cost her more than she cared to remember. She did have to admit, however, as she cast a glance at him slouched in the passenger seat beside her, that his outfit was a definite improvement over the discarded jeans and sweatshirt he'd been wearing since St. Louis. His lithe body was clad in tan slacks and a lightweight jacket over a knit shirt.

The clothes made him look respectable. Unfortunately, since they hugged him in all the right places, they also emphasized his lean masculinity. Ellie had trouble concentrating on the road.

He had been quiet since they'd left Homer just before noon. She knew he had to be regretting the time they'd lost because of the breakdown, that he must be more anxious than ever to reach Joel. He was clear and relentless about his objective. That hadn't changed. It was she who was no longer certain of anything in connection with Noah Rhyder. Her confusion about him, and, yes, her feelings toward him as well, had deepened since that newscast, promising her some difficult decisions. They would reach North Carolina before nightfall. What was going to happen when they arrived? And what was she going to do when it did happen?

It was mid-afternoon, and they were nearing the mountains, when Noah startled her with a sudden, "Stop the car!"

"What is it?"

"Stop the damn car!" he insisted.

There was a pull-off for a scenic overlook at the side of the road. She braked the van and coasted into it. When they were parked, she turned to him in alarm, waiting for him to give her an explanation. Without a word, he grabbed the keys to prevent her from taking off without him and scrambled out of the van. He never looked back as he headed for the low stone wall that framed the overlook.

Bewildered, Ellie followed him. There was excitement on his face when she caught up with him at the wall. "Look!" he said.

She followed his gaze. He was staring at a building perched alone on a knoll just across the narrow, wooded valley. The red brick structure had a domed roof and was fronted by a white-columned portico.

"You scare me out of my wits and almost cause an accident just because of that?" she said. "It's a house."

He was indignant. "It's not just any house. Don't you know what we're looking at?"

She glanced at him. He hadn't taken his eyes off the structure. "Maybe it's a little familiar. I suppose because it reminds me of a Greek temple. What do you want me to say? It's very pretty, okay?"

He snorted with disgust. "Just pretty, she says. How can anyone say *just pretty* about a genuine Thomas Jefferson? One of his original house designs was supposed to have been built right here in east Tennessee, and I bet anything this is it."

"How long have you had this love affair with Thomas Jefferson?" she asked him in wonder.

"Since I discovered he was a lot more than just a statesman. That he could create perfection like that. Look how pure the lines are. Everything is in balance, everything works."

He had the same awe in his voice, as he rhapsodized about the house, that she had when she was passionate about a painting. She was seeing a new dimension in him, and her appreciation of it both pleased and worried her. It also made her curious.

"What made you become an architect? Were you always interested in it?"

He answered her without removing his gaze from the

house. "I was a street kid, Ellie. I wasn't interested in much of anything but a fast motorcycle and looking for trouble."

"And girls."

"Yeah, girls, too." He smiled in memory. "I must have been eighteen, nineteen, and I was dating this hot redhead, a student at St. Louis University. She dragged me along with her on some assignment to the Gateway Arch. It was the last place I wanted to go."

"Let me guess. It ended up changing you forever."

"Something like that. I mean, I'd never been near the arch before, but suddenly here was this thing soaring into the sky over my head. It blew my mind. I kept going back there to visit the exhibits."

"With or without the redhead?"

"Without. I wasn't much fun by then. Too busy wanting to know who built this thing and why. That's when I learned all about Eero Saarinen and how he designed the arch as a memorial to Thomas Jefferson. A tribute from one architect to another."

"If I remember," Ellie gently corrected him, "the arch commemorates Jefferson not because he was an architect on the side but because he was the president who acquired the Louisiana Purchase, which made St. Louis the gateway to the west."

"Yeah, well, you look at history your way, and I'll look at it mine. All I knew was that I wanted to build structures of my own. Not arches maybe, but buildings that were beautiful and useful."

"Is that when you put the motorcycle away in the garage?"

"Hell, no, I needed it to take me back to school."

"It couldn't have been easy."

"It wasn't, but I didn't let that stop me."

She could imagine what, as a troubled teenager from the streets, he'd had to overcome to become a qualified architect. It must have involved sacrifice and a long struggle.

He turned his head to look at her, sensing the direction of her thoughts. "It isn't what you give up along the way that hurts, Ellie. It's what it costs you when you get there."

"I don't understand."

"I didn't want to be just an architect. I wanted to be a *successful* architect. You don't get that without money."

The Buchanans. He was talking about marrying into the Buchanan wealth.

"I told myself I loved Jennifer, and I did, but I wasn't *in* love with her. I did a pretty good job, though, of fooling myself I wasn't marrying her for the money and influence that came with her. It wasn't until afterward that I looked at myself and saw the truth." There was regret in his voice. "I think it was the same for her. I think she only wanted me because I was somebody she wasn't supposed to want."

Ellie eyed him as he stood there staring pensively at the house. He'd shifted his weight from one leg to the other, leaving a hip stuck out at a negligent angle. With his hands hooked into his back pockets, he offered an unconsciously sexy pose.

She could picture him looking like that in his youth, probably wearing black leather and maybe with his tough, rangy figure straddling a motorcycle. He would have been the image of every girl's fantasy. The wild, dark-eyed rebel representing danger and excitement.

Oh, yes, she could imagine how hard Jennifer Buchanan must have fallen for him and how much her father had opposed the match.

"Marriages like that aren't supposed to work," he said. "Funny thing is, ours wasn't bad. Maybe because I lived with what I'd done by being the best husband and father I could be."

"And there was Joel," she pointed out.

"Yeah," he said, his voice tender, "there was Joel. So it wasn't bad, except when her father interfered. It might have been even better if Jennifer hadn't gotten sick."

He was silent for another moment, and then he turned away from the wall with a resolute, "Let's go."

Ellie followed him back to the van, wishing they had never stopped. Wishing she hadn't just learned that this man had the poetry of architecture in him. Why did he have to make it so difficult for her? She wanted to go on thinking of him as a rough lout attractive to women only because he had a pair of predatory bedroom eyes. Instead, hour by insidious hour, Noah Rhyder revealed to her the layers of his character. Teaching her his sensitivity, his humor, and, worst of all, his irresistible sexiness.

She was blinding herself to the truth. He couldn't be any of those things. He had to be the merciless killer the law said he was.

That was what she told herself when she climbed behind the wheel. That was what she needed to believe. But as they pulled away from the overlook, he looked again at the house on the knoll. There was longing in his expression and a little smile of loss on his mouth, and she sensed his unspoken certainty that he would never again have the chance to execute one of his own designs. It was the smile that tugged at her. As she gazed at him, she lost all her resolve, and her heart along with it.

Oh, dear God, it couldn't be true! She couldn't be falling in love with him! But she feared it was already too late.

Chapter Eight

Ellie had been aware for some time now of the change in her passenger. He was a stranger again, silent and with a brooding expression on his lean face. She guessed what that look conveyed. Understood the intensity in him that seemed to deepen with each passing mile.

But she didn't want to face what was coming. She avoided the inevitable by distracting herself with the scenery. It wasn't difficult. They were deep in the mountains by now, and the views on all sides were breathtaking.

Rank after rank of lushly forested billows stretched to the horizon. The soft haze that lingered on the summits had given these ancient ranges their names. The Great Smokies to the south, the Blue Ridge Mountains to the north. Except they weren't blue in this serene light. The sinking sun had tinted their flanks in shades of deep rose and delicate pink, leaving the troughs between the peaks in purple shadow.

She knew that no artist's brush could replicate such a spectacle. The result would be garish, a poor substitute for the original. Sunsets were better left to nature.

"It's no use, Ellie."

His voice biting into the silence jarred her, forcing her attention away from the mountains. She knew what he was talking about, but she didn't answer him.

"You going to make me say it?" he demanded. "All

right, I'll say it. We passed the state line five miles back. This is it, North Carolina. You can't put it off any longer. Either you give me the address, or—''

"What?"

"It's a big state. I don't see us wandering up and down the highways until you decide to stop holding out on me."

"What makes you think I'm going to tell you now what I wouldn't tell you in St. Louis?"

"Still protecting your friend Buchanan? Or is he much more than a friend? Are you sleeping with him, Ellie?"

The twisting mountain road was dangerous. This was no place to lose her temper. She held her anger in check, refusing to answer him until a safe situation presented itself. She found what she was looking for within a half mile down the highway. Another scenic overlook. She pulled into it without hesitation, stopped the van, and swung around in her seat to vent her resentment.

"Once and for all, I am not having an affair with Brett Buchanan. But if I *was,* it would be none of your damn business. And I'll tell you something else. If you figured there was a way to get that address out of me, this isn't it."

What was she going to do about him? He was as mercurial as a Missouri wind. Just when you thought you knew what to expect of it, when it was warm and friendly and made you long to embrace it, it suddenly turned cold and forbidding. Noah was like that. In another mood this afternoon, he had revealed the vulnerable facets of himself. *Loving* qualities. But he had closed up since then, leaving her nothing but this harshness. His face was rigid and cruel in the hard light of the vanishing sun.

He wanted Joel's address. And she couldn't give it to him. She didn't dare because, the truth was, she still didn't trust him. Not when it came to Joel's welfare. She had no right to endanger the child, even if she had fallen in love with his father.

She feared that love. Feared that it might blind her to the reality of Noah Rhyder. Because nothing had changed. He was still a man on the run, and she had yet to be convinced he hadn't murdered Howard Buchanan.

"Oh, I'll get it out of you all right," he promised her, his voice laced with fierce determination. "I told you back in St. Louis that, before I was through with you, you'd tell me what I wanted to know. I meant it then, and I mean it now."

"How?" she challenged him recklessly. "Brute force?"

"Maybe I've got a much better idea. I think I can buy that address."

"Oh, you don't seriously think that I could be bribed into—"

"Not my money, Ellie. *Yours.*"

What on earth was he talking about?

"Yeah, I think so. We're gonna start spending, Ellie. We're gonna take those credit cards of yours and wear them out. If putting you in debt is what it takes to make you give in, then I'll do it. Starting now. Both of us can use a bath and a real bed. We're stopping for the night. A nice place. An expensive place."

"I won't sign the credit slips. Not this time."

"Wanna bet?" He produced the revolver from a deep pocket in his jacket, holding it up in the ruddy light to remind her of its existence. "Of course, I could be bluffing. Maybe I didn't keep the bullets after I removed them. Maybe I didn't reload this thing when you slipped out of the van to get rid of the wrappings from our carryout supper in that last town."

He popped open the swing-out cylinder, permitting her a glimpse of its loaded chambers before snapping it shut. "What do you know. I *wasn't* bluffing. Shall we go now, Ellie, and look for that nice place to spend the night?"

She didn't argue with him, but not because she was afraid he would actually shoot her if she refused to obey him. The knowledge she had gained of him since St. Louis persuaded her he wouldn't deliberately hurt her, however desperate he was to reach Joel. Of course, because he was such an enigma, she couldn't be absolutely certain of this, but it wasn't her reason for submitting to his will.

The truth was, she was exhausted from long hours behind the wheel, two nights of inadequate sleep, and the tension of being on the run with a wanted man. She also longed for a hot shower and fresh clothes. It would be dark soon, and the thought of spending another night in the open without facilities was unbearable. Yes, taking a room somewhere was an appealing idea. Time enough in the morning for a serious showdown with Noah.

Without another word, she put the van back on the winding highway. The lights of a village were winking down in the valley, where it was already dusk, as they descended the mountain. The place was called Sutter's Gap. She had noticed the name the last time Noah had consulted the map.

If only he knew how close Joel is now, she thought. She had looked at the map, and Sutter's Gap was less than ten miles away from the town that was the mailing address for the estate Brett Buchanan had rented. Its proximity made her nervous.

She was surprised that Noah wasn't uneasy himself, though for a different reason. He was taking a chance putting them in a lodging for the night where they would encounter other people. Someone could get suspicious, even recognize him from photos that might have been circulated, though that wasn't so likely this far from Missouri and with his altered appearance.

She might have known he had every intention of minimizing the risk. He made her pass up the chain motel on the western edge of Sutter's Gap, as well as the bed and-breakfast prominently located in the center of the village. Not until they were a mile east of the community did he find what he wanted.

There was a discreet sign mounted at the entrance of a wooded drive bordered by split-rail fences. The Mill Inn. Ellie knew the accommodations would be charming, private, and depressingly pricey.

"Separate cottages available," Noah read. "I think we're in business, Ellie. Let's go see if the Mill Inn likes your credit card."

The inn, a rambling stone structure with a terrace bar overlooking a picturesque millpond, was happy to accept her credit card. And, yes, one of the cottages was vacant for the night. They were given a key and directions. The tiny place was located under the trees several hundred yards away from the main lodge. The van could be parked out of sight. Noah was satisfied.

When they reached the frame cottage and removed what they would need for the night from the van, he locked it and pocketed the keys. A flagged path carried them to the door of the cottage. This, too, he locked behind them.

Noah went around turning on the lamps, checking the interior to be sure it was secure. The place consisted of a bed-sitting room and an adjoining bath. There was a stone fireplace and an enormous four-poster.

"Cozy , huh, Ellie? Looks like maybe we got the honeymoon cabin. Shame to waste it just sleeping the night away."

He gazed meaningfully at the four-poster. It was the only bed in the cottage. She tried not to think about the necessity of sharing it with him. What he couldn't achieve with the threat of the revolver, he was capable of trying to win in another way. She had already learned that on more than one occasion.

"I'd like to take a shower," she said as matter-of-factly as possible. "*Alone,* if you don't mind."

He considered her request. "Guess that would be all right. There are no windows in there. But leave the door unlocked."

She took her things and fled into the bathroom before he decided to change his mind. Minutes later, she stood under a hot shower, lathering herself with the shampoo and fragrant soap provided by the inn. After a night spent in the back of the van and another in the hayloft of a barn, the shower was more than just a relief. It was pure luxury. Even the towels were wonderful, thick and soft and extra large. She refused to remember what these simple pleasures were costing her.

The first thing she noticed when she emerged from the bathroom, wrapped in a terry-cloth robe, was the absence of the telephone. He had unplugged and removed it from the night table, concealing it somewhere in the cottage. That didn't surprise her. What she didn't expect was his intention to leave her alone in the bedroom while he took his own shower. She couldn't believe it when he ducked into the bathroom and shut the door.

She should have known he was only playing another game with her. Before she could consider the possibility of locating that missing telephone and using it, he snatched the door open again. There was a thoughtful expression on his face as he stood there in the opening.

"Oh, gee, I was forgetting, wasn't I? You still don't trust me, which means I can't trust you. I suppose I could make you come into the bathroom and sit on the seat while I take my shower. But with me occupied in the stall, there's nothing to keep you from sneaking out." He leaned against the jamb and stroked his jaw, pretending to consider the problem. "Guess we don't have a choice about it, Ellie. Guess you'll have to come back under the shower with me."

"I don't think so."

"You must have forgotten what I told you back at that rest area in Illinois. You know, about us not being separated, including the two of us standing under the same spray. Remember?"

"Suppose I refuse."

"Suppose I drag you in there." He nodded slowly. "Like I say, no choice. Let's go, Ellie."

She was tempted to call his bluff, except she feared it wasn't a bluff and that if she resisted he *would* physically haul her into the shower. It seemed they were back to where they had started in St. Louis. No, not quite. This time as she obeyed him, slipping by him into the bathroom, her body burned with anticipation. An excitement she wanted to deny and couldn't. How could he have made her feel like this in a brief span of two days?

Mistaking the hot flush on her face for embarrassment, Noah took pity on her as he followed her into the bathroom. "If you want to be modest about this, Rembrandt, then wrap yourself in a towel. Won't matter since you've already had your shower."

The room suddenly felt very small when he closed the door. It felt even smaller as he began to remove his clothes.

"The same won't work for me, though, will it?" he said. "Afraid I'm going to have to get down to the skin. Wanna help?"

It wasn't safe to answer him. She turned her back and reached for a towel. Opening her robe, she managed to tuck the towel around herself before she dropped the robe to the floor.

"I'm ready, Ellie." She didn't dare to turn around. He laughed softly. "You planning on backing into the shower?"

Clutching the towel to make certain it didn't slip down her breasts, she turned in his direction. She kept her gaze lowered, looking at nothing but his bare feet.

"Think we can both fit in there?" he asked, indicating the tiled shower stall. "Let's find out. You first."

Scuttling into the stall, she squeezed into a corner, keeping her face turned to the wall. She felt like a fool. A helpless one. He joined her, and she heard the door click as he dragged it shut. A second later she felt the spray pelting her.

Ellie tried to make herself as small as possible. It didn't work. His naked body kept brushing against her as he twisted and turned under the stream of water. A jolt went through her every time his slick flesh came in contact with her.

"Here, take it," he said, catching her hand and pressing the bar of soap into it.

"What—"

"I need you to scrub my back. There's always that one spot you can never comfortably reach."

She knew he was only playing with her again. She could have refused. But she didn't want to refuse. Whatever her objections about the situation, she wanted to touch him.

Her breath quickening, she turned away from the wall. The sight of his hard body, licked by water through the mist of steam, was riveting. He presented his back to her. She began to lather it, her hands caressing his taut, muscled flesh.

He uttered a rumble of deep satisfaction. "I've just decided," he said. "Having a shower partner is a damn good idea."

She didn't resist when he turned slowly, offering more than his back. She found herself slowly, sensually stroking his hair-roughened chest. Through the slashing waters, she was aware of his arousal.

"Ellie," he muttered thickly. "Ellie, I think maybe..."

It was when he leaned toward her with his searching mouth, when his hands started to grope for the soaked towel plastered to her body, that she realized the serious mistake she was about to make. She couldn't! She couldn't let him make love to her, not when she felt about him the way she now did! She was a woman unable to separate the physical from the emotional, and if she allowed this to go any further she would destroy herself. Because there could be no tomorrows with this man, only the heartache of loss when he was gone from her life. Better to leave it here while the hurt was still bearable.

Abruptly pulling away from him, she informed him in a hoarse voice, "I'm not going to be intimate with you."

Then, before he could stop her, she shoved the bar of soap at him and fled from the shower stall. He didn't follow her. She snatched up her robe and left the bathroom. Back in the bedroom, she raked through her suitcase for something to wear.

She had managed to slip into panties and a sleep shirt when he appeared in the bedroom. Her breathing was under control by then, but the sight of him made her light-headed.

He'd slung a towel around his waist. The towel rode low on his hips, somehow emphasizing his masculine allure. His black hair was still wet and lay flat against his scalp. He stood there in the doorway, his face taut as he regarded her in silence. There was no humor in him now. He looked angry and dangerous.

"I don't give a damn whether you want to be intimate with me or not," he finally informed her in a cold voice, "but don't ever disappear again like that without asking. Because, naked or not, I'll come after you, and you won't like what happens when I catch you."

She said nothing. She was in no mood to verbally spar with him. Feeling weak in the legs, she sat down on the edge of a chair and avoided looking at him while he donned one of the sets of underwear acquired that morning.

He was no less tempting in clean briefs and a T-shirt, but at least she could face him now. He was still brusque with her, and that helped.

"You have any reason we shouldn't make this an early night?"

She shook her head.

"Good." He'd brought the familiar length of clothesline from the van. He dangled it in front of her. "I don't suppose you'd like to promise me that this isn't necessary anymore.''

She didn't answer him. She couldn't.

"No, I didn't think so," he said.

He motioned her to the four-poster, turned out the lights except for a single lamp on one of the night tables, and joined her on the bed. She submitted without argument when he lashed their wrists together with the cord. Then, drawing the quilt over them, he stretched out on his back beside her and closed his eyes.

Noah could feel her edging away from him as far as their bound wrists would permit. She doesn't have to worry about it, he thought bitterly. He didn't plan on trying anything. She had made it pretty clear under the shower that she didn't want him touching her again. What was the matter with him? Why couldn't he get it in his head that she wasn't going to believe him or trust him? That it was only his imagination she'd maybe started to care for him as he'd come to care for her.

It was his own fault. He'd gone and broken this morning's promise to himself to stay away from her, and now he was paying the penalty. When was he going to realize that, however she made him feel, he couldn't have her? Didn't dare to let her know how much she'd already come to mean to him.

If only she'd tell him where Joel was, he could end this misery before he lost his sanity along with all his broken dreams. He could learn to stop wanting her then. *Had* to stop wanting her.

Meanwhile, it was killing him having her here beside him on the bed. He could feel the heat of her body next to his, could picture the way she had looked under the shower with her long, slender legs and that wet towel molded to her breasts. He fought the images, willing himself to go to sleep, willing himself to forget...

ELLIE ONLY MEANT to convince him she was asleep when she settled down and closed her eyes. But she was so tired, both emotionally and physically, that her body betrayed her. Before she could prevent it, she drifted off.

It was Noah, tugging at her wrist as he stirred in his sleep, who awakened her. She lifted her head from the pillow. The lamp on the night table was still burning. Its soft glow permitted her to see the antique cottage clock on the fireplace mantel. Almost eleven. Assuming, that is, it kept correct time.

It was late, anyway, but not too late for her purpose, providing she could manage it. There was a good chance that she'd be able to free herself since she now had two advantages unavailable to her the night in the van when he had last roped them together. This time she had watched him tie the complicated knots. Better still, she had light now to guide her.

When she raised herself up a bit more in order to look directly down at him, it was just to make certain he was sound asleep. She didn't count on the tenderness that instantly welled up inside her at the sight of that strong face. He had the most amazing bone structure, making his features all angles and planes. They were softened in sleep, and so attractively vulnerable that she had to quell a powerful urge to stroke them.

She wanted to love him, not escape from him. She wanted to believe in his innocence, *longed* to, but she didn't dare. Not with Joel's welfare at risk. That was why she had to release herself. She needed to reach a phone. Brett Buchanan must be warned that Noah was here and intended to snatch his son. Must be prepared to prevent such an action.

It was a cruel decision, but what other choice did she have? Noah was blind in his determination to have his son. Unable to realize he would be subjecting the child to the mean existence of a fugitive, forever on the run, never free of the fear of pursuit and discovery. Joel didn't deserve that. He was too young, too helpless.

Noah would never forgive her when she told him afterward what she'd done. She would bear the anguish of his bitterness for the rest of her days. Because she would have to tell him. He would have to know so that he had a chance to get away before the local police came for him. Right or wrong, she intended to give him that much.

God help her, she couldn't turn him in herself. Not now, not feeling about him as she did. Whatever his guilt, she couldn't bring herself to do it. But she knew that Brett, as Joel's legal guardian, wouldn't hesitate to alert the nearest authorities the minute she ended their call.

Trying not to think any longer of the outcome and its consequences, Ellie concentrated on ridding herself of the binding that pinned her right wrist to Noah's left wrist. She knew it would be a slow, laborious process, requiring the awkward use of her left hand and made more difficult by the constant fear of disturbing him.

Exercising every care as she peeled back the top of the quilt on her side, keeping her right arm perfectly still, she began to pick at the knots. They were so tight and tangled that it seemed hopeless. She had to caution herself repeatedly to be patient, to persevere.

The only sounds in the room as she worked at the tough cord were the ticking clock on the mantel and Noah's steady breathing. She was aware of him every second. The clean scent of his body after his shower, the beat of the pulse in the hollow of his throat, the way he swallowed unconsciously in his sleep. Small, appealing things that did nothing to help her effort.

Her frustration mounted, but she continued to pluck at the tough cord. There, success at last! She had managed to loosen the first knot. But before she could attack the others, he moved restlessly. Catching her lip between her teeth, she held her breath and prayed he wouldn't try to roll over on his side. The action would drag her arm with him, either awakening him or putting her wrist out of reach.

No, it was all right. He remained on his back and was still again. She resumed her operation, fingers digging at the restraint. It seemed to take forever, but in reality was probably less than twenty minutes later, before she succeeded with the last knot and was finally able to slide her hand out of the loop.

For a moment she rested, testing her freedom, making certain that Noah was unaware of her escape. Then, inch by cautious inch, she squeezed away from him, lifting herself off the bed in slow stages.

The tension eased once she was on her feet, but it was nothing like relief. Not yet. Stealing across the room, she slipped into a pair of jeans, tucking her sleep shirt into the waistband. Grabbing up her shoes, she headed on bare feet for the door. She wasn't interested in finding the gun. Not this time. Nor would she hunt for the phone he'd hidden. Even if she located it, she wouldn't dare to use it in here. She needed a safe public phone away from this cottage. There was one in the lounge off the lobby where they had checked in.

She managed to unlock the door and open it soundlessly. She looked back toward the bed before she headed into the night. He was still sleeping. She felt like a fist was squeezing her heart at the sight of him lying there, unaware of what she was about to do.

"Forgive me," she whispered.

Then she went out into the darkness, closing the door softly behind her.

ELLIE PAUSED under the trees as she neared the brightly lit main entrance to the inn. A late-arriving tour bus was parked there, discharging passengers and unloading luggage. She decided it might be better to avoid this flurry of noise and activity. However small the risk, she didn't want to arouse any curiosity about her errand.

The flagged walk divided here, a sign indicating that the left branch led to the open-air terrace bar edging the mill-pond at the back of the sprawling building. She could gain access to the lounge from that side without mingling with the guests. The terrace probably wasn't occupied at this hour. Ellie headed that way.

Arriving at the rear of the inn, she discovered that on this end the terrace was screened by a thick, man-high yaupon hedge. An arch midway along its tightly sheared length offered an entrance to the stone-flagged terrace. She hesitated when she reached the opening. She wasn't alone out here.

There were lanterns in the trees above the scattered tables. They revealed the solitary figure of a man standing on the far side. He had his back to her and was smoking a cigar. He kept glancing impatiently in the direction of the door to the lounge. Obviously waiting for someone, he was unaware of her hanging here in the dimness of the archway.

There was nothing familiar about him. No reason why she shouldn't ignore him and continue on her way to the lounge door. But there were two things that bothered her and kept her lingering in the shadows. He had a grungy look about his clothes that made him seem an unlikely guest in a place this expensive. Also, there was a kind of tension in the restless way he puffed the cigar that she didn't like.

Ellie was glad she had trusted her instinct to be cautious when, a second later, the lounge door opened and the stranger was joined by another man. Before the arrival could spot her, she pulled back swiftly behind the cover of the hedge. Brief though her glance had been, she'd recognized that buzz cut and tough, meaty face. What was Brett Buchanan's driver and bodyguard doing here?

"Beginning to think you weren't coming," she heard the man with the cigar complain.

"I've got a job," Peaches said. "I can't just drop it and run because you pick up a phone and call me. I had to wait until Buchanan decided he didn't need me anymore tonight. What are you doing here anyway?"

"I'm not staying in the place. Just seemed like a good out-of-the-way spot to have a beer and talk."

"I don't mean the inn. I'm talking about North Carolina."

"Come on over here and sit down and I'll tell you."

They were headed in her direction. The wisest thing she could do was to make a swift, silent retreat before they detected her presence behind the hedge.

"This is about Noah Rhyder, isn't it?" Peaches said.

Ellie froze in astonishment. She knew now that she wasn't going anywhere. Not before she had some answers. But an explanation wasn't immediately forthcoming. There was a frustrating delay while they settled themselves at one of the tables.

She heard the scrape of metal against stone as they pulled out the wrought iron chairs; she smelled the odor of the cigar and knew that the table they had selected was directly on the other side of the hedge from where she stood. The yaupon was as solid as a wall. They couldn't possibly know she was here hugging the darkness and listening to them. Not as long as she remained perfectly quiet. That's what she told herself anyway, but she was ready to bolt at the first hint of discovery.

"You want a beer, Peaches? I'm buying. Waitress should be along again in a minute."

"Forget the beer. I'm still waiting to hear it, Lew. Noah Rhyder, right?"

There was a pause and then a mumbled, "Yeah, okay, I'm after Rhyder. He's still on the loose out there, and I want him."

"The department send you?"

There was no reply.

Peaches chuckled. "I didn't think so. They don't know you're here, do they? You're on your own. Bolling's gonna have your badge when he finds out."

"Not if I bring him Rhyder."

"Yeah? And what makes you think you're gonna find him in North Carolina?"

"Because his kid is here. I know that bastard. He won't go anywhere without his kid."

"That's bull. He can't get to him even if he was to learn Buchanan has him here."

"I figure he does know he's here," Lew said. "I figure he's probably coming after him."

"How?"

"The Matheson woman. I think he's grabbed her."

Ellie wanted to seize a deep, steadying breath and didn't dare. In the silence that followed she could hear the waters of the millpond lapping softly against the stone wall that framed the terrace.

"You know that for a fact?" Peaches finally challenged him.

"Not for certain," Lew admitted, "but everything points to it."

"Okay, if it's true, then maybe he does know this is where Buchanan and the kid are. But how come you know it, Lew? Buchanan wasn't telling anyone where to find us, except a few people who had to know."

"Well, one of those had to be somebody in the department," Lew answered evasively, "because I didn't have much trouble getting the address."

There was another pause. Ellie could picture the bodyguard on the other side of the barrier leaning back in his chair as he suspiciously considered Lew's information.

"I don't know that I buy that," he said, "any more than I buy the rest. But if I was to buy it, what's all this got to do with me? You wanna explain that, Lew? Wanna tell me why you phone me on the sly and get me down here in the middle of the night?''

"Come on, Peaches, you know why. I need your help in getting Rhyder. You're in charge of security at the estate, so when he turns up—and he will—you'll probably be the first to know it. When that happens, I wanna know it, too. I wanna be there to personally collar him.''

"You think he's that dumb?''

"I think he's that desperate. I think he'll risk getting caught to snatch his kid.''

"Let's say that he does, and I'm ready for him. Only why should I make you a part of it?''

"Because the two of us working together have a better chance of catching him. And when we do, you stand to benefit.''

"How?''

"Your boss, Buchanan. He's loaded, right? You prevent his nephew from being kidnapped, he's gonna be grateful. Probably grateful enough to see that you get a bonus. Maybe a bonus generous enough for a down payment on that condo Ginger has been wanting.''

There was another thoughtful silence on the other side of the hedge. Ellie heard the click of a lighter. Lew must be lighting another cigar. A chair creaked as one of them stirred in it restlessly.

"It's an interesting proposition,'' Peaches said. "Real tempting. Kind of funny considering what I think about this guy.''

"What?''

"He isn't the one. Noah Rhyder isn't the one who murdered Buchanan's old man. Yeah, that's what I think. As a matter of fact, I felt from the start he was all wrong.''

"You trying to tell me you sympathize with the bastard?''

"I could care less. I'm just telling you he's not it. Remember how, when I was on the force, I had this sixth sense about suspects being guilty or not guilty and how it turned out I was right every time. Yeah, the more I think about it, I'm certain Rhyder didn't do it.''

''You're nuts. Who else was there?''

''For all I know, it was Buchanan himself. He's capable of murder, and there was no love lost between him and the senator.''

''No motive,'' Lew said, and Ellie could hear the anger in his gravelly voice. An anger directed at Noah. ''Rhyder had *all* the motives.''

''Maybe. But you know what else I think? I think that deep down in your cop's gut you're not convinced either that Rhyder did it. But you're not interested in his innocence, are you, Lew?''

''I'm interested in justice.''

''The hell you are. You never let it go, did you, Lew? You've kept that hate for the guy inside you all these years. It's got you crazy. That's why you want him so bad.''

''Look,'' Lew growled, ''are you gonna help me or not?''

''Sure, why not. Buchanan pays me well, better than the force ever did. And like you say, if we put Rhyder back behind bars, maybe he'll pay me even better.'' There was the sound of a chair being pushed back, someone coming to his feet. ''I gotta get back to the house. Let me know where you're staying so I can keep you posted if anything turns up.''

''I've checked into the Big Mountain Motel. They'll take messages for me if I'm out. I figure I'm gonna be busy scouting around the area. Trying to pick up something useful while we wait for Rhyder to show and make his move. You sure you don't want that beer?''

His voice faded along with the sound of their footsteps as the two men left the terrace. Ellie was alone. She went on standing there in the shadows, numbed by what she had overheard, her mind struggling to process the information. In the end only one thing mattered. A vast relief that left her glowing inside. However, on the outside...

She shivered, suddenly aware that she was cold. She hadn't realized until now how sharp the night air of autumn was coming off the millpond. Her bare feet were like ice against the stone flags. In her excitement she hadn't remembered to slip into her shoes after she left the cottage. She was still clutching them.

Nor did she bother now to put them on. She had something more urgent to do. Turning away from the hedge, she hurried along the path. She was no longer interested in finding a telephone.

Chapter Nine

Something had awakened him, and for a moment he didn't understand what it was. He lay there on his back, pushing away the fog of sleep that still clung to him. When he lifted his arm to rub his hand over his eyes, he realized there was no weight attached to it. There should have been a weight. That's when he knew something was wrong.

Suddenly alert, Noah shot up on the bed. The clothesline was still wrapped around his wrist, but Ellie wasn't at the other end of it. Gone. She had managed to loosen the knots without his awareness. And had escaped, vanishing into the night.

For a few seconds he experienced a frantic sense of loss that had nothing to do with a fear for his own safety. And then reality kicked in. Did he stand any chance of getting her back, or was it already too late?

He started to swing his feet to the floor, intending to get out of here before the cops arrived. He froze, his head swiveling toward the fireplace. That's what had awakened him. There was a blaze crackling behind the screen. What in the hell was—

The outside door opened. Ellie came into the cottage, her arms loaded with lengths of split log. She saw him there on the bed, staring at her.

"There wasn't enough wood in here to make a good

fire,'' she said. "They keep a stack just outside." She crossed the room and dumped her load on the hearth. Then she crouched down on the hooked rug and held her hands toward the flames.

Noah shoved himself to his feet and went straight to the fireplace where he hunkered down beside her. "You wanna tell me what's going on here?"

"I needed a fire. I was cold."

Bewildered, he watched her as she casually opened the screen to add wood to the blaze. Then she got to her feet, went to the sofa, and removed a pair of cushions, which she placed side by side on the rug near the hearth.

"We'll be more comfortable on these while we talk." She settled on one of the cushions, patting the other in an invitation for him to sit.

Noah went on squatting on the floor. "So let me get this clear," he said, eyeing her warily. "You get cold and decide you need to make a fire. Only to do that you have to work your way out of knots that would have anchored a battleship. Which, naturally, you manage to do without waking me. Then you sneak outside, not to disappear, mind you, but just to bring in wood. That what you asking me to believe, Ellie?"

"Well, of course, it's more involved than that. Are you going to go on squatting there like that? You'll get cramps in your legs if you don't sit, because we have a lot to discuss."

Irritated with her nonchalance, Noah shifted himself onto the cushion beside her. "Satisfied?"

"Would you like me to remove that rope from your wrist?"

"Are you trying to stall me while—"

"You can relax. No one is coming to arrest you. Are you sure you wouldn't like me to—"

"Forget the damn rope. I'll untie it myself. Just tell me what I've got to worry about."

"Nothing. At least not tonight."

While he unfastened the length of clothesline with impatient fingers, she explained her intention to phone Brett, how she had been halted, and all that she had overheard on the terrace.

He had freed himself of the rope by the time she was finished. He held it with both hands, his thumbs absently stroking it as he stared at her intently. "You never made that call?"

"No."

"You came straight back here?"

"That's right."

"Are you trying to tell me, Ellie, that everything's changed because of what you heard? That you believe me now?"

"I guess I am saying just that," she said softly, and with a kind of wonder over her own certainty.

"Maybe what you heard doesn't mean a thing. Maybe I've been lying to you all along and I am guilty of killing Howard Buchanan."

"But you weren't, and you aren't."

There was a simple conviction in her voice and such sweet relief inside him at hearing her unquestioning faith in his innocence that he wanted to take her in his arms, hold her tightly, and shout his gladness. But he restrained himself as he noticed her expression. She was gazing at him with a new fear in her eyes.

"What?" he demanded, tossing the rope aside.

"That man, Lew," she said anxiously. "Who is he?"

"You heard. He's a St. Louis cop. Lew Ferguson. The detective who questioned and arrested me. He was moved off the case a day or so after I was brought in, something about mismanaged evidence. I can't say I was sorry they replaced him."

She shook her head. "It's more than just that. Noah, he

hates you. It has to do with the past, long before the murder. What happened between the two of you?''

"Nothing. Ellie, I never met the guy before that afternoon they picked me up outside the zoo. Never even heard of him.''

She frowned. "I'm sure I didn't get it wrong. I'm sure that's what Peaches said, and Lew Ferguson didn't deny it. It must be something.''

"I don't know. It doesn't make sense. Anyway, it doesn't matter.''

"It does matter,'' she insisted. "If St. Louis doesn't know he's here, then he's risking his job to personally get you. There's something creepy about that.'' She shuddered. "He's mean, Noah. And Peaches strikes me as a cold brute. The two of them are dangerous.''

"It could be worse. If Ferguson had told his department whatever he learned about my heading out here, I'd never get near Joel. Cops would be swarming all over the place waiting to take me. This way I stand a chance of grabbing Joel and putting distance between us and North Carolina.''

"How, when Peaches and the detective will be watching for you every minute?''

His face wore a stubborn look. "I'm not leaving here without my kid.''

She leaned toward him from her cushion, appealing to him. "Then get him back legally. If your enemies aren't sure of your guilt, and I've been convinced of your innocence, there's hope now to reopen the case and clear yourself.''

"You're dreaming, Ellie. Nothing has changed. If I turn myself in, I go straight to Boonville with no detours on the way. And Buchanan gets to keep Joel. You want that after what you heard on the terrace?''

Brett. She'd forgotten for a moment what Peaches had said about Brett. "Capable of murder,'' she murmured. "You tried to tell me that back in Ridley, that Brett could have killed his father. But how, when he had a solid alibi? And why?''

Noah ran a distracted hand through his sleep-tousled hair. "I don't know. And since at this point it isn't gonna do me much good to speculate about it, I don't care. All I give a damn about is getting my son away from Brett Buchanan.''

She gazed at him, amber eyes widening in concern. "He wouldn't hurt Joel. He has no reason to touch him.''

"You wanna take that chance, Ellie?'' he asked her softly.

The thought of Joel sharing a fugitive existence with his father was still abhorrent to her, but she could no longer argue Noah's intention. Brett had become a threat, but without evidence, the court would never agree to remove the child from his care.

"I'll help you to get Joel,'' she promised him quietly. She refused to think beyond that, to recognize that then he and his son would disappear. Would no longer be any part of her life. The ache of that loss—

"No,'' he said decisively. "All I want is the address, and the first thing in the morning when it's light I'm gone. Then you're out of it.''

"It's too late for that,'' she said, angry that he was already dismissing her. "I'm involved. However he found it out, Lew Ferguson knows I'm with you.''

"He has no real proof of that. You can turn around and drive back to St. Louis. You can say you were in the Ozarks, just where you were supposed to be, and nobody will question it.''

"I see,'' she said, her voice like ice. "In other words, once I give you the address, I've served my purpose. Not only am I no longer useful to you, I become a burden if I stick around. Is that it?''

"Close enough,'' he said, his voice equally cold. "Sorry, Ellie, but after tonight I just don't need you anymore.''

She held his hard gaze for a long moment, searching his face. "You're lying."

He had no answer for her. She went on challenging him with her eyes. In the end his gaze softened in helpless surrender.

"Damn it, Ellie," he said, his voice gruff with emotion, "I want you safe. I want you back with your easel and your brushes in that homey house in Webster Groves. I want to know I haven't permanently hurt you and that you can pick up your life where it was before I bulldozed my way into it."

She reached up and placed a hand against his beard-roughened cheek. "It isn't that easy. It's different now."

"Are you telling me— What *are* you telling me?"

"Figure it out."

She watched his face. She could see him remembering what she had told him when he had joined her by the fire. "You weren't going to turn me in when you left here to phone Brett. You were coming back afterward to let me know you'd warned him. Giving me a chance to get away, you said, even though you weren't sure then that I wasn't guilty. Why would you do that, Ellie?"

"You know why."

"Yeah, I guess I do." He caught her hand where it still rested on his cheek, turned it over, and pressed a kiss against her palm. "But you and me...it's not smart, Ellie."

"Everything considered, you're probably right. It's probably a big mistake. What can we do about it?"

He went on holding her hand, using it to draw her slowly toward him. "Talk ourselves out of it?"

"We could do that."

His parted mouth closed on hers in a deep, lingering kiss that left her completely defenseless.

"Or could we?" she whispered when his sensual mouth finally lifted from hers.

"Maybe not."

"Maybe instead we should just make the most of tonight," she suggested recklessly, refusing to remind herself that it could be their last, "and worry about arguments in the morning."

"Yeah, let's do that," he growled, unable to resist her invitation.

Hands framing her face, he began to kiss her again. A series of warm, wet kisses on her nose, cheeks, throat. Then his mouth settled once more on her lips, his tongue seeking and receiving a willing entry into her mouth. She clung to him, whimpering with need as his tongue stroked her seductively.

Long seconds later he was puzzled when she broke the kiss, pulling back from him.

"What?" he demanded, his voice thick and raspy.

"There's something I need to be sure of," she said, her own voice sultry and breathless. She scanned his face in the flickering light of the fire. "Yes, it's true."

She could see the sudden concern in his dark eyes. "What's wrong? What are you looking at?"

"This," she murmured, her finger lightly tracing the side of his jaw. "You have a muscle here that's been twitching at the oddest moments ever since St. Louis."

"I'll be damned."

"It's throbbing like crazy right now," she informed him solemnly, "which confirms it. Whenever you're seriously aroused, that tiny muscle gives you away."

"You ought to be flattered then, you little witch. It's been doing a number on me since the night I broke into your house."

"Oh, so you are aware of the problem."

"Why do you think I wore a beard for years before that night I shaved it off? I had to cover up this twitch. It was forever getting me in trouble."

"Women took advantage of you, did they?"

"Hell, yes. They were all over me."

"Uh-huh. Then you wouldn't want *me* to—"

"C'mere," he commanded, hauling her into his arms. "No more games."

He claimed her mouth with another blistering kiss.

No more games, she silently agreed as his hands dropped to her jeans, freeing her sleep shirt from the waistband. His fingers impatiently burrowed under the folds of the shirt, sliding up to her breasts, molding their fullness.

She couldn't have said just when he peeled the sleep shirt over her head, when his eager mouth replaced his fingers on the taut buds of her breasts. Didn't know at what point she rid herself of her jeans. Had no actual awareness of his casting aside his briefs and T-shirt so that she could touch his body without any barriers.

It was all a sweet blur of lush sensations: The glow from the fire licking their naked flesh as they stretched out side by side on the cushions. Their hands and mouths caressing each other. Their breathless murmurs communicating a raw, mutual need.

"It has to be now, Ellie," he rumbled, his voice desperate and hoarse as he strained his swollen hardness against her thigh. "If I'm going to stop, it has to be right now. Tell me to stop before it's too late."

"I won't," she whispered. "I can't."

"Then tell me exactly what you want."

"You, just you..."

He gave her that, answering her plea when he covered her with his strength, his arousal gently, slowly probing an entry into both her body and her soul. In the end, unable to hold back, he completed their joining so deeply and forcefully that she gasped with stunned pleasure. Then he rested, permitting her a moment to adjust to him, to marvel with him at their oneness.

"Hold me," he commanded.

She clasped him tightly with her arms and legs. He groaned and began to stir inside her. She answered his rhythms as, together, they spun an elemental magic. There were endearments from him between his long, powerful thrusts. Blurred love words that she didn't dare to define as anything more than an expression of his passion, but which she cherished all the same.

Then the words were gone, consumed by the urgency of their bodies searching for a pinnacle. Reaching it. Surging over the top. Tumbling into a blinding oblivion.

They were silent in the long, languid aftermath, savoring the joy they had found in each other. The fire burned on, its light casting a mellow glow on their flushed, sated bodies.

It was Noah, after an exaggerated clearing of his throat, who finally ended the silence. "Speaking of flaws on jaws..."

She blinked in surprise. Whatever he was talking about, it wasn't what she expected to hear on the heels of intense lovemaking. "Were we?"

He grinned at her outrageously. "You picked on me first with that twitch thing. Now it's my turn."

Propping himself up on his side, he reached out with one finger and slowly stroked the line of her jaw.

"You've got this small, white scar right here on the side of your chin. Been fascinating me since Missouri. Gotta be an interesting explanation for it."

What was he doing? she wondered. Defusing what could be a dangerously emotional moment with a playful interlude? Avoiding the risk of a commitment that, under the circumstances, just wasn't possible? If so, she had no right to complain of his tactic. She had known what the consequences would be, *had* to be, when she invited his first caress. Now all she could do was hide her ache and join his game.

"There is," she said gravely. "The scar is a souvenir of something that...well, it's too painful to talk about."

"A tragedy?"

"Almost one. I shudder to think what would have happened if I hadn't been there."

"Where?"

"In Arizona visiting my parents. They're retired there. I was out in the desert that day hunting for gemstones."

"Say again."

"Gemstones. When I'm not painting, I create jewelry. There were these men camped at the bottom of an arroyo. I was up on top, so I saw it coming."

"What?"

"A flash flood. I had to rush down to warn them and—"

"Uh, hold it, Ellie. These guys are down in an arroyo, and a flood is coming, and they don't know enough to get out?"

"They didn't have to be smart. They only had to look spectacular, which they did. Didn't I mention this was a company of exotic male dancers on their way to their next gig?"

"Wow. Lucky for them you were right there."

"Yes."

"Let me guess. In racing down to rescue them, you fell and cut your chin on a gemstone."

"Exactly. The point is, I did save them, and they were very, very grateful."

"I don't want to hear any more *verys,* if they mean what I think they mean."

"I'm in trouble with this scene, huh?"

"I'm giving you thirty seconds to revise it."

"All right, but the truth isn't much fun. I split my chin falling off the back of Stan Hooser's bike when I was ten, which I guess makes ol' Stan the first boy who ever dumped me. Satisfied?"

"Not yet." He snuggled down beside her, cradling her in his arms. "Tell me the rest."

"What rest?"

"Everything," he said, his voice earnest this time. "I want to know about Ellie Matheson. All the vital stuff."

So she told him how her father had been a high-school coach and her mother had arranged flowers for a local florist. Her parents really were in Arizona now and wanted her to come out and be another Georgia O'Keeffe, but Ellie preferred the solid, old-fashioned life-style of the Midwest. And she told him about her career-driven ex-husband and how he had wanted them to wait to have children and how eventually she'd realized David didn't want children at all, and that's when they'd drifted apart. Then she told him of her ambition to hang a show in a major art gallery, but she was far from ready for that...

Noah listened with both interest and sympathy, but she didn't deceive herself. She knew the real purpose behind these stories about herself was to avoid the reality of tomorrow. Anything to keep from discussing their unavoidable parting once he'd recovered Joel and was forced to disappear and leave her behind.

The fire had died to a bed of glowing embers and Noah was asleep when she finally ran out of things to tell him. Lifting herself on one elbow, she gazed down at him with a bittersweet longing. She noticed the small tattoo of the sword wrapped in flames on his upper arm. She had meant to ask him about that tattoo, as he had asked her about the scar on her chin. Now she would never know.

With the fire down, the room was growing cool again. Ellie was careful not to disturb him as she slipped away from his side. She brought the quilt from the bed, stretched out beside him again on the cushions, and tucked the cover around both of them.

She closed her eyes and tried not to think that by this time tomorrow Noah could be gone from her life. He would take a part of her with him, because he had stolen her heart. But there was no comfort in that.

Knowing this might be her last time to share any physical

intimacy with him, she put her arms around him and held him close. Only that way could she finally join him in sleep.

"ROSEBAY," she told him.

"Rosebay," he repeated, searching the map spread open across his knees as she started the van and drove away from the inn where they had spent the night.

"It's just south of here," she indicated.

"Got it," he said, locating the town on the map as they passed the split-rail fences that bordered the drive. "Man, it can't be more than ten miles away! All this time—"

"Joel was close by, yes, and I couldn't tell you." She turned onto the highway headed south.

"What's the rest?"

"Ten-twenty-one Settlement Road."

He was silent for a moment, and she knew he must be savoring the relief of finally having secured the address. Of knowing at last just where his son was located. Then, sensing her concerned expression, he turned toward her.

"You haven't made a mistake by telling me, Ellie. I promise you that Joel—"

"No, it isn't that. I know I've done the right thing."

"Then what is it?"

"Lew Ferguson. Are you forgetting he's out here somewhere watching? He could be on the road now, and if he spots this van and the Missouri license plate...

"You shouldn't be with me. You should let me go on alone."

She shook her head emphatically. "We settled all that last night. It's not me I'm worried about."

"There's nothing we can do about Ferguson."

Other than be very careful, she promised herself, remembering just how eager the detective was to get Noah.

In an effort to ease her tension as they sped toward Rosebay, she tried to interest herself in the scene outside the van's windows. It wasn't difficult. The mountains that loomed on both sides of the valley were majestic, shimmering in the clear light of an early morning sun.

The fall colors on their lush slopes had reached their peak. Ellie could hardly believe they were real. The flaming scarlet and blazing orange of sugar maples, the gold of birches, the russet of oaks. So brilliant that they hurt the eye. It was almost a relief to find momentary distraction in the ranks of evergreens with their somber greens.

As they neared Rosebay, she asked the question that had been nagging at her since they'd left the inn. "Have you *any* idea just how you'll get Joel away from the estate?"

"Not yet. I'll know better after we scout the place. I don't suppose Brett provided you with any directions?"

"Just the address. I think we'll have to stop somewhere and ask."

"It's either that," he agreed, "or risk drawing attention to ourselves by searching up and down every back road."

Minutes later, they halted at a four-way stop at the edge of Rosebay. "How about trying in there?" Ellie asked, indicating a general store on the opposite corner.

"Looks like it's been there since the Civil War," Noah said, judging the sagging building with the critical eye of an architect. "Which means whoever runs it probably knows every house in the valley. Go for it."

He made no objection when she urged him to remain in the van while she tried her luck in the store. Both of them realized that, unless it was absolutely necessary, he shouldn't be seen in the area.

Ellie was immediately intrigued when she entered the building from the porch stretched across its windowed front. The general store, crammed with merchandise of every description and smelling of another era, was the genuine article and not the tourist version, although there were displays appealing to travelers. Fried apple pies and fresh cider, locally made baskets, whimsical carvings of a true rural character, even a board advertising cabins to rent in

the region. Under other circumstances, she would have lingered and explored the place.

Rounding a potbellied stove, she arrived at a wooden
counter near the rear of the store. Here the twentieth cen-
tury had intruded in the form of a computer. A woman with
a lined face and silver hair that needed taming looked up
from the screen she'd been consulting.

"Help you?"

"Yes, please. I need directions to an address. Settlement
Road."

"That's not a town road. It winds off into the country.
Goes for miles. You have a number?"

"Ten-twenty-one."

The woman didn't immediately answer her. She looked
surprised. "You sure that's the place?"

"Yes."

"Take the next turn to your left and just follow the road.
There should be a mailbox with the number on it."

Ellie thanked her and left the store.

Noah was waiting for her impatiently. "Any luck?" he
asked as she slid behind the wheel of the van.

She told him what she'd learned. Beginning to think she
had imagined the woman's reception, she said nothing
about the storekeeper's odd expression when she'd mentioned the number of the address.

Fifteen minutes later, as they sat in the parked van on
the edge of Settlement Road and gaped in silence at the
structure far above them, Ellie understood the storekeeper's
curiosity.

Brett Buchanan's Appalachian hideaway was no ordinary
retreat. Nestled on a high terrace against a thickly wooded
mountainside was a Scottish-style baronial castle complete
with crowstepped gables, turrets with conical roofs, and
corbeled battlements that looked as though they were intended to defeat an invading army. To Ellie, the place

seemed more like a fairy tale than a house. Noah viewed it differently.

"It's a fortress," he said angrily. "He's got my kid locked up in a damn fortress. Why is all this security necessary?"

Ellie had no answer for him, but she could see what he meant. Across the road from where they were parked, a stream coiled around the foot of the mountain. It was like the moat of a castle, only the drawbridge that crossed it was a stone span.

Iron gates sealed off the entrance to the drive on the other side of the bridge. Above the bank of the stream, on either side of the stone gate piers, was a cyclone fence topped by strands of barbed wire. A formidable-looking obstacle that probably enclosed the entire property.

"Place has to be costing him a fortune," Noah muttered. "But then he always was an extravagant bastard."

She glanced at him, understanding his immense frustration. He'd been excited when they left Rosebay. Tense with the anticipation of finally nearing the objective he'd traveled a thousand miles to reach. But now what he was so desperate to recover was behind seemingly impossible barriers.

She knew he wouldn't be defeated, though. One way or another, he would get his son back. He'd somehow overcome the challenges of this place, whose lofty arrogance must make him feel it was more imperative than ever that he get Joel out of there.

Ellie gazed again at the castle perched on its ledge far above them. It was a beautiful Gothic absurdity, and it made her nervous.

"Let's move on," she suggested, "before someone up there spots us."

"You're right. There's no way in from this side unless I'm invited, and somehow I don't think that's going to happen. Let's see what the fence looks like up ahead. Maybe I can find a way around it.''

But there was no break in the fence as the van crawled slowly along the road that paralleled the stream. Even if there had been one, the waters prevented them from reaching it.

The castle was well out of sight behind them, concealed by the unbroken mass of the woods, when Noah, searching the perimeter of the estate, called out to her.

"Stop!"

She pulled off on the shoulder of the road and looked where he pointed. One of the massive trees on the other side had fallen across the stream, offering a footbridge over the waters.

"Time to check out that fence," he said. "I want to see if I can climb it."

"You're not going to try to go up to the house in broad daylight?"

"Guess that wouldn't be smart. I'll come back after dark, but I need to know now just where I can get in. Stay put, Ellie."

He was out of the car in a flash and across the road. Ellie parked the van out of sight among the trees. By the time she joined him, he was already edging his way along the fallen tree. Hearing her behind him, he turned his head and scowled at her.

"I thought I told you—"

"You might need help climbing that fence. Don't argue about it."

"All right, but you're staying on the ground."

She had no intention of tangling with the wicked-looking barbed wire that topped the fence. As a matter of fact, though she didn't say so, and he wouldn't have listened to her if she had, this whole business was beginning to feel like something out of an unlikely combat movie. There had to be a safer, saner method for reuniting Joel with his father. The trouble was, she couldn't think of one.

Ellie followed him over the bridge. With careful balancing, it wasn't difficult to cross since the trunk was broad and the bark rough. The high bank on the other side was thick with underbrush and drifts of fallen leaves. They climbed it, wading through the tight growth to reach the fence.

Excluding the barbed wire, the fence was probably a good ten feet or more in height and solidly constructed. She watched in silence as Noah evaluated the barrier, scanning its length in both directions.

"There," he said, "that's what I want."

He moved off to the right. Puzzled, she went after him. When she caught up to him, he was gazing at the bough of an oak which extended out over the fence just inches above the barbed wire.

"The fence itself is no problem to climb," he explained. "It's the angled barbed wire that's going to stop me. Or it would if it weren't for that branch up there. I can use it to swing myself over the top."

"Will it support you?"

"Let's find out."

Securing easy holds for his hands and feet in the stout wire mesh, he began to scale the fence.

"Careful," she warned him.

"After climbing out of a deep well, this is a piece of cake," he teased, inching his way upward.

He was clinging to the top of the fence with one hand, and reaching for the limb with the other, when she heard it. A scrabbling sound in the deep woods behind the fence.

"There's something up there," she hissed.

"You hearing wild boar again?" He had succeeded in grasping the bough.

"It's headed this way. Come down," she insisted.

Even Noah couldn't mistake the noise this time. There

was an animal bounding through the undergrowth, streaking directly toward them down the mountainside with the instinct of a predator. And behind it, still a safe distance away but approaching rapidly, was another figure crashing through the thickets on the slope and shouting after the animal.

"Caesar, get back here!"

Ellie knew that chilling voice. She had heard it last night on the terrace of the Mill Inn. Panic seized her. They were about to be discovered!

Noah needed no urging this time. He released the branch, one of his hands finding a fresh grip on the mesh as he prepared to scramble down the fence. But when he started to lower his other hand, the sleeve of his jacket caught on the barbed wire. She watched in horror as he tugged at it repeatedly, cursing under his breath.

He was still struggling to free himself seconds later when the dog, some kind of a large hound with a vicious temper, hurtled through the trees. Leaping and snarling, it attacked the fence where Noah was trapped. Ellie knew that the dog's master, still shouting after him, would be here in another minute.

"Noah, hurry!" she pleaded in a frantic whisper.

With one fierce shove against the fence where the hound still fought to reach him, he succeeded in tearing his sleeve from the barbs. But the effort cost him his hold on the mesh. He came slamming to the ground, landing so hard that he lost his footing. His body went tumbling down the steep bank into a dense tangle of witch hazel.

Ellie, without hesitation, dove after him.

Chapter Ten

The witch hazel was spangled with tiny autumn flowers. Yellow flowers. Peering through their thickness, Ellie could see the burly figure of Peaches behind the fence above them. He carried a shotgun.

She hugged the damp earth under the shrubbery, aware of Noah pressed close beside her. Both of them were flat on their stomachs, not daring to move or to speak.

She prayed that the dog wouldn't get under the fence. He was pawing at the ground below it, whining and straining at the mesh. He knew they were here in the witch hazel. Mercifully, Peaches didn't. Not yet, anyway.

"What is it, Caesar? What are you after?"

Ellie held her breath as the bodyguard ducked his head, his sharp gaze searching the area where they were concealed. Could he possibly detect them? It seemed forever until he straightened.

"There's nothing there now. It was probably a squirrel, and we've got better things to hunt. Come on, you cur." The animal resisted. "Come on, I say."

Gripping the hound by the collar, he dragged him away from the fence. Caesar went reluctantly. A moment later, shouldering the shotgun and with the dog at his heels, Peaches climbed back through the woods.

Ellie and Noah waited until there was no sight or sound

of them. Then, releasing her breath in a long sigh of relief, Ellie rose cautiously from the shrubbery.

"That was too close for—"

She broke off, alarmed by the sharp hissing sound from Noah as he climbed to his feet. When she turned to him, he wore a grimace of pain.

"What's wrong?"

"My damn ankle. When I went to put weight on it...hell, I must have injured it somehow when I hit the ground."

She wasn't surprised. He had come down like a boulder. "Can you make it out of the shrubbery so we can look at it in the open?"

Refusing the arm she tried to offer, he hobbled through the witch hazel, sinking down on the grassy bank. She knelt beside him, removing his shoe and sock. Bending low, she examined the ankle.

"What do you see?" he demanded. "And will you recognize it if you do see it?"

"Maybe. I did have a course in first aid. It was required when I qualified to take children into my home."

"Good. So how bad is it?"

"There's no abnormal angle, which would indicate a fracture. But I'll need to rotate it to know better. I'll try to be careful."

He made no complaint as she gently tested the joint, but she knew by the way he sucked in air that the ankle was agonizingly tender.

"I'm pretty sure it's not broken," she reported.

"Then I just twisted it, huh?"

"It's more than that. It's a bad sprain. Noah, it's already swelling like a melon."

"You mean I can't walk on it?"

She shook her head. "I'm afraid you're not going to be rescuing Joel either tonight or in the next few days."

He swore savagely. She sympathized with his anger and

frustration, but he had to understand that his injury needed attention.

"You should see a doctor. If the ligaments are completely torn—"

"No doctor. Do you know what kind of risk that would be? There must be some other way to treat it."

"There is. You'll have to keep off it as much as possible. It needs to be elevated, and it needs ice and compression to reduce the swelling."

"What else?"

"It's going to hurt. A lot. Sprains are more painful than breaks."

"So I'll take aspirin. Ellie?"

"What?"

"It's going to be fun getting me back across the log to the van."

It wasn't fun. In the end, unable to balance himself on the trunk, Noah had to crawl across its length on hands and knees. By the time they reached the other side, his male pride was no longer a consideration. He accepted her support with grim resignation.

She was relieved when they finally arrived at the van. Noah was white with pain and exertion as she helped him into the passenger seat. Anxious to get them away from the scene as quickly as possible, she climbed behind the wheel, swung the van onto the road, and sped back toward Rosebay. Noah had no comment until they flashed past the gates to the estate.

"The way you're driving, I'm guessing you've got a destination in mind."

"The general store. The place is bulging with stuff. We need to get you an ice bag and an elastic bandage."

There was something else she wanted from the store, but she didn't tell him about it. Not yet. Though a plan had already formed in her mind, she had to build a solid ar-

gument before she shared it with him. It was not going to
be easy to convince him.

Even suffering as he was from the sprain, she should
have known he was too perceptive not to realize that her
mind was seething with more than just concern over his
injury. But he waited until they parked in front of the general store before he demanded an explanation.

"Let's have it, Ellie."

She was ready. She came straight to the point. "They
have a notice board in there with vacation rentals listed on
it. Some of them are isolated mountain cabins. There's
nothing you can do now for the next several days but heal
that ankle, and you need someplace safe to do it."

She could see by the grim tightening of his jaw how
much he hated his situation, but he grudgingly accepted the
necessity of a temporary hideaway. "Okay, so we hole up
for a couple of days in a cabin."

"*You* do," she corrected him. "I'm going to be with
Joel in that ridiculous castle."

"The hell you will!"

There was an explosive expression on his face. She ignored it and went on with her proposal.

"Noah, I can make this work. Brett gave me the address
because he wanted me to visit them at the estate. All right,
he'll probably be surprised when I suddenly turn up at his
door, but he'll welcome me as his guest."

"You think so?" he said angrily. "You think his bodyguard isn't going to question what you're doing there when
Ferguson told him I'd grabbed you?"

"He has no real proof of that. You said it yourself last
night. Brett will believe me when I tell him the Ozarks
didn't work out, that I decided to accept his invitation and
paint the mountains here. If I'm asked, I never saw you. I
don't know anything about where you are, and I'm just as
shocked as everybody else that you escaped and are still
on the loose."

He opened his mouth for another stern objection, but she cut him off. "No, listen to me. It all makes sense. You can't be there yet for Joel, but I can. I can watch over him for you, I can make sure that he's safe. Then when the time comes, when your ankle is no longer a problem, I can bring him out to you. Your intention to sneak in there and run with him wasn't a good plan, anyway, but this way—"

"No! It's too dangerous! You forgetting that Buchanan could be a killer?"

"He has no reason to harm me. I'm not a threat to him. It isn't as if I'm going in there to snoop. Though, of course, there's always the chance that I might learn some answers just by being there. Don't look at me like that. I know how to be careful."

He stared at her for a moment in silence. Then, maddened by his helplessness, he brought his fist down hard on the padded dash. "This isn't what I wanted," he said. "Once we'd located Joel, I wanted you to turn around and go home. I wanted you safe and sound where I wouldn't have to worry about you."

She could understand what he was feeling. He was essentially a man of action, and now he'd been taken out of the game. Forced to sit on the bench and watch while she carried the ball. Even though his removal was a temporary one, it drove him crazy.

She leaned toward him, appealing to his emotions on another, softer level. "Please, Noah, let me do this for you. Let me do it for Joel."

His son's welfare was something he couldn't ignore. In the end, he surrendered to her argument.

"All right," he grumbled, "but if this doesn't work out, if Buchanan should get suspicious of you in any way at all, I want your guarantee that you're out of there."

She gave him that promise before she left him in the van and hurried into the general store.

The elderly storekeeper was happy to provide her with

everything she requested, including an available cabin that was secluded but equipped with the essentials. She was thankful the woman asked no questions. If she wondered why Ellie wanted the rental, or who else might be occupying it, she kept her curiosity to herself.

Ellie came away from the store armed with two bags of groceries that also contained an ice bag and an elastic bandage, a key to the cabin, and directions to its exact location. Her credit card had taken another beating, but she would worry about that later.

Noah, however, expressed his concern over the subject the moment she rejoined him in the van. "I've put you through a lot, Ellie, but I'm damned if I'm going to leave you in debt as well. When all this is over and Joel and I get relocated, I'll find *some* way to repay you."

For a moment she was angry that he should regard the money as important when, compared to everything else, it didn't matter at all. But she said nothing, knowing this was his male pride talking again. She wished, though, that he could see all of this—the money, her being here for him, her wanting to help him in any way she could—for what it was. An expression of her belief in him—of her love.

But what if he did recognize that love and was afraid to acknowledge it? Afraid he would hurt her because he didn't share her feeling? They had never discussed this aspect of their relationship. Not in specific terms. She longed to know, but there had been no time.

Nor was there any time now to pursue the subject. She needed to concentrate her thoughts on the job ahead of her. The rest must wait. But the longing wouldn't go away. The nagging hunger to know that she meant something to him, even if a future together was impossible. Because if she had that much, his love to cherish, then when he and Joel left her behind she could somehow endure the pain of their separation.

She had to stop this! Had to focus on the here and now!

To divert herself as well as Noah, she began to rapidly describe their destination as she drove in the opposite direction of the Buchanan estate, crossing the valley to the mountains on the west.

"The cabin is in an open hollow up there. They call them coves around here. The Cherokee River runs right through the cove. In fact, the cabin's back door opens practically on the water. There's a raft there, so you can fish if you'd like. I think you could manage that. But she said to be careful because there are some bad rapids not far downstream…"

Noah listened without comment. She knew he wasn't interested in fishing. He was struggling to maintain his self-control in a situation he loathed.

A deserted back road carried them up through the forests to a fold between the mountains. When they topped the ridge, the trees opened briefly, affording them a glimpse of the small, weathered cabin tucked beside the rushing river far below. Then the narrow track descended through the woods along a series of zigzags.

They had emerged into the clearing on the level floor of the cove before they saw the cabin again. This time it was only yards away, a picturesque, split-log structure sheltered under a sourwood tree, so brilliant a crimson it glowed like a torch.

It was a lonely setting. An ideal hideaway for Noah while he recovered from his sprain. Maybe too lonely. By the time she settled him inside the compact cabin, she began to regret the necessity of leaving him here on his own.

"The ankle," she said.

"Keep off it as much as possible, keep it elevated, keep the ice on it, keep the elastic bandage on it. I know, Ellie."

"The groceries—"

"I watched you put them away. I can find them."

"The remote for the TV—"

"Right here beside me."

"There are plenty of books, anyway. But no phone. Why didn't I think to ask if there was a phone?"

"Ellie ?"

"What?"

"Stop worrying about me. I can manage."

"Of course." But they both knew she was unconvinced. "I'll try to come back first thing tomorrow, if I can get away. They'll expect me to go out painting. No one should question it."

He took her hand, drawing her down until her face was level with his own where he sat in a deep easy chair. "This stinks, doesn't it?" he said, his voice low and husky in that slow rumble that never failed to tug at her insides.

She didn't know what to say. Their parting was even more difficult than she'd anticipated. "I'd better go," she murmured. "I'll have to find a phone back in Rosebay. I can't just show up at the castle without calling first."

"Yeah." He took her face between his big hands. "Uh, watch yourself with Buchanan, will you?"

"I know."

"No, you don't. The guy has a way of getting to women."

Her gaze searched his dark eyes. What she saw there left her glowing. He was jealous. Aside from his major concern about Brett, he was jealous at the thought of her being near him. But she was afraid to attach too much meaning to that jealousy.

"I'll remember that," she promised him solemnly.

"Okay, but just in case you're tempted to forget…"

His reminder came in the form of a potent kiss. Mouth melding with hers, he branded her with his lips and tongue. It was a deep, thorough kiss that rocked her senses, leaving her breathless when he finally released her.

"What have you gone and done to me, Rembrandt?" he asked her, his voice rough with emotion. "And, come to think of it, *for* me? My kid, too. How am I supposed to thank you for all of it?''

"We'll find a way," she promised him, keeping her voice light and playful. It was the only way she could find the will to turn and leave the cabin without him.

THE IRON GATES were no longer a barrier. Ellie was expected. The phone call from Rosebay had taken care of that. All she had to do was identify herself from her lowered window at the speaker mounted in a stone pier. The gates swung inward, admitting her van.

She was aware, as she rolled up the drive, that the electronic gates were promptly closed behind her. The estate was being very careful about its security. She could guess why.

The long, smooth drive ascended the wooded mountainside along a series of switchbacks that brought her at last to the castle's front door. Turning off the engine, she gazed up at the sprawling structure. It really was an extravagant stone pile, but she couldn't deny its magnificence.

She went on sitting there at the wheel, giving herself a moment to steady her nerves. Playing a role as an ordinary houseguest was a tough challenge. Deceit didn't come easily to her. She would need to be careful at every turn.

Reminding herself that what Noah so desperately needed was somewhere behind those lofty walls and that she had the means to give it to him, she summoned her courage and climbed from the van.

Brett himself, blond and handsome, came down the wide stone steps to meet her in the drive. "Welcome to North Carolina's version of Balmoral."

She clasped the hand he offered, forcing a cheerful, "You look right at home playing the local laird."

He laughed, displaying perfect teeth. "I have to admit I'm having fun with it, but I draw the line at wearing a kilt. Come on inside and see the place."

She accompanied him toward the front door. "It's brazen of me to arrive here like this, but it's like I told you on the phone—I was all set to paint mountains in autumn, and when the Ozarks didn't work out I thought—"

"No apologies. I couldn't be more pleased that you're here."

Not wanting him to get the wrong idea, she defused his enthusiasm with a quick, "Well, I missed Joel."

They paused under the archway of the stone porch that sheltered the door. She turned to him. "Where is he, by the way?"

"Inside, working with a retired kindergarten teacher I hired from Rosebay. She was willing to come out half days to tutor him."

"He's not attending public school then?"

Brett shook his head, his expression turning grim. "He isn't setting foot off the estate until Noah Rhyder has been caught. I suppose you know he's on the loose out there somewhere."

"Yes, I heard it on the news," she murmured. "But you don't think that he'd try to—"

"Probably not. He must still be in Missouri, but I'm not taking any chances. The boy remains inside the estate and protected until Noah is back behind bars."

It was not going to be easy then delivering Joel to his father, Ellie thought. She was relieved about one thing. Peaches couldn't have revealed to his employer Lew Ferguson's opinion that Noah had kidnapped her. Brett wouldn't have welcomed her here if he had.

"How is Joel doing?" she asked him solemnly.

"He seems content, but to tell you the truth, I think he's lonely. He misses you too. It'll be good for him to have you here."

"Has he been told about..."

"Yes, I explained to him about his father. Don't ask me what he's feeling. He still doesn't want to discuss it, and I haven't pushed it. Maybe you can get him to open up. I'm putting you in the room next to his. I hope that's all right."

"I'd be disappointed if you hadn't."

He led the way into the castle. Seconds later, Ellie stood beside him in a cavernous banquet hall with immense fireplaces and a barrel-vaulted ceiling. Everything but tartan on the walls, she thought.

"How do you like it?" he said, pointing out a piper's gallery overhead.

She was aware that he was too close to her, his arm brushing her side. She glanced at him, noticing something she'd never observed before. There was arrogance in that good-looking face. She remembered Noah's warning. Brett Buchanan was not to be trusted.

Uneasy with his closeness, she started to move away. And found herself dealing with another threat. There was a sudden pressure against her leg. Alarmed, she looked down to see the hound, Caesar, who had arrived without warning in the hall. He was pushing against her calf, sniffing at her suspiciously.

Ellie went very still, fearing that the dog was about to recognize her from this morning. If he regarded her as an intruder, there was the possibility that, aside from taking a chunk out of her leg, his unfriendly behavior would result in his master asking some awkward questions.

Brett, finally noticing the animal, glowered at him. "He won't hurt you, but he's not supposed to be in this part of the house." He lifted his voice in a shout, calling for his bodyguard. "Peaches!"

Ellie kept her wary gaze on the dog, but out of the tail of her eye she saw Peaches appear in a doorway across the hall.

"Get this mutt out of here," Brett instructed him.

The bodyguard snapped his fingers, and Caesar trotted obediently to his side. The hound had lost interest in her.

But Peaches, discovering her presence in the hall, eyed her shrewdly.

Ellie nervously wondered if she was about to be challenged, but he remained silent. Maybe Peaches didn't want his employer to know he'd hooked up with Lew Ferguson. Or maybe he simply felt that, if she had been kidnapped by Noah as the detective claimed, then she wouldn't be casually turning up here on her own.

Whatever the explanation, she knew she would have to watch herself around the bodyguard. He was a potential enemy.

Acknowledging her with a polite nod, Peaches turned his attention to Brett. "You asked me to remind you about the conference call with Chicago scheduled for one o'clock. You want me to cancel it now?"

"No, I'd better go ahead with it." Brett glanced at his watch, then favored her with one of his dazzling smiles. "Ellie, will you excuse us? One of the staff will be along to help you with your things and see that you get settled. Just make yourself at home, and I'll see you later."

He disappeared with Peaches and the dog. Ellie, uncomfortable with the idea of being waited on, went out to the van to collect her luggage on her own. She had unloaded her two cases when she was startled by a yelp of excitement from the direction of the front door.

Looking up, she saw the small figure of Joel tearing down the steps. He'd obviously been informed of her arrival. Released from his lessons, he had rushed to meet her.

She was clutched in a fierce hug. Their reunion would have been emotional under any circumstances, because the child had captured her heart from the start. But now, feeling as she did about Noah, knowing this was his son she embraced, she felt a protective tenderness for Joel that threatened to result in tears. To prevent that, she held him away and gazed into his small, earnest face.

"I missed you, sweetheart."

"Me, too." He grinned up at her happily, but she thought she detected a shadow of sadness in his dark eyes. Noah's eyes.

"So now we don't have to miss each other. Only there's a small problem."

"What?"

"Where am I going to sleep?" she wondered, pretending she didn't already know.

"Next to me. Come on, I'll show you." He tugged impatiently at her hand.

"Whoa, I have to bring in my suitcases."

"I'll help."

He insisted on taking one of the bags. She reluctantly handed him the smaller of the two. Lugging it manfully up the steps and into the castle, he led the way down a broad corridor. They weren't midway along the passage when he began to puff with the effort.

"Why don't I take it the rest of the way?" she suggested.

"I can do it."

He stubbornly moved on toward the stairway at the end of the corridor, the case banging against him. Ellie worried about him, fearing that the load would be more than he could handle on the massive staircase. A solution presented itself when they reached the bottom of the flight.

"Just like in a hotel!" she said, exaggerating her amazement as she indicated the elaborate iron gate stretched across a paneled cubicle in the wall beside the staircase.

She thought he would be delighted by her surprised discovery of the small elevator, but Joel had no response.

"Aren't we going to ride up in style?" she wondered. "Or are you going to make me haul my suitcase all the way to the bedroom?" Again he had no answer. "Joel, doesn't the elevator work?"

"Uh-huh."

"Then why don't you want us to use it?"

"I like the stairs," he murmured, offering no other explanation.

He clearly had a dislike of the elevator. She could see it in his manner, in the way he edged away from the gate as though he feared he might be trapped behind it. It was an odd phobia for a boy who, otherwise, was fascinated with machinery. Back in St. Louis he had forever asked her questions about such things as cranes and bulldozers. But this subject agitated him to the degree that he was unwilling to discuss it.

"Then I like the stairs too," she said firmly.

His relief was evident. They mounted the stairway in easy stages. Ellie pretended a need for frequent pauses to rest her load so that he wouldn't be tired by his own heavy burden.

The matter of the elevator was unimportant, a concern she would have dismissed if she hadn't recalled Joel's aversion to the fanciful slide in her home. Come to think of it, he had also avoided any contact with the old-fashioned laundry chute outside her bedroom. Was there a similarity here, a connection of some kind? Maybe it had to do with height in enclosed spaces.

"I just remembered something," she said brightly when they reached the landing. "You and your Uncle Brett had a plane ride out here to North Carolina."

"Two planes," he corrected her cheerfully. "A big one first and then a small one."

"I've never been up in a small plane. I'm not sure I'd like it."

"I did. It was great."

That couldn't be the problem then. And did it really matter? Children often had funny likes and dislikes about unrelated things. She forgot about it. Joel was eager to show her their bedrooms.

They went along another passage to the front of the mansion. He led the way into a spacious, elegantly furnished room that overlooked the valley.

"This is yours," he said, depositing her bag at the foot of the bed. "And here's my room in here."

He showed her how the two rooms connected, pointing out the bathroom they would share.

"This is wonderful," she said, admiring the accommodations. "I'm going to feel very spoiled staying here."

"Will you stay for good? I want you to stay for good, Ellie."

"Sweetheart, I'm only here for a short visit. I thought you understood that."

"Oh."

She looked down into his face and saw disappointment. "Joel, aren't you happy living here?"

"It's okay."

"Just *okay?*" she asked him gently.

He thought about that for a second. "I've got a pony. He's out in the stable with Uncle Brett's horse."

"Wow, your own pony! Will I get to meet him?"

"You want to go now? Hobo can come with us." Without waiting for her answer, he raced into his bedroom and returned bearing the clown puppet to which he had become attached back in St. Louis.

"Hello, Hobo," she greeted the sad-faced tramp. "Are you ready to see the pony?"

Minutes later, they were on their way to the stables with Joel chattering beside her as they descended a walk through terraced formal gardens.

"Jonnie takes care of the horses," he informed her. "Jonnie's my friend and is teaching me how to ride."

"You like Jonnie, huh?"

"Jonnie's nice."

They reached the stables at the bottom of the gardens. Jonnie turned out to be a young woman with skin the color of dark mahogany and a warm, glowing smile. Ellie liked her immediately. She seemed very fond of Joel.

The pony was led out and presented to Ellie. She was busy admiring him when she was startled by what sounded like an explosion from the stall behind them. Swinging around, she saw a large black horse tossing its head restlessly as it bumped against the half door of the stall. There was a wild look in its eye.

"That's Sultan," Joel said. "He's mean."

Ellie's gaze met Jonnie's. The young woman sketched a shrug, murmuring a soft, "Mr. Buchanan's horse. I don't know why he bought him. He's a handsome brute, but he has a bad disposition."

Ellie cast a glance in Joel's direction.

Jonnie noticed her concern. "Don't worry," she quickly assured her. "Joel knows he's not supposed to go anywhere near Sultan, and I'm always careful to keep the door latched."

Ellie and Joel were on their way back to the house when she decided to introduce the sensitive subject of Noah. She longed to tell the boy that his father was close by, that he loved and wanted him, but she didn't dare. Not yet. What she could do was to learn just how much Joel cared. That was vital if she was going to risk reuniting him with Noah.

"Joel, can I ask you a question?"

"Uh-huh."

"Do you miss your father?"

He didn't answer her. When she looked down, he was tightly clutching the puppet, slowly stroking the top of its head.

"Sweetheart," she coaxed, "it's all right to talk about him."

Still no answer. She tried again.

"He didn't go away because he stopped loving you. It was something he couldn't help, and if he could I bet he'd have you with him right now."

She waited for his response, *any* response, as they climbed up through the gardens, but Joel had shut down like a trap. Why? she wondered. Why was the subject something he still refused to discuss? Did he resent his father because he believed he had abandoned him? Or was there another reason for his silence?

She thought about it. Remembered that, no matter how carefully Joel had been shielded, the murder and its aftermath had been a terrible experience for him. Maybe his young mind simply couldn't handle it anymore, so he had taught himself that if he didn't talk about it, then none of it could be true.

That was what Ellie wanted to believe. But another thought occurred to her, one she struggled to resist. What if Joel was afraid of his father, convinced he was dangerous? What if, when the time came, he wouldn't want to join him?

The awful possibility was still with her late that night. Joel was asleep in his room next door. Ellie, alone in her darkened bedroom, knelt on the window seat and gazed across the valley. A single light winked high on the slope of a distant mountain.

She knew it couldn't be a lamp shining from the cabin where Noah was hiding. The cove that sheltered the cabin was out of sight somewhere behind those hills. But in her loneliness for him she pictured him out there, sleepless as she was, worried as she was, with a solitary light burning at his bedside like that one.

She hoped he was managing all right with his ankle. She also wondered, when she saw him again, whether she ought to tell him about Joel's silence and her fear of what that silence might convey. It would devastate him if he thought Joel didn't want to be with him. No, she couldn't tell him. Not unless it became absolutely necessary.

The light on the mountainside vanished. It had been turned off.

"Good night, love. I'll see you tomorrow," she promised, whispering her message into the blackness of the night.

Chapter Eleven

Ellie was eager the next morning to keep her promise to Noah. But first she had to find a way to slip away from the castle so she could visit the cabin in secret.

They were seated in the sumptuous dining room, bright with sunlight. She waited until Brett finished helping himself to more coffee. Then she declared her intention in a casual voice.

"Would you mind if I spent the morning away from the estate? I want to scout picture locations. I may even do some painting if anything irresistible turns up."

"I'd love to be out there with you. So would Joel." Brett sipped his coffee and nodded in the direction of a back parlor that had been designated a schoolroom. "He already made a fuss having to go off to his lessons with Mrs. Connelly. It's too bad neither one of us is available for you this morning, but I promise to be more attentive as soon as I wrap up some pressing business."

Ellie did her best not to look relieved. It was all working out, and she was satisfied that Joel would be safe while she was gone. She had met his teacher before breakfast. The woman seemed devoted to him. He would be with her until lunch, and by then Ellie planned to be back at the castle. Besides, even if Brett was involved somehow in the death of his father, there was no reason to suppose he was any threat to the boy. Anyway, what choice did she have? Joel was forbidden to leave the estate, and she had to meet with Noah.

Brett regarded her thoughtfully. "I imagine you'll be in and out of the place a lot. It's probably a good idea if you have an automatic opener of your own for the gates."

He trusted her. Perfect, Ellie thought. She could come and go without being monitored, and when the time came to remove Joel from the estate…

She felt a hard gaze on her. Peaches. He sat across the table from her. When she looked at him, she could see it on his face. He didn't want her to have that gate opener. But he was in no position to offer any objection when Brett instructed him, "Peaches, will you see to it that Ellie gets one of the spare openers for her van?"

Peaches nodded without comment. He was supposed to be Brett's driver and bodyguard, but he was more like a factotum. He didn't seem to resent it, nodding again when Brett stood and added a quick, "After that I'll need you in the library. It's going to be a full morning."

This was something else Ellie wondered about. She'd gathered that Brett was dealing with a tense business matter. There had been a veiled reference to it between him and Peaches shortly after her arrival yesterday and again last night at dinner. It evidently had to do with a series of phone calls between here and Chicago. Brett was supposed to have been in Chicago the day his father died. Maybe there was a connection between all this and Howard Buchanan's murder. Or maybe not. Ellie would love to know, but right now her need to join Noah at the cabin was a priority.

SHE NOTICED IT in her rearview mirror just seconds after she pulled away from the gates. A dark blue sedan directly behind her. She had no reason to be worried by its presence.

After all, this was a public road. Why shouldn't other vehicles regularly use it?

But Ellie had an uneasy feeling about this particular car. It seemed to have appeared out of nowhere. Nor did it make any effort to pass her, even when she slowed the van to an aggravating crawl on a pretext of admiring the scenery.

Maybe her situation was making her paranoid, or maybe she had a real concern here. She kept a watchful eye on the rearview mirror as she continued along Settlement Road. The dark sedan, like some sinister phantom, shadowed her through every turn and dip.

Ellie decided long before she reached the crossroads where the general store was located that she was definitely being followed. And though her pursuer maintained just enough distance between them to prevent her from catching more than an unsatisfactory glimpse of him at the wheel, she was certain of his identity.

Noah's enemy, Detective Lew Ferguson. It had to be him. Nor had his rental sedan just happened to be there outside the gates when she emerged from the estate. Peaches must have contacted him when he'd left the dining room to fetch the gate opener. Ferguson had been waiting for her.

Ellie understood now why the bodyguard hadn't objected to her sudden arrival at the castle yesterday. He regarded her as an opportunity. Because if he and Ferguson were convinced she was the key to Noah, they must be hoping she would lead them to his hideout.

She couldn't go to the cabin. She couldn't go anywhere near it. When she arrived at the crossroads, she turned left toward Rosebay. It was the opposite direction from the route to the cabin.

She was on the highway now. There was traffic here, and it thickened as she neared the center of town. Maybe she could lose the detective, find her way to the cabin after all... Not a chance. Despite the congestion or the twists and turns she executed as she pretended to explore the town, the dark blue sedan stayed with her. Relentless and unnerving, determined to wear her down.

Ellie's anger and frustration mounted. He was keeping her from Noah, and there was nothing she could do about it. Yes, there was one thing. She could demonstrate the innocence of her outing, make the effort to convince her pursuer that she had no connection with the man he wanted. Even that she was unaware of being tailed, or at least not troubled by it.

She found a place to park along the main street, conscious of the sedan doing the same just down the block but ignoring it as she struck out on foot.

Rosebay was a bustling community supported by a large furniture factory. She strolled along the sidewalk, gazing into the windows as though she had nothing more important to do. There was a paint store that carried art supplies. She went inside, browsed through its merchandise, and bought a tube of watercolor that she didn't need. She didn't see him, but she knew that Lew Ferguson was somewhere close by.

There was a bank on the corner, and when she came away from the paint store she decided she had a legitimate reason to use it. She had secured emergency traveler's checks in St. Louis for her trip to the Ozarks. Noah would need funds to get away, and when that moment arrived there would be no time or means to secure them. He didn't know it yet, but she intended to finance his flight from North Carolina.

Ellie went into the bank to turn the checks into cash. When she emerged a few minutes later, Lew Ferguson was waiting for her on the sidewalk. The sight of him standing there in her path disarmed her for a second. Then, remembering that she wasn't supposed to know who he was, she started to move away from him, hoping that she had betrayed no sign of recognition.

He stopped her with a raspy-voiced, "Ms. Matheson?"

Ellie turned to face him, registering her surprise. The surprise was genuine. She hadn't expected him to reveal himself. He must have grown tired of playing cat and mouse with her, realized that it was getting him nowhere and decided to risk a bold confrontation.

"Yes," she said hesitantly, "I'm Ellie Matheson, but how did you—"

"Detective Lew Ferguson from the St. Louis P.D." He displayed his identification for her.

Ellie glanced at his credentials, then smiled at him sweetly. "How nice. Someone else from home. Are you here on vacation too, Detective?"

His gaze narrowed, warning her not to play games with him. "It's business, Ms. Matheson, not pleasure."

But not *official* business since his department didn't know he was here, and for that reason alone she was prepared to resist him. "I see. Well, actually, I don't. Did you want to ask me something, because you still haven't said how you knew who I was?"

"A cop has his sources."

And we both know you have no intention of disclosing this one.

"As a matter of fact, Ms. Matheson, there *are* a couple of questions you could answer for me." He leaned back against the parking meter behind him. "In connection with Noah Rhyder."

She gazed at him directly, careful to maintain an expression of innocence. "Then he's still on the loose?"

"Afraid so."

She nodded sympathetically. "Which, of course, is why you're here in North Carolina. I can understand that now. I just can't understand how I could possibly help you to find him."

"I figure maybe you might, Ms. Matheson." She didn't like him. Even if he wasn't relentlessly after Noah, she wouldn't have liked him. He had ashes on his clothes, he stank of cigar fumes, and he was smug. "Like to know why I figure that?"

"Please."

"Because I think you've been with him recently. I think he busted into your house back in St. Louis, grabbed you, and forced you to take him to North Carolina so he could snatch his kid. Maybe I'm wrong, Ms. Matheson, but that's what I think."

"That's quite a theory, Detective. Uh, how did you—"

"Arrive at it? Well, now, see, it's more than just a theory. There's a matter of some evidence."

Ferguson went on to describe how her worried neighbor had let him into her house and how he had discovered the discarded jail coverall in the basement, traces of dark hair in the bathroom sink, and the smashed door in the kitchen.

Ellie was impressively appalled. "You're serious? He was actually inside my house? If it was ransacked, I've got to call home."

"He wasn't in there for that reason, Ms. Matheson. All he wanted was his kid."

"I can't imagine why he thought he'd find him there. The house was empty. Joel was with his uncle, and I was gone on my trip."

Ferguson shoved his hands into his pockets and nodded slowly. "Then you weren't home when Rhyder broke in, so he couldn't have grabbed you."

"I don't see how it's possible, Detective. Do you?"

"No, not if you were already on the road, like you say. But it's a funny thing about that break-in. Nothing was damaged except the kitchen door, which means he entered from the garage. Now how did he get into the garage after you were gone? No windows in there, no entrance except for the garage door itself. That was down, and it being automatic, he couldn't have raised it from the outside. See what I mean?"

"That is funny. How *did* he get in? Unless…" She broke off in flustered realization. "I'm afraid I have a bad habit of forgetting to punch the opener when I'm distracted."

"Which you happened to be that night."

"Must have been. I was probably trying to remember whether I'd packed everything when I pulled away. I suppose I forgot to hit the button on my visor. If the garage was wide open, all he had to do was walk in and lower the door after him."

"You really think it happened that way?"

"I'm sure it did. Don't you?"

"No, I don't. I still say he abducted you and that maybe along the way you fell for him, and now you're protecting him. Where is he, Ms. Matheson?"

"I think I've answered enough absurd questions, Detective Ferguson."

"Just one more. Why are you here in North Carolina?"

"To visit a little boy I'm very fond of, to paint in the mountains, and because Brett Buchanan invited me. All solid reasons for being here. Feel free to check them out." She started to turn away. Then she stopped and faced him again with a challenge of her own. "By the way, shouldn't you have had a search warrant to go into my house without my permission?"

He flushed, his florid face turning an even deeper red. An *angry* red.

"Don't worry, Detective. I don't plan to file a complaint. *This* time."

Ellie left him there on the sidewalk. She was fairly certain that he wouldn't dare to approach her again, not when he had no authority to be here. But she knew better than to think she'd seen the last of him.

He hadn't believed anything she'd told him. As tenacious as a pit bull, he would continue to follow her, confident that she would eventually lead him to Noah. Why? Why did he have this abnormal obsession to punish Noah?

She didn't bother checking her rearview mirror when she drove away from Rosebay. She knew the dark blue sedan would be somewhere not far behind her, but there was no point now in trying to shake it. It made no difference, because the morning was almost gone. She had no choice but to return to the castle.

Joel would soon be finished with his half day of lessons. She had promised herself that when his teacher departed she would be there for him. Though she trusted the boy with Mrs. Connelly, she didn't trust him with either Brett or Peaches.

The situation was maddening. Lew Ferguson had cheated her of seeing Noah, and she damned him for it. Now her need to be with the man she loved would have to go unsatisfied for another twenty-four hours. She couldn't safely try again until tomorrow morning.

Noah would be frantic when another day passed without contact from her. He had to be worried, wondering what was happening, maybe even imagining the worst. But what else could she do? If only there were a phone at the cabin...

ELLIE PARKED THE VAN in a wide gravel area at the side of the castle. She was about to head for the front door when she heard the sound of voices behind the tall hedge that bordered the drive. One of them belonged to Brett. The other was a woman's, punctuated by lilting laughter. They were coming up through the gardens from the direction of the stables.

Not wanting to intrude if Brett had a guest, Ellie started to turn away. Too late. He had already appeared in the narrow archway in the hedge and discovered her standing there.

"Ellie!" he called to her. "Look who turned up this morning to join the party!"

He came on through the archway and stepped aside, permitting his companion to reveal herself in the opening. For a second Ellie didn't recognize the stunning redhead. It wasn't until she smiled that she remembered her. It was a smile as blinding as Brett's. She had met it once before in her driveway back in St. Louis.

"Look at her face," the tall redhead teased in her low, throaty voice. "She's as surprised as you were, Brett, when I landed at your gates."

Hand outstretched, the woman came forward to greet her. Ellie shook the offered hand, murmuring a polite, "It's Sandra O'Hara, isn't it?"

"Bless you for remembering. Most of the time I get, 'Oh, it's the lady from Family Services.'"

"I didn't forget that part either. You were Joel's case-worker there at the very end when he was turned over to Brett." Ellie had a sudden concern about that. "Is something wrong? Is that why you—"

"Arrived out of nowhere? No, it's nothing like that. I'm not here in any official capacity. I had to take some vacation time or lose it. I remembered Brett's tempting descriptions of the mountains here, so I thought, why not? I could have my holiday and at the same time stop in to check on Joel's progress."

"More than just stop in," Brett said. "I've convinced Sandra to be my guest while she's in North Carolina."

"Isn't it awful? He only had to ask, and I moved right in. Who could resist this place?"

"I've been showing her Sultan while we waited for Joel to finish his lessons."

"Isn't he an impressive animal?"

The redhead linked a proprietary arm with Brett's. The meaning of her words, and of her action, was not lost on Ellie. She had already clearly understood the situation. Sandra O'Hara wasn't interested in Joel's progress or the North Carolina mountains. She was interested in nothing but Brett Buchanan and had been from the start, back in St. Louis. If she in any way regarded Ellie as a rival, she was far too self-assured to let it bother her. Her manner toward her remained friendly, her smile radiant.

Sandra O'Hara didn't know it, but Ellie was grateful for her arrival on the scene. If the redhead kept Brett occupied—and he was behaving as though he wouldn't object to her attentions—then Ellie herself was safe from him. He'd be too involved with Sandra to get familiar with her or be curious about her activities.

"There's our boy now," the redhead said, lifting her hand in a cheerful wave.

Ellie turned to see Joel at the window of his schoolroom. Though he politely returned Sandra's wave, his greeting lacked enthusiasm. He probably doesn't even remember who she is, Ellie thought.

Joel was shy with the social worker when they all sat down to lunch a few minutes later. She asked him questions about his schoolwork and his pony, and he answered her in monosyllables. Ellie didn't blame him for his spiritless manner. Sandra's incandescent smile and eager conversation wore a bit thin after a while, though Brett seemed fascinated by both.

Ellie revised her opinion about Joel's quiet mood when they escaped to his bedroom after lunch. Probably Sandra had nothing to do with it. He was looking a bit flushed.

"Sweetheart, are you feeling all right?"

His shoulders lifted in a little shrug. "I dunno. I guess."

She felt his forehead. It was slightly warm. She wondered if he was running a fever. "Why don't you lie down," she suggested, "while I see if I can find a thermometer. I'd like to take your temperature."

He didn't object. He crawled up on his bed and cuddled Hobo. Ellie checked the bathroom. No thermometer. Leaving their rooms, she went in search of one.

The house was quiet. The staff were all in the service wing, and Sandra had disappeared into her own bedroom to unpack her things.

Ellie was passing the library when she heard Brett's voice behind the door that stood ajar. She raised her hand to rap on its surface, intending to ask him where she could locate a thermometer.

Then she realized he was talking to someone on the phone just inside, maybe Chicago again. When his voice suddenly lifted with impatience, his words becoming perfectly clear, she forgot all about her intention to announce herself.

"I'm telling you there's nothing to worry about. Listen, I don't care what my situation was six months ago. I can cover the debt without a problem. There's plenty of money now."

Ellie stood there, listening with growing dismay.

"No, it's true. My troubles are over. Never mind how. All you have to know is that I solved them. Even better, there's more where that came from, and before long…"

She was so involved in what she was overhearing that she failed to detect any movement behind her. It was only when a hand reached around her and quietly, firmly closed the library door, shutting off the conversation on the other side, that she realized she was no longer alone in the hall.

Ellie swung around to find the hulking figure of Peaches blocking her path. There was a menacing expression on his broad face.

"You wanna watch what you listen to, Ms. Matheson," he cautioned her, his voice low and tough. "Could be people will think you're snooping."

"Are you accusing me of eavesdropping?" Technically, that was exactly what she had been doing, but she resented the bodyguard's implied threat.

"Me? No, I wouldn't go around insulting Mr. Buchanan's guests like that. He wouldn't like it. On the other hand, he might like it even less if he was to learn somebody had overheard one of his private calls."

"You go ahead and tell him what you want," she informed him boldly. "And while you're at it, let him know that the only thing I was *snooping* for was a thermometer to take Joel's temperature."

She pushed past him without another word. He didn't try to stop her.

Less than twenty minutes later, as Ellie gently drew the coverlet over Joel's sleeping figure, there was a soft tap on the bedroom door. She went to answer it. Brett stood in the hallway, looking concerned.

"Peaches said you needed a thermometer for Joel. Is he ill?"

She shook her head. "One of the help did finally come up with a thermometer for me. I took his temperature. It's normal, and he isn't complaining of anything. I think he was just tired. He's napping now."

"If you're sure he's okay, then I won't come in and disturb him. Sandra and I are going riding. Why don't you join us?"

"Thanks, but I think I'll just sit with Joel a bit."

"You don't have to. One of the staff will do that."

"I'd like to," she assured him. "It will give me a chance to catch up on my sketching."

"Well, if you won't change your mind..." She thought he would leave then, but he went on standing there. He was watching her, wondering maybe just how much of his sensitive phone conversation she had managed to hear. Peaches must have told him she was there outside the library. Would he challenge her?

In the end he merely smiled, told her he would see her later, and left. Relieved, Ellie shut the door behind him and settled on the rocking chair beside Joel's bed. Her thoughts were on that phone call.

Just how important were those fragments she had overheard? Important enough that her knowledge of them might be dangerous to her? Important enough to provide a motive and explanation for Howard Buchanan's murder? The trouble was, none of it was clear, none of it was definite.

She needed to share all of this with Noah, to discuss it with him carefully. There were possibilities here, particularly concerning Joel, that she feared to examine without him. She missed his strength and decisiveness. Longed to be with him again.

Tomorrow, she promised herself. One way or another, she would go to him tomorrow.

SUPERINTENDENT Hamish Bolling looked up over the top of his slipping glasses. The slim figure of Officer Judy Belucci stood there in the open doorway of his corner office in the St. Louis Homicide Division.

"What?" he asked.

"Sir, there may be a lead for us in connection with Detective Ferguson and the Rhyder case."

"About time," he grumbled. "What is it?"

"There's this woman down in holding. They picked her up last night for rolling a drunk in the bar where she works. Her name is—" she consulted the slip of paper in her hand "—Ginger Zukawski. She says you know her."

"Do I?" He thought about it for a second. "Yeah, maybe I do. From back when I was working vice. This isn't Ginger's first arrest either."

"That's what she told me when they called me down. She's afraid this time they'll throw away the key. She's asking to talk to you personally."

He nodded his grizzled head, immediately understanding the situation. "Ginger wants to cut a deal. Only how come she's got information to trade?"

"She says her boyfriend is an ex-cop who worked with Lew Ferguson before he left the force. He and Ferguson are still buddies."

"That would be Peaches. It's all come back to me now. So she knows something."

"That's what she claims, sir."

"All right, Judy. Have them bring her up. We'll see if what she's got is worth anything."

Officer Belucci departed to handle the request. While Ham waited at his desk for her return, he thought about Ginger Zukawski's boyfriend. He hadn't much cared for Peaches, either as a human being or as a cop. He suspected the guy had been on the take, though no accusation had ever been leveled. In his estimation, Peaches was no loss to the department.

Minutes later, Officer Belucci led Ginger Zukawski into his office. The blonde still had a figure, but her face had suffered from years of the wrong kind of living. A night spent in a holding cell hadn't helped. Ham waved her to a chair in front of his desk.

Ginger cast a glance around his cluttered office as she settled herself. "Your place looks as bad as my apartment, Superintendent."

"We'll talk housekeeping later, Ginger. Let's hear what you know."

"Yeah, but first—"

"Uh-uh, you know how it works. No promises. You talk, and if it's worthwhile, I'll see what I can do for you. That's all the guarantee you get, Ginger."

She hesitated, then nodded with resignation as she crossed her legs. "Word on the street is you got a detective missing. I know where he is, Superintendent. And if that ain't worth a lot to you, then I bet getting Noah Rhyder back at the same time is."

Bolling and Officer Belucci traded looks. Ginger didn't miss their exchange. Satisfied, she went on to explain that Peaches, who worked now for Brett Buchanan, had trusted her with the confidential North Carolina address and how Lew Ferguson had threatened her to get that address.

"Buchanan has Rhyder's kid," Ginger said. "And Rhyder won't disappear without his kid. That's the way Lew figures it. He's gone to North Carolina to nail Rhyder when he turns up to grab his boy.''

Bolling leaned toward her earnestly. "Are you telling me that Detective Ferguson is that determined to personally collar Noah Rhyder?"

"Damn right. He's positively weird about it. Peaches told me why when Rhyder was arrested. Lew hates him. It's because of this girl that was part of the motorcycle gang Rhyder ran with years back. I guess she was sort of wild. Peaches didn't know the particulars, just that she ended up getting herself killed and that Lew was crazy about her. Peaches said she was probably the only human being he ever really cared about, though he bet the girl didn't feel the same. Anyway, Lew blames Rhyder for her death.''

"Revenge?" Ham asked.

Ginger shrugged. She had disclosed all she knew, and now she was interested in nothing but escaping a jail sentence. Bolling, after obtaining Brett Buchanan's address from her, assured her he would use his influence on her behalf.

When Ginger was returned to holding, he adjusted his slipping glasses and spoke to Officer Belucci.

"If everything Zukawski told us is true, then Lew Ferguson is one hell of a loose cannon. I want the North Carolina authorities alerted. Tell them that Ferguson's presence out there is unauthorized and that if he shows himself and interferes in the Rhyder manhunt, he's to be apprehended.''

Meanwhile, the superintendent wondered, after Belucci had departed to fulfill his instructions, where was Noah Rhyder? Could the fugitive have somehow reached North Carolina? Or was Lew Ferguson simply delusional in his conviction that Rhyder would go to any lengths to recover his son?

There was one thing Ham Bolling was certain about. This case had gotten to be one sweet mess.

NOAH STOOD in the open doorway of the cabin, resting his weight on a crude crutch he had fashioned for himself out of a length of hickory. The ankle was still throbbing, but he ignored it.

He watched the sun go down in a fiery glow over the mountains beyond the river. He knew now that Ellie wasn't going to come. All day he had waited for her anxiously, spending the long hours restlessly examining books and maps of the area he had found in the cabin. The maps, anyway, were of value. He might have to depend on them when the time came to get away.

He hadn't seen a soul. No one had come near the cabin. That made him lucky, he supposed, but he was lonely. God, how he missed Ellie!

Better get used to it. You can't take her with you when you leave here. You've hurt her life enough as it is.

He knew that's how it would have to be, but the thought of an existence without her was killing him. Forget it. He had more immediate concerns. Why hadn't Ellie come? What was happening in that castle up on the mountainside? It was driving him crazy not knowing. His uselessness was even worse.

The sun had vanished, leaving pink banners in the sky. He turned away in disappointment, shutting the door. The cabin was already in thick gloom. He hobbled toward the refrigerator with the intention of making himself supper, though he wasn't hungry. But it was something to do.

It was going to be another long night. He'd do better to spend it resting the ankle instead of worrying about what he couldn't help. He told himself that Ellie and Joel were all right, that there had to be a good reason why she hadn't come today. That she would get here as soon as circumstances permitted.

That's what he told himself. But he also promised himself fiercely that if she didn't appear tomorrow, he was going after her. He wouldn't let this damn ankle stop him either. If he had to, he'd crawl all the way.

Chapter Twelve

Ellie sat at the breakfast table, listening in silent relief to Brett's proposal.

"Peaches is driving us down to Asheville to spend the day. I promised Sandra we'd tour Biltmore," he said, referring to the famous Vanderbilt estate.

This was the opportunity Ellie had been waiting for. Now she could visit Noah without fearing for Joel's safety in her absence. Leaving him behind had been a major concern to her after what she had overheard yesterday outside the library. But with Brett and the surly Peaches off to Asheville for the day, the boy would be all right.

Joel was feeling perfectly well this morning. He was down at the stables now visiting his pony before his tutor arrived. Ellie knew that she could entrust him to Mrs. Connelly for a few hours. Also, his friend, Jonnie, the capable young woman in charge of the horses, would be close by to look out for him.

"You're going to come with us, aren't you, Ellie?" Brett urged her.

She shook her head in feigned regret. "I promised myself I came here to paint, and so far I haven't produced much of anything. I think I'd better spend the day with my brushes."

"Sure you won't change your mind?" Sandra tempted her.

"Thanks, but I plan to hang around the castle. No need to go out at all, with so many pretty views right here."

Her casual announcement was for the benefit of Peaches, who sat eyeing her from the foot of the table. Hopefully, he would relay her intention to Lew Ferguson, convincing the detective it would be pointless to wait for her this morning outside the gates.

Sandra looked disappointed by her refusal. Ellie knew she wasn't though Brett's disappointment seemed genuine enough.

Changing into the overalls, her favorite garb whenever she painted outdoors, Ellie waited impatiently until the car bearing the Asheville-bound party headed down the drive. Then, making sure that Joel was secure in the schoolroom with Mrs. Connelly, she loaded the van with her art supplies and started for the cabin.

She was less than a mile from the castle's gates when she saw it in her rearview mirror. The dark blue sedan. Her spirits plummeted. She should have known that neither Peaches nor Lew Ferguson would have trusted her to remain at the castle.

The detective was going to follow her wherever she went. She couldn't stand it. She had to reach Noah. She refused to subject him to another day without contact from her. But how was she going to escape that sedan?

No solution occurred to her as she drove aimlessly in a direction away from the cabin, her frustration mounting. In the end, knowing she couldn't just wander up and down every back road and hoping to persuade her tail that her outing was a legitimate one, she pulled into a county park on a height overlooking the valley.

As a painting site, it wasn't bad. The scene far down in the hollow offered an excellent subject in the shape of a white clapboard church, an overgrown graveyard adjoining it, and yellow poplars hugging a fenceline. Except that Ellie had no intention of undertaking a painting here. Something requiring that much gear wouldn't permit her a quick get-away, should the chance present itself. But a drawing involved only paper and a pencil.

Sketchbook in hand, she climbed from the van. She was aware of the blue sedan that had trailed her into the wooded park, but she pretended to ignore it. He parked on the other side of a grove occupied by picnic tables, well away from the van but close enough to monitor her every move.

Ellie settled under a gold tulip tree on a point of land overhanging the valley. Open pad on her knees, she began to sketch the country church below her.

Ferguson knew better than to try to approach her today. Across an open gulf on her left was another tongue of land. He took up a position there, leaning against a pine as he patiently smoked one of his eternal cigars. His persistence was unnerving.

Striving to convince him that his presence didn't matter to her in the least, she concentrated on her drawing without bothering to glance more than once in his direction. But all the while she could feel him watching her as she searched her mind for a method to outwit him.

The day was mild, with a clear sun and the aroma of autumn in the air. Mourning doves called to each other from the shrubbery, and chipmunks chased across the grass. The setting demanded nothing but serenity, and outwardly that's how Ellie played it.

Inwardly, she seethed with the need to reach Noah. The day was creeping toward mid-morning. If she didn't start soon for the cabin, it would be too late. How was she going to defeat that blue sedan? There had to be some way of losing it.

She was dealing with the steeple of the church when, minutes later, the park was invaded by a pair of yellow school buses. The lumbering vehicles pulled between her van and the blue sedan. The tranquility of the morning vanished in an explosion of chatter and laughter as sixth-graders bound on a field trip streamed from the buses.

Ellie, scrambling to her feet, blessed their arrival. The buses, and the noisy crowd they discharged, had the sedan effectively boxed in. Her van was clear and pointed in the right direction. She lost no time in reaching it.

Sliding behind the wheel, she spared a fleeting glance for her pursuer. He had raced to his own vehicle and was shouting at the mob to move. If they heard him, they weren't impressed by his urgency.

As she sped down the hill toward the main road, Ellie could gleefully hear the furious barking of Lew Ferguson's horn. The blue sedan was still trapped, unable to work its way through the mass of sixth-graders, and she was free.

Thank you, Rosebay School District.

She continued to be grateful as she traveled toward the cabin along the maze of country roads. There was no glimpse now of the rental sedan in her rearview mirror.

NOAH WAS OUT on the raft with a fishing pole when she arrived in the cove. By the time she rounded the cabin, he had paddled to the riverbank and was hobbling toward her, supporting himself with his makeshift crutch, which he recklessly abandoned when they met under the brilliant sourwood tree. It clattered to the ground as he caught her in a savage embrace.

The kisses that he lavished on her face were just as ferocious. Between them, he muttered snatches of his longing and desperation.

"Thought you were never coming...imagining every kind of calamity...don't ever put me through that kind of suffering again, Rembrandt..."

Ellie managed to insert a few breathless explanations among his alternating kisses and accusations.

"I tried to come yesterday...couldn't shake Lew Ferguson…followed me whenever I left the estate…convinced I'll lead him to you…it's all right, I lost him this time…"

His kisses grew more forceful, threatening to escalate into something intimate and intense. Had there been more time, she would have welcomed a sensual interval. Maddeningly, there wasn't. In the end, she reluctantly disengaged herself from his wild embrace.

"Noah, I've only got an hour or so, and we have to talk."

He nodded unhappily. "Joel," he demanded. "Is he all right? Tell me about Joel."

"Your son is fine, and I'll tell you everything. *After* I look at that ankle of yours."

"Forget the damn ankle."

"Sit," she ordered, indicating a bench against the cabin wall. "And that's not an option."

Grumbling, he lowered himself on the bench. Ellie knelt and gently removed the elastic bandage in order to examine the sprain. There was still swelling, though not as much, and an angry bruise in the stressed area.

"It's improved," she decided, "but you're going to need at least another day before you can put any kind of weight on it for more than a few minutes."

He didn't argue with her, but she was afraid that he still resisted his condition. Deciding not to press the issue, she handed him the fallen crutch.

"Interesting," she said as she observed the length of hickory. "And resourceful."

He grinned at her. "Like Tiny Tim, huh? Hell, I had to do something halfway useful in my boredom. Anyway, whittling is a tradition around these parts, isn't it?"

"Speaking of local crafts…" She got to her feet. "Noah, do you mind if I paint while we talk? If I don't produce something before I go back to the castle, it's going to look suspicious. So far, Brett and the others are willing to accept that's why I come out on my own, and I want to keep it that way.''

He glowered over the subject of Brett Buchanan. "Just how friendly has he been with you?''

She smiled at his jealousy. "You'll be happy to know that Brett has a far more willing diversion to keep him occupied." She explained about Sandra O'Hara. For the first time since her arrival in the cove, Noah looked pleased.

She left him on the bench and went off to the van to collect her supplies. Minutes later, she was seated at a small table she had dragged out of the cabin, a sheet of watercolor paper pinned to her board. She began rapidly sketching a scene of the Cherokee River, framing it with a corner of the log cabin and the flaming sourwood tree. Noah, watching her from the bench while she worked, rested his ankle and listened to her account of all that had been happening since they'd parted.

She described in greater detail her efforts to shake Lew Ferguson and her confrontation with the detective yesterday in Rosebay.

"It worries me he's following you like that," Noah said, his face grim. "If he's convinced you're involved with me, and he can end up proving it, then you could be charged with aiding and abetting an escaped felon.''

"That won't happen," she insisted. "I know how to be careful." Satisfied with her pencil rendering of the landscape, she began to mix her colors.

"I don't like it. I don't want you to end up paying a price for helping me.''

They had been over this territory before, and she wasn't going to argue the subject again. She made an effort to divert him as she applied splashes of vermilion and cadmium yellow to produce the autumn foliage of the sourwood tree. "Have you been able to come up with any reason why Ferguson has it in for you?''

He shook his head. "Nothing.''

She glanced at him. She could tell from the rigid line of his jaw that in another second he would start in again about how she was risking herself for him. To forestall him, she talked about Joel and his existence at the castle. He was eager to hear about his son, and this time he listened without interruption while she built up her layers of paint, controlling the colors with quick, deft strokes.

She told him about Joel's lessons with Mrs. Connelly and his attachment to the puppet, Hobo. It reminded Noah of a battered stuffed elephant that had never left his son's side when he was an infant. There was such a glow of paternal love and longing in his gaze as he spoke of the memory that Ellie's heart ached for him.

She couldn't bring herself to tell Noah that Joel refused to discuss his father. It would devastate him if he thought his son feared him now. But it worried her. If Joel didn't want to be with his father, was perhaps even frightened of him, how could she help Noah to take him away?

But for Joel there might be no other choice. In fact, his life could depend on it. She could no longer delay sharing with Noah what she had overheard yesterday outside the library and how worried she had been ever since.

The sourwood tree and the logs of the cabin were finished. She started on the river with tones of olive.

"Noah," she said slowly, "I think I may have stumbled into a motive for Howard Buchanan's murder. And if I have, then it's very possible Brett did kill his father, or at least arrange for it, since he was supposed to have had an alibi for that day."

He leaned forward on the bench, his body tense. "Have you been taking chances? I thought I told you— All right, don't look at me like that. Just tell me what you learned, and how."

"It seems that Brett wasn't as independently rich as we thought. Or, anyway, that he was in financial trouble before his father's death, and now he isn't. Which, I'm assuming, means that he inherited a large portion of his father's fortune. As for how I discovered this…''

She went on to explain about the phone conversation she had overheard. Noah was silent when she finished, his eyes as hard as jet.

"If it's true," she said softly, "then you *were* framed for the murder."

He nodded, his voice harsh. "But what good is it going to do me? Without hard evidence, I don't stand any chance of clearing myself. I'm still where I was."

She was afraid he was right, but she tried to offer him a hopeful, "Maybe something will turn up yet."

He didn't respond. They both knew there was little chance of that happening. She began to prepare a wash for the sky, mixing cerulean and French ultramarine blue.

"Noah, there's more," she said with difficulty. She hated having to tell him this part, but it couldn't be avoided.

"Let's have it."

"Just after Brett assured whoever was on the other end of the phone that he had plenty of money now, he stressed there was more where that came from. He—well, he implied that before long he'd be able to get his hands on it."

She waited for Noah's explosive reaction and was surprised when it didn't happen. Surely the terrible significance of her information hadn't escaped him. She glanced up from the sky she was filling in. He was frowning.

"What are you suggesting, Ellie?"

"Joel. Didn't you tell me that, as Howard Buchanan's grandson, he inherits a fortune?"

"Right. The estate was divided equally between Brett and Joel, and the court controls Joel's half until—" He broke off, staring at her in understanding. "You're thinking that if Brett did kill his father for the money, Joel could be next."

"It's a terrifying possibility. I didn't want to believe Joel was in any danger from him, but now…''

Noah shook his head. "It's not a motive, Ellie. Because if anything should happen to Joel before he's of age, his half of the estate doesn't pass to Brett. It goes to various charities. Howard Buchanan's will was clear about that. Brett doesn't get a penny of Joel's money. All this was eventually established at my trial when the prosecution tried to suggest I had an eye on my son's half of the inheritance."

"Then Joel isn't at risk." She breathed deeply in relief. "Thank God. I've been imagining every kind of horror and afraid to tell you the worst."

She completed the sky and began to define and highlight the details of her painting.

"That doesn't mean my kid isn't threatened," he insisted. "There's something there. I can feel it. I have from the start."

"But why, if no motive exists?"

"I don't know. I just do. Call it parental instinct. Hell, Ellie, why was Brett so eager to get custody of Joel? And why come way out here with him and rent some isolated estate? I've got to get my son out of there."

She was inclined now to think he was exaggerating Joel's situation, but she understood his frustration. He was a father, and his child was under someone else's control. Someone he had every reason not to trust.

"Noah, you will get him back, but you have to be patient just a little longer. The ankle—"

"I'm fed up with being patient! The damn ankle has kept me here long enough!" Flinging the crutch to one side, he surged to his feet. "Look. Good as new."

Before she could stop him, he placed his full weight on the ankle and started toward her, determined to demonstrate his recovery. He'd taken no more than a few steps when the injured leg started to buckle on him as he cursed in pain.

Ellie jumped up from the table and went to help him. He

shook her off and staggered back to the bench, collapsing on it heavily.

"Are you all right?"

He nodded, silent with helpless rage.

"Noah, I know it's infuriating, but you have to accept it. The ankle simply isn't ready to bear your weight, and it certainly isn't up to anything as punishing as your running away with Joel."

He didn't answer her, but she knew he reluctantly bought her argument. The painting was finished. She went back to the table and began to gather up her supplies.

"I have to leave. Joel will be finished soon with his lessons. I want to be there with him before Brett and the others get back from Asheville."

She took her things and tossed them in the rear of the van, placing the wet watercolor flat on the floor to dry. Then she went back to the yard to return the table and chair to the cabin. By the time she emerged, Noah was on his feet again. This time he was wisely using the crutch.

"I don't know how I'll manage it," she promised him, "but one way or another I'll be back tomorrow. We'll decide then just when and how I'm going to bring Joel out to you. Is there anything you need?"

"No, I'm fine. And if willpower has anything to do with it, when you see me again the ankle will be fine, too."

She hesitated, jangling the car keys in her hand.

"What?" he urged.

"It's nothing important. Just something I've been wondering about Joel." She explained about his son's irrational fear of the slide and laundry chute in her home and the elevator at the castle.

"This is news to me," he said, his brow knitted in puzzlement. "I've never known him to be nervous about anything like that. And he won't talk about it?"

"Not to me. He probably will to you when you see him." She glanced at her watch. "I'd better go."

"Take care of my kid. Hell, I know you will. The thing is, will you take care of yourself? You'd better."

He emphasized his warning by leaning down and placing a long, possessive kiss on her mouth. She wished he hadn't. It made it all the harder to turn away and leave him there in the yard of the cabin.

MUCH TO HER RELIEF, Ellie saw no sign of the blue sedan on her way back to the estate. But when she arrived at the castle, there was an unfamiliar sports car parked in the drive close to the front door. Wondering who was here, she pulled in beside it.

Before she could remove her painting gear from the van, the front door opened. Jonnie came down the steps, accompanied by a tall man with skin the color of polished ebony and carrying a bag. The young woman called to her. Ellie joined them at the bottom of the steps.

"This is Dick Sherwood," Jonnie introduced her companion. "He practices medicine in Rosebay. We're good friends, which helps when you need a doctor on the spot."

From the warmth in her voice, Ellie guessed he might be more than just a good friend. The doctor shook her hand.

"What Jonnie is trying to say is that I don't make house calls, but since young Joel can't leave the estate, I was willing to make an exception."

Ellie was instantly alarmed. "What's wrong? Has Joel—"

"Ellie, it's okay," Jonnie assured her. "He's had a little accident. If it had been anything serious, rule or no rule, I would have called for an ambulance to take him to the hospital. I just felt Dick should have a look at him to be sure he didn't suffer a concussion or something."

The doctor added his own assurance. "He's fine. Nothing more than a lump on his head. He's resting in his room with an ice bag and one of the house staff reading him a story. Just keep an eye on him to be sure nothing develops. Not that it will.''

''But what happened?''

Jonnie explained it to her. ''Mrs. Connelly had to leave a bit early for an appointment. Joel was supposed to wait in the house until you got back, but he took off without telling anyone. Hobo was missing, and you know how crazy he is about that puppet.''

''Where?''

''Down to the stables. He'd forgotten Hobo there when he visited his pony this morning. The thing I can't figure out is how the puppet got on the shelf in Sultan's stall.''

''Oh, no, he didn't go into that stall!'' Ellie exclaimed, shuddering over the image of Joel under the deadly hooves of Brett's temperamental horse.

''Not quite that bad, but something almost as risky. He climbed up on the half door. He was sure he could reach the shelf from there. I was on the phone in the tack room. I didn't even know he was out there until I heard him yelling.''

''Sultan didn't—''

''It was the door. I don't know how it got left unlatched. I'm always so careful about that, and Joel swears he never touched the hook. He didn't expect the thing to swing open, but with his weight pulling on it, that's just what happened. By the time I got there, he'd been flung off and cracked his head against a post.''

''It could have been worse,'' Dick comforted her.

''I know. Sultan was wild over the incident, and if he'd managed to get out of that stall before I got the door shut... Anyway, I feel so responsible.''

''Why should you?'' Dick said. ''You've done nothing wrong.''

No, Ellie silently agreed. Jonnie wasn't to blame for what might easily have been a tragedy. But someone was. Someone had placed the puppet temptingly on the shelf, just out of reach. Someone had unlatched the stall door.

It could have been unintentional, a result of simple carelessness. Or—chilling thought—had it been meant to harm Joel and look like an accident? Was Noah right? Was his son in danger? But why? It made no sense if Brett couldn't touch his inheritance.

"I just hope Mr. Buchanan understands why I called in Dick," Jonnie said.

"You did the right thing," Ellie assured her. "Look, I'm going on up to see the patient."

She felt an urgent need to be with Joel, to remain protectively beside him. She wasn't ready to put it into words. It wasn't a conviction yet, but the fear lurked there just under the surface. Someone in this house wanted Joel dead. In her eagerness to reach him, she forgot about her painting gear in the van.

"THE BITCH GAVE ME the slip this morning," Lew growled, leaning forward to make himself heard above the country and western music blasting from an old-fashioned jukebox.

He and Peaches shared a cramped booth in a bar on the edge of Rosebay. The place was as dim and dingy as a cave, which must have been appealing since it was packed with a noisy, late-night crowd.

Peaches leaned his arms on the scarred tabletop that separated them. "Face it," he jeered, "she's too smart for you."

"We'll see about that. She's not gonna get so lucky the next time. The next time I don't lose her. She's gonna lead me to Rhyder if I have to hire bloodhounds to track her there."

"Maybe that won't be necessary," Peaches said mysteriously. "Could be there's another way to locate his hideout."

"Like?"

"See where this leads you." From a pocket inside his jacket, he produced a sheet of thick paper that he had folded into a fraction of its size. He spread it open on the table between them, indifferent to the creases that spoiled it.

"What the hell is this?" Lew demanded.

"What's it look like? It's a watercolor. One of *her* watercolors. I had to move her van out of the way this evening so I could get Mr. Buchanan's car into the garage. This was on the floor in the back."

"And how's it supposed to help me?"

"She went out painting this morning, didn't she? Well, this has to be what she painted, because it was still damp when I lifted it."

"Yeah, I get it. She maybe painted this where Rhyder is holed up, which could mean..." Interest aroused, he bent his head to study the picture. "Not much here to go on, though."

"Not for you or me. But one of the locals might find enough in it to recognize the spot."

"It's worth the effort," Lew agreed. "If she doesn't show up outside the gates tomorrow so I get another shot at following her, I'll start showing it around. The thing is, if she misses it before then—"

"She won't. She's too worried about the kid to think of anything else." Peaches sat back in the booth, picking at his teeth. "I dunno. Maybe none of this is worth anything. Maybe, like she claims, she never even saw Rhyder."

"Oh, she knows where he is all right." Nothing would shake Lew's certainty about that. "And before I'm finished with her..."

ELLIE CAME AWAKE in the middle of the night. Her brain was so dull with sleep that for a moment she didn't understand what had aroused her. Then she heard it. A low, keening sound from the room next door. Joel's room.

Shaking off the last shreds of sleep, she was out of her

bed in a flash and racing toward the communicating door of their connecting rooms. She'd left the door open after tucking him in last evening in case he should need her. It seemed now that he did.

Alarmed by what might be happening to him, she rushed toward his bed, guided by the night-light. To her relief, there was no one else in the room. When she leaned down over his small form huddled under the covers, she realized that what was threatening him was a bad dream. Probably a result of his accident earlier.

Joel was still mewing in his sleep like a frightened little animal as Ellie lowered herself on the edge of the bed and gathered him in her arms. He came awake at once and clung to her, flushed and trembling.

"It's all right, sweetheart," she soothed him gently. "It was just a dream. But an awful one, huh?"

"Yes," he muttered, face buried against her breasts.

"Does your head ache?" she asked him, checking to be sure he wasn't suffering any aftereffects of the episode at the stables.

He shook his head.

"That's good. Would you like to tell me about the dream? Would that help?"

He didn't answer her.

"I bet I can guess," she encouraged him. "I bet it was about Sultan. He scares me, too."

He drew his head back. "It wasn't about Sultan, and I'm not scared of him. It was about the bad place," he blurted.

"The bad place? What bad place?"

He stiffened, as if suddenly realizing his mistake. She put her hand under his chin and looked down into his thin face.

"Joel, have you had this dream before?"

"Sometimes."

"Then don't you think it's time to share it with me?"

He didn't answer her.

Sensing that the nightmare was something she needed to understand, she tried to penetrate his reluctance. "We're friends, aren't we, Joel? Good friends."

"Yes."

"Then you can trust me to know about your dream. I promise not to tell anyone else about it. Maybe I can make you feel better about this imaginary bad place."

"It isn't a pretend place," he insisted. "It's a real place. It's this box thing, and I'm inside it, and I can't get out because it keeps getting smaller and smaller. It's squeezing me, and I'm real scared to be stuck in there because the bad guy is coming for me."

"What happens next?"

"I don't know." He hesitated, then confided in an earnest voice, "That's just in the dream, a'course, because when it happened for real I wasn't stuck. I got out, and I got away, and the bad guy never came to hurt me like he hurt Grandpa."

Ellie was seized by a sudden chill as a horrifying suspicion occurred to her. Keeping her voice calm and patient, while seething with an inner urgency, she coaxed him to give her the rest. "Sweetheart, this is very important. I want you to tell me all about this—this box thing. Does it have a name?"

"Uh-huh. Dumbwaiter. That's what Carmen called it."

"Carmen is the housekeeper at your grandfather's place back home, isn't she?"

"Uh-huh. Carmen told me I wasn't ever to mess around with the dumbwaiter."

"But you did play in it," she guessed.

"Just the one time," he confessed.

"When was this?"

"That day Carmen took me to the zoo. Only I never got to see the tigers. Carmen got one of her bad headaches right after we got there, so we had to go straight home so she could lie down."

"Did your grandfather know you were back home?"

He shook his head. "Carmen said we shouldn't bother him, because he was working in the library. But I think she was afraid to tell him we got home real early. Once before, he hollered at her for falling asleep in her room when she was supposed to be watching me."

"What happened next?"

"She told me to play quietly in my room while she rested. But there wasn't anything to do all by myself, and I was bored. That's when I figured out about the dumbwaiter."

"What did you figure out?"

"How to ride it up and down between floors. It was easy. I'd scrunch up inside it, and then I'd reach around outside and press one of the buttons just before the door was all the way down. The motor would start whirring, and away I'd go. It wasn't spooky then. It was fun."

"When did it become spooky, Joel?"

She could feel his reluctance again. She didn't urge him this time. She gave him a moment to think about it, then he went on. "When I thought it would be a good idea to surprise Grandpa. I was gonna pop out and scare him. I thought he'd laugh about it. I thought he wouldn't be mad about it like Carmen."

"I guess that means the dumbwaiter opened in the library on that floor."

"Yes, in this corner place."

Ellie thought he must be referring to an alcove. "But you didn't pop out and surprise your grandfather, did you, Joel?"

"I would've, 'cause the dumbwaiter got there just like I planned, and I got the door up, too. I was real quiet about it so Grandpa wouldn't hear. I would've surprised him all right."

"Why didn't you?" Ellie already knew, but she had to hear it from him to be certain.

"Because Grandpa wasn't alone. There was someone with him. Grandpa was mad and kept hollering."

"Could you see them?"

"No, they were around the wall where the fireplace is."

"Did you hear what they were saying? Joel, this is important—did you recognize the other voice?"

"I couldn't tell. It was real low and hard to hear. Only Grandpa was loud. Then there was this funny sound, and Grandpa came down on the floor. I could see part of him. I could see his head. It was all bloody, and everything got quiet."

Dear God, the child had witnessed Howard Buchanan's murder! And if the killer *knew* Joel had been hiding there in the dumbwaiter—

"Sweetheart, I know this is very hard to talk about, but you need to tell me what happened after you saw your grandfather on the floor. Did you make any sound? Did this other person who was in the room find out you were in the dumbwaiter?"

"He didn't see me. I didn't let him see me. I put the door down. I pushed the button and put the door all the way down. Then when the dumbwaiter got down in the kitchen I got out and ran. I was afraid he'd come after me so I hid in Carmen's bathroom until she woke up."

The murderer must have heard Joel lowering the door of the dumbwaiter, must have heard the whine of the motor carrying him away to another floor.

"Joel, have you told anyone else what you've just told me? Did you tell Carmen afterward?"

"No. Ellie, do I have to talk about it anymore? I don't want to talk about it anymore."

He was trembling again, his young mind terrified by the confusing mixture of nightmare and reality. No wonder he had been afraid of the slide and the laundry chute in her house and the elevator here. They were all confined places dealing with movement between floors, all of them associated with his shocking experience in the dumbwaiter.

"No, sweetheart, you don't have to talk about it anymore." She held him close and rocked him comfortingly. "I'm sorry I made you tell me. But I had to know so I can do something to make these bad dreams go away."

"What will you do?"

"I have to figure that out."

He was quiet for a moment. Then he asked in a small, worried voice, "Ellie, will I get in trouble because of the dumbwaiter?"

"You won't be in trouble, Joel. You did nothing wrong. Here, take Hobo. He looks lonesome all by himself."

She reached for the puppet on the bedside table and put it into his hands. Seconds later, clasping Hobo, he drifted off in her arms. She lowered him carefully onto his pillow, drawing the cover over him.

She was shivering. Not just because of the frightening implications of what Joel had told her. It was cold in the room. One of the windows was partly open. She could see the curtains stirring in the breeze. She went and shut the window, then crossed to the hall door to make sure it was locked. Satisfied, she returned to the bed, checking the clock next to the night-light. It was after four. She had a lot of thinking to do, decisions that had to be made before daybreak.

Perching on the edge of the bed again, she watched Joel as he slept. His story had jolted her, but it was time to put that impact behind her. Time to calmly evaluate the situation.

Joel was in danger. There was no longer any reason to question that. Noah had been right to sense, as he had all along, that his son was threatened, even though he hadn't been able to identify a motive. Well, now the motive was very clear.

Howard Buchanan's secret visitor in the library must

have realized, if not immediately, then eventually, that Joel had been hiding there in the dumbwaiter. The killer couldn't be certain that the child could identify him, but must have realized that it was possible. Therefore, Joel had to be eliminated before his young mind sorted it all out, before he understood and found the courage to tell what he had either heard or seen.

Not in St. Louis. There would have been too many questions asked if something happened to Joel right there in St. Louis. So Brett—because it had to be Brett—had managed to win custody of his nephew. Then he had removed him from the scene, taken him far away to a remote mountainside where an accident, such as a careless moment with a wild horse, wouldn't be suspicious enough to be too carefully investigated.

That had to be the explanation for everything that had been happening, even if it did leave a few unanswered questions. There was simply no other way to account for it.

There was something else that was even more certain. Every moment Joel remained in this house, he was in jeopardy. The local police? No, she couldn't trust them to protect Joel, not when Brett was so rich and influential, and not with the unpleasant Lew Ferguson perhaps able to exert his own authority. There was only one person who would move heaven and earth to safeguard Joel.

Sitting there in the dim, chill hours of the morning, with the house as silent as death around her, Ellie reached a vital decision. She wouldn't wait another day. She would take Joel and run with him now. She wouldn't stop to examine the morality of what she was about to do, either. Nor would she worry about what might happen to her because of her action. She was beyond any previous hesitation, because only one thing mattered. Joel had to be delivered immediately to his father.

Chapter Thirteen

She regretted having to wake Joel again, but it was necessary. They had to be far away from the estate before the house stirred. Ellie knew what would happen when she and the boy were found missing. There would be a widespread alarm and an immediate search for them. But by then she planned to have Joel with his father. As for what would follow...well, that was up to Noah. Once she had brought his son to him, her essential work was done. She could breathe a sigh of relief and let Noah take charge. That couldn't come soon enough. But in the meantime...

"Sweetheart," she called to him softly as she leaned over him and shook him gently.

He stirred and turned over on his back.

"Joel, you have to wake up. It's very important."

This time he opened his eyes and hunched up against the pillows. "It's still dark out," he objected in a sleepy voice.

"I know, but I have to talk to you. Are you listening?"

"Uh-huh."

She took his hand and held it. "You have to get dressed. Both of us have to get dressed. We're going to leave."

"Why?"

She decided it was best to be honest with him. "Because I don't think it's safe for you in this place."

He was an intelligent child. He understood at once. "On account of what I told you about the dumbwaiter?"

"Yes."

"Where are we going?"

This was the hard part. His unbroken silence about his father had worried her from the start. If he resented Noah, even feared him... But there was no other choice.

"We're going to your father, sweetheart. He's only a few miles from here waiting for you."

He stared at her, his eyes wide with disbelief, his chin trembling. "Daddy is here?" he whispered.

"Yes, and very worried about you. He wants you with him." Was she doing the right thing? She prayed that she was. "Joel, it will be all right. He loves you very much, and you'll be safe with him."

He didn't ask her how his father could be nearby, or why. Those were mere details that were unimportant to his five-year-old mind. All that mattered was Noah's presence close by. She held her breath and waited for his reaction.

He smiled. The smile widened to a grin. For the first time since she had known him, he was genuinely happy. She breathed again in deep relief.

"Can we go now, Ellie?" he asked her eagerly.

"Just as soon as we're ready." He started to scramble off the bed, but she delayed him for a moment. "I have something I'd like you to tell me first, and then we'll go."

"What?"

"About your daddy. If you love him, if he's the most important person in the world to you, and I can see now that he is, why wouldn't you ever talk about him?"

He went very still, gazing at her uncertainly.

"I've been worried about that," she appealed to him. "Can't you tell me, since you've told me all the rest?"

He was undecided for another few seconds, and then he made up his mind to trust her again. "It's because I was scared to talk about him. I thought if I said anything about him, someone would find out I was in the dumbwaiter and make me say I heard Daddy kill Grandpa, and then Daddy would have to die instead of just go to jail, like in this movie I saw once on TV. But Daddy didn't kill Grandpa, did he, Ellie? It wasn't his voice in the room with Grandpa. I would have known Daddy's voice.''

She took him in her arms and hugged him reassuringly, distressed that all this time he had been carrying such an awful burden. No wonder he had never mentioned to anyone the episode in the dumbwaiter.

"No, sweetheart, he never killed anyone, though there are people who think he did. But no matter what they think, he isn't going to die. That was just an old movie, not real. What's real is that you're going away with him. Only now we have to hurry."

She considered packing a suitcase with some of his clothes, but decided in the end it would only prove to be a hindrance, especially if they encountered any difficulty in their flight. The one thing Joel refused to leave behind was Hobo, and she didn't argue with that.

Minutes later, dressed in warm clothes, with Joel clutching the puppet and Ellie her purse, they slipped away from their rooms. She could sense his excitement as they crept cautiously toward the staircase, guided by the weak glow of the few night-lights that were left burning throughout the castle.

There was silence in the house as they made their way to the first floor, Joel clinging to her side. It was too early for anyone to be up yet, but Ellie was tense, half expecting a harsh challenge from the shadows as she led them toward a French door in the dining room.

She had selected this particular exit because it opened off the side of the house, close to the driveway where her van was parked. Fumbling with the lock, she succeeded in opening the door. Seconds later, they stood on the stone terrace where she paused a moment to get her bearings.

The morning was still dark, although there was a hint of daylight off to the east. A clamminess penetrated the air. Not surprising, considering there was a mist down in the valley. If it thickened into a serious fog, which it threatened to do, it could be a problem for them on the road.

"Let's go, Ellie," Joel whispered, tugging impatiently at her hand.

"This way," she murmured, leading them through the shrubbery at the edge of the terrace and across the drive to her van.

She had her key out as she slid behind the wheel after making certain that Joel was securely belted on his side. Her concern at this point was for the sound of the van's engine when it came to life. Would it alert someone inside the house?

It was an insignificant problem. There was something far more important for her to worry about. It revealed itself just before she inserted the key in the ignition, when she suddenly remembered to check the visor overhead. The gate opener should have been clipped there. It was gone.

Peaches, she realized immediately. He had borrowed her car keys the evening before to move the van. He must have removed the gate opener to prevent her from leaving the estate anytime during the night when Lew Ferguson wouldn't be out there waiting to shadow her. Without the gate opener, she and Joel were trapped.

"What is it, Ellie? Why aren't we going?"

"The zapper for the gates isn't here. I'm sorry, sweetheart, but until I can figure a way for us to drive out of—"

"I know how to get another one without going back into the house."

"Where?"

"From Uncle Brett's car in the garage. It's easy to get into the garage. Come on, I'll show you."

"Did anyone ever tell you that you're a smart little boy?" she asked as she followed him out of the van.

"Sure, *you* did," he responded with the same pluck and humor that she had experienced so often in his father.

"All right, smarty-pants, lead the way, and let's hurry."

She regretted the frustrating delay. It was already growing lighter in the east.

"The door is through here," he explained as they rounded the house and reached the gate of a fenced yard attached to the side of the wide garage.

When Ellie started to unlatch the gate, there was a startling movement inside the enclosure. Something rushed at the gate, snarling furiously. Alarmed, she leaped back. It was Peaches's bad-tempered hound, and he had no intention of letting her inside the fence. Front paws up on the gate, he growled a warning at her.

Joel giggled. "It's just Caesar, Ellie."

"He's vicious without Peaches to control him. I don't see how I'm going to—"

"You wait here, Ellie. I'll get the zapper."

Before she could stop him, he had shoved Hobo into her hands and was clambering over the gate like an agile monkey.

"Joel, no! The dog is dangerous!"

"Caesar wouldn't hurt me. Would you, boy?"

He dropped into the yard, and the hound was all over him. To her relief, Caesar's attack involved a furiously wagging tail and an ecstatic tongue that licked every portion of the boy's face he could reach. Joel pushed him off and raced toward the door of the garage, disappearing into its depths with the dog at his heels. Seconds later, he reappeared, triumphantly bearing the gate opener.

"You're not only smart, you're *very* smart," she praised him as he climbed back over the fence and handed her the opener.

Caesar decided to be a menace of another sort as they started toward the van. Realizing he was being abandoned, he leaped at the fence, barking wildly. Someone inside the house was bound to hear him. There was no time to lose. Grabbing Joel's hand, she began to run.

PEACHES WAS a light sleeper, which suited his role as a bodyguard. Caesar's barking awakened him almost immediately. He lay there for a moment, listening attentively and wondering if the dog's clamor was worth his investigation. Then he heard another noise. The sound of a car engine.

He was off the bed in a flash. His room was adjacent to Brett's at the front of the mansion. By the time he reached the window overlooking the valley, the taillights of the vehicle were disappearing into the first switchback that descended the mountain in a series of long swoops. Brief though his glimpse had been in the murky light, he was certain it was the Matheson woman's van.

He wasn't worried. She couldn't leave the estate. He had sneaked the gate opener out of her van last night, and if she had managed before leaving the house to locate the master opener in the service passage, the gates would have already opened. But he could just make them out far below on this side of the bridge, and they were tightly closed.

Peaches waited at the window to be certain. There was a fog developing in the valley. One of those infamous fogs that cursed this region in the fall. It was drifting like smoke over the stream, threatening to obscure his view of the gates in the slowly strengthening daylight.

There! He could see the lights of the van again as it emerged from around the wooded corner of the last switchback. As it neared the approach to the bridge, the gates swung slowly inward. Peaches swore savagely. The bitch had managed to find another opener.

The fog closed in around the van, swallowing it completely as it crossed the bridge to the turning. He leaped for the telephone beside his bed, stabbing in the numbers for the Big Mountain Motel.

Lew's voice was groggy and irritable when he answered

seconds later. Peaches rapidly explained the situation. "If you hurry, maybe you can still catch her where Settlement Road joins the main road into Rosebay. She was headed that way, but this fog has got to slow her down."

"I'm on to it," Lew promised, fully alert now.

LESS THAN twenty minutes later, unshaven and looking more unkempt than usual in clothes he had flung on in haste, Lew arrived at the intersection. He had driven with reckless speed through the fog in order to intercept the van. He was too late. She had beat him to the crossroads. He could see the back end of her vehicle receding into the fog on a main road that swung off to the right.

Lew didn't hesitate. Racing through the turn at a dangerous angle, he chased the van up the highway. There was no other traffic at this early hour, but his pursuit was hopeless. The fog was thicker than ever, a choking wall of eerie gray. He lost her taillights almost immediately, and though he continued to search the highway, he failed to overtake her. She could have turned off on any of a half dozen side roads.

Cursing in frustration, he pulled off on the shoulder. He found a cigar and lit it, smoking in tense puffs as he examined the situation. The bitch had to be on her way to Rhyder. But why, at this ungodly hour? He sensed it was something major this time, something he needed to prevent. But how? He could wander these roads all morning and never find her.

Then he remembered the painting that Peaches had given him in the bar last night. It was still on the back seat where he had tossed it when he'd returned to his motel. If he could find one of the locals able to identify the setting in that picture…

The nearest possibility was a dilapidated general store back at the intersection on the edge of Rosebay. He had passed it many times. He'd begin there.

Stubbing out the cigar, Lew turned the sedan and traveled toward Rosebay. He was in luck when he reached the crossroads. As early as it was, there were lights at the rear of the sagging building. He figured whoever operated the store must live on the premises. He didn't hesitate to march around to the back where he found another entrance.

The woman who answered his knock had a seamed face and a sour expression that told him she wasn't happy to have a visitor hours before her store opened. He displayed his identification, explained he was in the area on police business, and showed her the watercolor.

"Any chance, ma'am, that you recognize where this might have been painted?"

She scarcely glanced at the picture before informing him flatly, "I ought to. It's one of the rental properties I handle."

Lew couldn't have been more pleased. A break at last! "Could you give me directions to the place?"

She hesitated, poking at wisps of her untidy silver hair. "I don't know about that. There are renters there. I wouldn't like them disturbed."

"This is an official investigation, ma'am."

"Meaning I don't have a choice about it, huh?"

The elderly storekeeper reluctantly provided him with directions to the cabin. After closing the door on him, she was uneasy about what she'd done. She watched from a window as he departed in the blue sedan. Badge or not, she hadn't liked him. A cop from St. Louis. That's what his identification had claimed. What was a St. Louis cop doing this far from home? Maybe it was something she shouldn't ignore. Maybe his visit to her should be reported.

Turning away from the window, she went to the phone on the wall and dialed the Rosebay police.

THERE HAD BEEN an anxious moment, just after they passed through the intersection where the general store was located, when Ellie feared she was being tailed again. She'd glimpsed headlights in her rearview mirror. But when she took the next turning, they vanished somewhere behind her in the fog.

Convinced it couldn't have been Lew Ferguson after all, she concentrated on her driving. The fog was a relentless hazard, so heavy in places that the headlights were barely able to penetrate it. She had to crawl along the highway, losing precious time.

It was hard to tell in the fog, but she figured it must be full daylight by now. The household would be stirring back at the castle. Maybe they had already discovered that she and Joel were missing. But she couldn't worry about that. She had to keep her mind on getting Joel to his father.

They were climbing the high, wooded ridge now that separated the valley from the deep cove that sheltered the cabin beside the Cherokee River. The fog was less dense up here but still thick enough that it made the narrow, twisting lane difficult to negotiate. The hemlocks seemed to close in on them, their wet, drooping boughs slapping like ghostly hands at the sides of the van.

Joel had been silent through most of the drive as he held Hobo on his lap, but she could feel his mounting anticipation. He was excited about joining his father. Their arrival at the cabin would bring a new beginning for him.

But for Ellie it would mean an ending, a separation so wrenching that it already filled her with a profound despair. Once she had delivered Joel, she had no choice but to let both father and son go. She and Noah had never discussed the possibility, but she knew he would never permit her to sacrifice her life in St. Louis, to join them in their harrowing fugitive existence. They would leave without her, disappear from North Carolina, and she would forever lose the man she loved.

Battling the anguish that threatened to overwhelm her, Ellie brought the van to the crest of the ridge. They began the long descent to the floor of the cove, following the zigzags that carried them toward the river in easy stages. The fog was much lighter on this side of the mountain. She was able to catch glimpses of the cabin below through gaps in the trees. Joel saw the structure, too.

"Is that where Daddy is waiting, Ellie?" His voice was breathless with longing.

"Yes, sweetheart."

Noah must have heard the sound of their engine. By the time they arrived in the clearing he was out of the cabin and moving toward them as swiftly as his injured ankle would permit. He wasn't using the crutch today, but he was limping, which could be a problem in their flight from the cove.

Ellie had scarcely brought the van to a halt before Joel was out the door and tearing toward his father. She remained at the wheel, not wanting to intrude on their reunion. They met under the sourwood tree, Noah sweeping up his son in a fierce embrace.

Any small, lingering doubt she might have felt for stealing Joel from his guardian was obliterated as she watched father and son in their emotional bonding. Tears threatened her when Noah's gaze sought hers over Joel's head, his eyes expressing a loving gratitude to her for bringing him his son.

Climbing from the van, Ellie joined them under the sourwood tree. There was a wonderful joy on Noah's lean face when he caught one of her hands and raised it to his lips, tenderly kissing her fingers.

"You've given me back my son. There aren't enough thank-yous in the world for that. But how did you—"

"I managed. I had to," she said with a catch in her voice. "Joel had to be where I knew he'd be safe."

"Trouble?" Noah's smile melted away. "Come on inside and tell me everything." His hand still clasping hers, he started to draw her toward the cabin.

Ellie pulled away. "No, there isn't time."

While they went on standing under the tree, she rapidly filled him in on all that had happened since she'd left him yesterday. Joel added his own bits and pieces.

"Noah, you and Joel have to leave now," she urged him. "They must already be out searching, and if they find this place—"

Noah held up a hand, silencing her. "I think maybe they already have," he said grimly. "Listen."

She heard it then, too. The sound of a car engine high on the ridge above them. Turning, she searched the distant woods where the fog still trailed in long bands above the treetops. Seconds later, she caught a glimpse of dark blue through the drifting layers of mist.

"It's Lew Ferguson's car! That must have been him behind me at the crossroads! Noah, you can't confront him! He'll be armed, and maybe he's not alone!"

"I don't intend to risk Joel with any encounters, not if I can help it. We're getting out of here before Ferguson arrives."

"How? The road dead-ends here. There is no other route. Oh, you can't be thinking of running for it on foot! Not with your ankle!"

"Give me credit, Ellie. There are all kinds of books and maps inside the cabin, and I've spent two days studying them. The river is going to take us out of here."

The raft! He meant to escape down the Cherokee on the raft! "But there are rapids!"

"Nothing I can't handle. I've been practicing. We're wasting time. He'll be here in a few minutes."

Taking Joel by the hand, he hurried them in the direction of the river. He had been inactive long enough. This time he was taking control of the situation, making the decisions, and she was happy to let him.

She spared a frantic glance behind her. No sign of the blue sedan yet arriving in the clearing, but she could hear its approach along the zigzags. Grasping both her purse and the puppet she'd brought with her from the van, she turned and ran.

By the time Ellie reached the riverbank, Noah had Joel already settled in the raft and was buckling him into a life jacket. The inflated raft was plastic-coated nylon, supported by a steel frame and equipped with a pair of aluminum oars. There was adequate room between its cross tubes for two adults and a child.

"Where do you want me to sit?" she asked.

"You're not coming with us, Ellie. There's still a chance for you to avoid any charges. It's all I've got to give you, and I want you to have it. You can tell them I broke into the castle and took you hostage when you caught me snatching Joel. You can say I forced you to drive us here. Ferguson might know otherwise, but this way, by letting you go now, he'll never be able to prove it."

"You're not leaving me behind. Think of Joel. How can you possibly manage the raft in white water and at the same time make sure he's not swept overboard?"

It was a plea for which he had no argument.

"I can still say I was a hostage, that you chose to release me *after* the raft landed."

The moment was too urgent for any further delay. The blue sedan had already emerged from the woods less than a mile away.

"Get in," he commanded her tautly.

Ellie wasted no time scrambling into the raft. Slipping into a life jacket, she settled into the stern compartment where she held the small figure of Joel between her legs.

"I'll hang on to you," she instructed him, handing him the puppet, "but it's your job to hang on to Hobo."

Joel nodded, clutching the puppet on his lap as Noah shoved the raft from the bank, hopped aboard when it was afloat, and seized the oars with confidence.

By the time Lew Ferguson trotted around the corner of

the cabin, Noah's powerful rowing had carried them out into the middle of the Cherokee's yellow-green depths. Immediately spotting the raft bearing the man who was once again eluding him, the detective raced down to the riverbank.

Reaching the shore, he shouted something after them. Ellie didn't understand what it was, because by then they were rounding the first bend. The clearing, together with the cabin and Ferguson, were suddenly, mercifully lost to view. There was only the river now and the steep wilderness areas that bordered it on both sides, where wisps of fog steamed through the dark evergreens. Their thick ranks were broken here and there by rioting maples that scattered their leaves on the drifting river.

Noah drove them steadily downstream. Ellie huddled there in the bottom of the raft, wondering what threats Ferguson had been shouting at them from the riverbank and whether there was any possible way that he could still pursue them. But she had no chance to worry about that in earnest. There was a much more immediate concern. The first cataract was just ahead of them.

Ellie, hearing the thunder of the boiling waters where the river narrowed and dropped on a treacherous, rock-studded bed, gripped Joel with her hands and legs and prayed that Noah knew what he was doing.

"Don't worry," he called out to her, sensing her alarm, "we'll be fine."

He didn't speak again after that, needing to concentrate on his maneuvers. As they neared the rapids, he pivoted the raft with a skillful stroke of a single oar. Now he was facing downstream and rowing against the current, slowing the craft in order to choose a safe passage through the savage waters.

Twisting her head around, Ellie watched him search the constricted river for the channel he needed. Seconds later, he directed them toward a dark tongue of water between a pair of massive boulders, where only slight riffles disturbed the surface.

As they neared the chute, he corrected their position with a slight feathering of the oars. Then he calmly rested on the oars while Ellie caught her breath and braced herself. The raft seemed to hang suspended for a moment, like a roller-coaster car hesitating on the pinnacle. Then the current grabbed it, rushed it forward, and hurled it into the funnel.

They came charging down into a churning chaos of rock and water. The hydraulics on all sides were spectacular. Torrents that leaped and surged and spumed, beating at the raft, soaking its occupants. Ellie, clutching the grab line with one hand and Joel with the other, heard both herself and the child yelling above the tumult as they caromed from boulder to boulder.

Noah was kept busy as he fought to keep the raft from broaching and overturning in the jumbled crosscurrents. At the same time, with the craft weaving and bobbing from one side of the stream to the other, he continued to find safe passages for them through the obstacles.

At long last they tumbled through the last chute and came to rest in a quiet pool. The turbulence was behind them, the raft swaying on a gentle current.

"Everybody okay?" Noah asked, releasing the oars in their locks.

"Still here," Ellie assured him, amazed that they hadn't swamped in what had seemed like a deluge. But there was a good reason for that. The raft was a self-bailer, allowing any collected water to flow back into the river through a series of grommet holes.

"Are there gonna be more rapids, Daddy?"

"A few of them," he answered carelessly, taking up the oars again.

"Please tell me," Ellie pleaded, "that we have just passed through the worst of them."

His only reply was a diabolical grin. She and Joel exchanged startled looks.

"Daddy is just having fun with us, sweetheart."

She was to regret her casual assurance a half mile later when they heard the ominous roar of the Cherokee's next cataract. Before she could object, Noah launched them through another chute into a seething cauldron of spewing foam and enormous standing waves that punished the careening raft from every side.

The channel was worse here, not just because it was clogged with rocks but because it occurred on a bend in the river. The current was so furious in its velocity that it swept them to the outside of the bend. It was a dangerous place to be since there were obstructions in the form of fallen trees.

Before Noah could avoid it, they were slammed against a massive trunk with wicked snags. Ellie heard a sickening crunch, and then they were free and racing on toward the next funnel.

She thought no more about the collision until a moment later when, after slicing through the last drop, they were suddenly pinned behind a huge slab of submerged gneiss. She heard Noah curse as he struggled to stabilize the spinning raft.

"What is it?" she called above the violent swells.

"Backroller," he shouted. "A spot where the current piles up on itself and actually runs back upstream. Or tries to."

"Is that bad?"

"It's like a whirlpool. It can trap you for hours."

It was Joel who informed them that the situation was even more hazardous than that. "Daddy, the raft is leaking air."

He was right, Ellie realized. The raft was beginning to shrink slowly on its steel frame.

"One of the snags on that tree must have punctured it," she said.

"Looks like we have just minutes to break out of here, and not hours," Noah said grimly. "Ellie, do you see the air pump down there? Can you keep us afloat long enough for me to try to get us safely to shore?"

The air pump, with its hose already attached to the nozzle, was a bellows variety that was worked with the foot. Ellie pumped it vigorously while Noah battled to release the raft from the backroller.

By shifting their body weights as he commanded, and with his intense exertions at the oars, they finally escaped the suction. The battered raft was settling in the water, threatening to sink in spite of her efforts with the pump, as he ferried them across the current at a forty-five-degree angle.

The cataclysm at last behind them, they reached the riverbank. The raft was rapidly shriveling on its frame when they crawled ashore, wet but safe.

"What now?" Ellie wondered, regarding the useless raft from which she had rescued her purse and Joel's beloved puppet.

"We walk," Noah said. "Looks like a trail here that follows the river."

There were no complaints as they started along the path. They were glad to be out of the Cherokee. Even Noah admitted as much when the river became more untamed as they hiked along its edge. It was below them now, trapped between the sheer walls of a gorge that deepened as they followed the thread of the trail. Ellie shuddered when she glanced at the wild waters far below, gushing and foaming over rocks as sharp as teeth. The raft could never have survived them.

Noah didn't object when she finally pleaded a need to rest. He would never have suggested a stop for himself, even though she knew the ankle must be suffering by now since his limp had grown more pronounced. But she could read the relief in his eyes when they settled on a massive log.

Joel, exhausted, dozed in his father's arms as he cuddled the puppet. Fog continued to smoke through the scarlet and gold of the trees around them. There was an interval of silence, and then she asked Noah what she had been wondering about since boarding the raft back at the cabin.

"I take it you have a destination in mind?"

He nodded. "There's some kind of small wilderness park up ahead. We should reach it in another mile or so. A footbridge crosses the river at that point. At least I hope the bridge is still there. It was an old map."

"And from there?"

"The trail on the other side of the bridge winds down the mountain to an airfield in the valley."

"What will you do when you reach the airfield?"

He shrugged. "Hijack a plane out of here, if I have to."

"That won't be necessary." She opened her purse, extracting a wad of bills which she extended toward him. "I cashed traveler's checks at the bank in Rosebay. There's enough here to hire a plane to take you and Joel a safe distance away."

"I can't take that money."

"You don't have a choice about it. You know it's crazy to talk about hijacking a plane. You don't even have the gun with you anymore, thank God. Noah, be sensible. Think of Joel."

He smiled. It was a sad smile. "What am I going to do about you, Ellie Matheson? Every time I think I've got you licked, you hit me where I'm vulnerable." He accepted the money with reluctance, thrusting it into the pocket of his jeans. "I'll find a way to send every penny back to you, just as soon as I'm able to."

"I know."

They didn't speak about the separation that would occur

when they reached the airfield. They didn't talk of their feelings for each other and what they would lose when they came down off the mountain. Perhaps for Noah those feelings weren't everything, as they were for her. Ellie didn't know. Maybe she would never know. Convinced that silence was less painful, he probably wouldn't tell her.

All she did know for certain was that she had to bear their parting, and she worried whether she had enough courage for that.

THEY STOOD THERE on the edge of the gorge, gazing at the footbridge with glum expressions on their faces.

"Sorry," Noah mumbled. "The map didn't bother to mention that this thing was a rope bridge."

"Are we gonna cross it, Daddy? It looks kind of scary."

Joel was right, Ellie thought. The rope bridge was an extremely narrow, flimsy-looking affair suspended above a sickening drop to the river over a hundred feet below. She tried to tell herself it was the fog that made them so nervous about the structure. It was so thick now that the bridge completely vanished into the stuff less than halfway across the chasm, leaving an uneasy impression that the other end of the span hung there in midair without support.

"It must be safe," she said, trying to feel as confident as she sounded. "Otherwise, they would have closed it off or removed it."

Noah nodded. "You're right, but let's not trust it with both of us on it at the same time. I'll take Joel and go first. Wait until we're on the other side before you follow us."

She had no argument with his plan.

"I can walk across on my own," Joel objected when his father lifted him into his arms. "I'm not afraid."

"I know you can, sport, but this time humor your old man."

Ellie watched him start across the bridge, one arm bearing Joel, his other hand on the stout rope that served as a rail. The stretched cables creaked under their combined weight, the flexible span bouncing and swaying as Noah progressed carefully, slowly across its sagging length.

She watched them disappear into a bank of fog that seemed more solid than the bridge itself. The long seconds passed without a sound. The silence seemed unnatural, eerie. Were they safe yet on the other side? She suddenly felt very lonely waiting here on her end.

Ellie was so intent, peering into the fog, trying to catch some glimpse of them where the bridge was anchored across the yawning gorge, that she failed to detect any sound or movement behind her. It was not until the muzzle of a service revolver was shoved into her back that she knew their enemy was suddenly, alarmingly there.

"Did you think I was such a fool I wouldn't figure out where to find you?" he growled so close to her ear that she could smell his sour breath. "I can read maps, too."

And those maps, she realized with a sense of despair, must eventually have directed him into the park from which the path to the bridge originated.

"Turn around," he commanded her roughly. "And keep your hands at your sides."

She pivoted slowly until she confronted Lew Ferguson's livid face.

"Where is he?" he demanded, nudging her with the gun.

"He's gone. Long ago. You'll never find him in this fog."

"You're lying. He wouldn't abandon you. He and the kid are somewhere close by. Get out on the bridge." She hesitated. "Do it!"

Ellie turned and edged her way cautiously onto the lip of the bridge. The detective followed close behind her, urging her forward with the revolver. She tried not to think of the frightening drop beneath them.

"That's far enough. We'll do our negotiating from here." He lifted his voice to a shout. "Rhyder, I know you're out there and can hear me. Your girlfriend is here with me on the bridge. It's a long way down to the river. You wanna keep her from having any accidents, you'd better come back here and give yourself up.''

She hated Ferguson, not because he was holding her at gunpoint, but because he was cheating her of any lingering goodbye with the man she loved. She had to send Noah on his way here and now without any last glimpse of him, without so much as a tender word of parting across the gap that separated them.

"Noah, don't listen to him!" she cried into the void. "You have to go on thinking about Joel! You have to get him out of here! Ferguson won't touch me! He wouldn't dare!"

"You think I'm just bluffing?" Lew laughed into the fog. A demented laugh. "Remember Teresa Marcos, Rhyder? Remember how she died? How *you* killed her? I haven't forgotten it. I'm remembering it now."

There was silence again as they waited tensely on the bridge. The fog licked at them. Ellie could taste its clamminess in her mouth. She clung to the rail and prayed that Noah had already taken Joel and vanished into the woods.

On the other side of the bridge, shrouded by thick fog, Noah stood there in an agony of indecision.

Teresa Marcos. What did Lew Ferguson have to do with Teresa Marcos? Noah had known her years ago in his motorcycle days. A black-eyed, rebellious girl. She had begged him to teach her how to ride a cycle. And he had taught her. *Safely* taught her. Then she had gone out with his bike and promptly killed herself. Did Ferguson actually blame him for her death? Apparently, he did.

What should he do? Noah frantically asked himself. If he surrendered to Ferguson, his son would be in Brett Buchanan's hands again. And if he didn't give himself up, he would be risking Ellie's life.

Joel, standing down at his side, tugged at his hand. "Daddy, is he going to hurt Ellie?"

His son's frightened, urgent whisper told Noah that he had no choice. He couldn't abandon Ellie. Joel would be all right without him. Ellie would move heaven and earth to make sure that he was safe.

"Joel," he instructed his son softly, "you wait right here. Ellie will come in a minute to get you."

Approaching the bridge, Noah called through the fog, "I'm yours, Ferguson, on one condition. You let the woman and the boy go."

"Done," the detective shouted back.

"No!" Ellie cried. "He's crazy, Noah! He'll execute you on the spot and say that you tried to make a break for it!"

"Shut up!" Ferguson snarled, dragging her back off the bridge in order to permit Noah to cross the span and join them.

She watched helplessly as his tall, sinewy figure emerged from the fog. He was sacrificing himself for her, and there was nothing she could do to prevent it.

"Joel is waiting for you over there," he told her when he arrived on their side and allowed the detective to frisk him. "Go to him, Ellie." She hesitated. "Go," he urged her.

She went, because Joel had to be protected. But the boy had disobeyed his father. He was already at the center of the bridge when she joined him. She froze at the sound of Ferguson's harsh voice, gathering Joel tightly against her side as she looked back over her shoulder.

The detective was waving his gun in their direction, taunting Noah as the two men stood there on the brink of the gorge. "What if they died out there, Rhyder? What if they fell to their deaths, like Teresa did? How would that make you feel, huh?"

Noah's response was immediate and physical. Disregarding the weapon in his enemy's hand, he launched himself at Ferguson with a savage roar. In the next second they were struggling on the perilous edge of the chasm. The gun went off, shattering the fog. Ellie screamed.

Then there were other sounds. The screech of tires on gravel just beyond the belt of trees. The slam of doors. Shouts and running feet.

Uniformed officers swarmed onto the scene. The police from Rosebay had arrived. Ellie didn't care to wonder who had alerted them. The two men, neither of them injured, were separated. Ferguson was disarmed, handcuffs slapped on Noah.

It all happened with such astonishing swiftness that she was too dismayed to move. She stood there numbly on the bridge, watching in forlorn disbelief as they led Noah away. Then, remembering her responsibility for Joel, she knelt beside him. There were silent tears streaming down his face.

Chapter Fourteen

A cold wind blew through the streets of St. Louis, a reminder to the city that winter was on its way. The dreariness of the gray day matched Ellie's mood as she sat facing Superintendent Ham Bolling in his office in the main police headquarters building on Clark Avenue.

"You're lucky, Ms. Matheson," he informed her in the severe tone of a school principal lecturing a wayward student. "No charges are being filed against you as an accessory, though you probably deserve them for helping Rhyder. You can thank the influence of the media for that. They've been sympathetic about you because of your conviction that the child was in danger and had to be removed."

He had already told her that Lew Ferguson, stripped of his badge, would face charges. At this moment Ellie was indifferent to both the detective's situation and her own. All she cared about was helping Noah, whose future looked totally bleak.

He had been immediately returned to St. Louis where he was being held in a cell in Prisoner Processing, awaiting transportation to Boonville Prison. Prisoner Processing was here in the same building, which meant he was close by at this very moment. But she hadn't been permitted to see or speak to him, a circumstance she found agonizing. But no matter how dismal the outlook was, she refused to give up hope.

"Brett Buchanan," she said, reminding the police superintendent of her primary reason for this visit as she leaned forward tensely in her chair.

Bolling poked at his slipping glasses before shaking his head. "It's all been thoroughly checked out, Ms. Matheson. Turns out that telephone conversation you overheard in North Carolina was completely innocent. Buchanan was in the process of buying some expensive properties, but his major funds had been tied up in short-term investments. Those investments had just paid off, freeing up large sums of money with more to come. He was independently rich before his father died, and he's just as rich now. No motive."

"But his alibi on the day of the murder—"

"Was solid then and still remains solid. He was in a business meeting in Chicago with a roomful of reputable investors who corroborate his statement. His bodyguard is equally blameless. Peaches was vacationing with his girlfriend in Florida at the time. Hotel confirms it. No, don't say it," he said, anticipating her next suggestion and forestalling it with an impatient wave of his hand. "Buchanan did not hire a killer. Contract killers don't eliminate their victims with fire pokers. Face it, Ms. Matheson. Noah Rhyder murdered his father-in-law, no one else."

Ellie refused to believe anything of the kind. But if not Brett—and she had no choice but to accept that now—then *who?* Who did kill Howard Buchanan?

"There's still Joel," she said desperately, "and what he witnessed from the dumbwaiter."

"Come on, the boy didn't actually see or hear the killer. In any case, I doubt whether a testimony at his age would be admissible in a court of law. You're clutching at straws, Ms. Matheson."

"And I'll go on clutching at them, Superintendent," she

promised him fiercely. "I'll do whatever it takes to prove Noah innocent."

"Guy really got to you, didn't he?"

"He's a decent, caring man. A loving father."

"That's the point," he said dryly. "He loved his son enough to kill for him."

"You're wrong, but I'm not going to argue with you about it."

There was nothing more to be gained from their conversation. Ellie got to her feet, but Bolling stopped her.

"Hang on a second." He pushed a slip of paper toward her across the desk.

"What's this?"

"Something that ought to make you very happy. It'll let you visit Rhyder in Prisoner Processing before he's removed to Boonville."

She snatched up the paper as though it were a lifeline, her eyes glowing with gratitude.

"Don't thank *me*," he said gruffly. "His lawyer pulled some strings to arrange for it."

But Ellie suspected that Ham Bolling could have prevented the visit if he'd chosen to, and that he was more sympathetic than he cared to reveal.

"What about Joel?" she asked. "I've been forbidden any contact with him since North Carolina."

"Don't push it, Ms. Matheson. The boy is safe and well cared for. That's all you have to know."

"Is he with Brett?"

"Not yet. But I imagine once his case has been reviewed by Family Services, he'll be returned to Buchanan."

Ellie wasn't satisfied with that. In her opinion Joel was still at risk because of what the killer believed he had witnessed from the dumbwaiter. But she could see that Bolling wasn't prepared to discuss that with her. He wanted her to leave.

She was on her way to the elevators, eager to reach Prisoner Processing, when someone called to her. Turning around, she saw the friendly face of Terry Goldman. The heavyset woman, who had been Joel's original caseworker, had just emerged from one of the offices along the corridor. It was no surprise to encounter her here. Understandably, Family Services had a lot of contact with the people in this building.

"I've been thinking about you, Ellie," she greeted her, with an expression of genuine compassion. "Hoping that…well, you know."

She liked Terry. The children under her direction had always been much more than just assignments. "I appreciate that, Terry. I guess you've heard that, after what's happened, Family Services probably won't be placing any more kids with me."

"Yeah, and I'm sorry about that. You were always so good with them. A natural."

"I can live with their decision. But Joel…Terry, they won't tell me where Joel is and what's happening to him. I've been sick with worry. If I could just know…"

"I shouldn't tell you. I shouldn't even be discussing him with you." She looked in both directions along the corridor, but there was no one to overhear them. "Oh, what the hell, with the kid's welfare being that important to you, you're entitled to know. He's been temporarily placed with Jan McCormick and her husband."

Ellie was relieved. She was familiar with the McCormicks and their home. She had shared foster-care classes with them. "He's in good hands then, and if you're his caseworker again—"

"Sorry, I'm not. It's Sandra O'Hara who's responsible for Joel. I guess she feels entitled to keep his case because she's the one who raised the alarm that morning she went to his room to check on him and discovered you'd taken him away from the estate. Except the way I understand it, it was some storekeeper out there who first called the cops.

Anyway, she claims the credit for looking out for his interests, and I guess the department agrees with her.''

"I was doing what I thought was best for Joel that morning,'' Ellie said, aggravated by Sandra's heroics. She knew perfectly well that the woman's only interest was in impressing Brett Buchanan, and had been from the start.

"I know, and Sandra can be…well, Sandra. I guess we shouldn't be too hard on her. She had a rough time of it a few months back. Boyfriend trouble,'' Terry said, lowering her voice to a confidential whisper. "Rumor was she was having this really hot affair with a rich, older guy who spent a bundle on her. I think she expected a marriage proposal. Instead, he got tired of her and broke it off. Sandra really suffered over that. I remember someone saying she wanted to keep as busy as possible to take her mind off of it. As a matter of fact, she requested Joel's case when it first came to us. But since her load was already full, they gave him to me. Of course, as you know, she did manage to handle him at the very end when custody was granted to his uncle. Hey, you okay? You look like someone just whacked you over the head.''

"I'm all right,'' Ellie assured her, struggling to control her sudden excitement. "This man who was Sandra's lover…who was he?''

Terry shrugged. "Beats me. She was always very hush-hush about him. The guy was probably already married. They always are, aren't they?'' The caseworker seemed to realize then that she was violating the ethics of her department by gossiping about a colleague. She quickly checked her watch. "I've got to run. I don't know that it'll do much good, but I'll put in a good word for you at Services.''

Ellie didn't try to detain her. She was anxious herself to hurry away in the opposite direction. She needed to see Noah immediately. Needed to share with him what she had just learned, because if she was right— But she was afraid to put it into actual words until Noah himself validated her startling conjecture.

Minutes later, she had been admitted into the visitor's area of Prisoner Processing. Seating herself where the guard indicated in front of the glass screen, she waited in a fever of impatience for Noah to be brought from his cell.

It seemed to take forever before he finally arrived on the other side of the divider. Her heart lurched at the sight of him. Even though he looked tired and gaunt in one of the blaze orange coveralls issued to all the prisoners, he would always be the most compelling man she had ever known. She longed to touch him, hating the glass wall that separated them and prevented any physical contact. But they could hear each other clearly through the stout mesh at the bottom of the screen.

Sliding onto the chair that faced her, he leaned forward, his dark eyes glowing with pleasure sharpened by concern. "Ellie, are you all right? They aren't threatening you with charges, are they? I've told them that you—"

"I'm fine," she interrupted him. "Noah, we don't have much time, and I've got something important to tell you."

"What is it? If it's Joel—"

"He's all right. They've assured me he's just fine." She didn't want to worry him before it was necessary. She needed his full attention. "Noah, when we were on the road to North Carolina, you talked about Howard Buchanan. You said something about him and Brett sharing the same taste in women."

He frowned at her puzzling reference to the murdered man. "Ellie, where are you going with this? What's—"

"No, just tell me, and then listen. What kind of women?"

"They were always younger than he was, usually on the flamboyant side."

Women like Sandra O'Hara, Ellie thought. "And he had affairs with them, right?"

"Some of them. I don't know a whole lot about it. He kept that part of his life pretty quiet. I suppose because of his position."

"And what if his latest lover, someone he'd been keeping a secret, visited him that day he died? What if she arrived at the house just after you left, hoping for a commitment from him? And what if, instead, he told her he was finished with her, and in a fit of rage—"

"She killed him. Ellie, what's going on? What have you heard?"

She pressed close to the glass, relating in a low, urgent tone everything that Terry Goldman had shared with her in the corridor. "It all fits, doesn't it? Sandra O'Hara killed Howard Buchanan and then left the house in a panic. But she must have realized Joel was there in the dumbwaiter. She probably figured that because she has such a low, husky voice, the child couldn't have understood what she was saying, and maybe he even mistook her for a man. And of course, she was right, which made her safe for the time being. But the possibility that in time the pieces would fall into place for Joel and that he would identify her must have gnawed at her constantly."

"So she had to get her hands on my kid to make sure he never talked."

"That's why she was so eager to get his case, and eventually she did. Only by then Brett had been awarded custody of Joel and was taking him to North Carolina where she couldn't reach him."

"Unless she turned up in North Carolina herself."

"Which she did. And, of course, I assumed she was there because she was after Brett and that Joel was just an excuse. But all along Joel was her target. She knew that Sultan was dangerous and if she put the puppet in the stall, there was a chance that Joel could be killed."

"And if that didn't work," he said angrily, "she could always arrange for another accident."

"Oh, Noah, am I crazy, or does any of this make sense?"

"Yeah, it does. It makes perfect sense. Trouble is," he said bitterly, "there's no way to prove it."

"There has to be! If we can convince—"

"Ellie," he stopped her, "I don't care about that right now. All I know is Sandra O'Hara still has access to my kid, and if we're right about her, Joel's in danger." His hands clenched into tight fists, an action that demonstrated his intense frustration. "And I'm trapped in here and can't do anything about it."

"No, but I can." Ellie got swiftly to her feet, her expression hardening with determination. "And I'm not going to waste time talking to either Superintendent Bolling or Family Services. Forbidden or not, I'm going straight to the McCormicks to beg them to keep Sandra away from Joel until we can get someone to act. The McCormicks are reasonable people. Somehow I'll convince them to listen to me."

"Ellie, be careful. The O'Hara woman must be desperate by now."

"Yes, but so am I."

She left him at the glass screen, his face wild with rage over his inability to join her.

THE MCCORMICK HOME was located less than a block from Forest Park, a short drive from the Police Headquarters Building. But Ellie, battling the city traffic, felt that it took her forever to get there.

Parking at the curb, she hurried to the front door of the neat brick bungalow. She rang the bell and waited impatiently, hoping to catch a glimpse of Joel's eager face at a window. But there was no sign of the boy.

It was Jan McCormick, an older woman with thinning hair and a benevolent face, who answered the door seconds later. She looked concerned to find Ellie on her front step.

She must have been instructed that Ellie was to have no contact with Joel.

"Jan, it's all right. I won't try to see him. I just need you to listen to me."

"You wouldn't be able to see him anyway. Joel isn't here right now. He's out with his caseworker."

Ellie's heart dropped like a stone. "Sandra O'Hara took him? Where? How long ago?"

"You know I can't tell you that."

Ellie fought a rising panic. "Jan, I don't have time to explain. Just trust me, please trust me to know Joel's whereabouts. I promise you it's vital."

The woman hesitated, wasting precious seconds. She must have been finally moved by the earnest, pleading expression in Ellie's eyes. "They've been gone just a little while. She took him over to the zoo. He's been withdrawn. She hoped he would open up to her in surroundings he liked. Ellie, what is this all—"

"I can't stop to tell you! I've got to find them! Jan, call the police!"

She hardly heard Jan's assurance that she would head straight for the phone. Nor, when she turned and rushed toward the street, did she return to her car. The free zoo was located on this side of the park. It would be quicker to reach it on foot than to deal with parking outside the gate.

Her heart hammered with fear as she raced along the sidewalk. Fear and a painful self-reproach. Why had she sacrificed time by visiting Noah? She should have come directly to the McCormick home. She would have been here before Sandra took him away. But she had been desperate for Noah's support, fearful of pursuing on her own what might have been nothing but a wild theory. Now, if anything happened to Joel because of that delay, she would never forgive herself.

The South Gate was just ahead of her. She flew across

the street, dodging cars whose drivers honked at her angrily. Paying them no attention, she reached the gate. The only attendant in sight was busy with a man in a wheelchair. She didn't feel she could afford to wait for help from that source.

Without pausing, she sped through the gate, ignoring the startled expression on the face of a woman she almost knocked down in her haste. But once inside the entrance, she came to a halt in the open area where routes branched off in opposite directions.

Which way? They could be anywhere in here, and if she chose the wrong route...

Where, *where?* she wondered frantically.

There was a mounted directory in front of her. She rapidly consulted the list, searching for a clue. Her gaze stopped at a sign pointing to the right: Big Cat Country. She remembered how Joel was fascinated by tigers and lions. It was her only hope.

She swung to the right, crossing the tracks of the Zooline Railroad, trotting past the herpetarium. Although a thin sun was struggling to shine through the cloud cover, it was still cool and blustery. Not a good day for visiting the zoo. The place was almost deserted.

Ellie kept straining for a glimpse of a redheaded woman and a little boy. Nothing. Had she made a fatal mistake? Chosen the wrong route?

It was outside the primate house that she spotted it. Joel's beloved Hobo—all alone and looking forlorn on a bench. Her discovery of the hand puppet was evidence that they had come this way. But Hobo went everywhere with Joel, and it worried her that he was abandoned on a bench. Was she too late?

Snatching up the puppet, she ran on.

Winded by the time she reached the empty show arena, with a stitch in her side whose pain she strove to ignore, she paused long enough to catch her breath. And it was from here, through a stand of shrubbery, that she saw them.

They were less than a hundred yards away, positioned in front of the open-air habitat of the Siberian tigers. The beasts prowled on rocks separated from the viewing rail by a deep moat. The woman and the boy were the only spectators in the area.

Joel in his eagerness had pulled himself up on the low rail for a better view. Sandra, who had probably encouraged him, stood close behind him. Looking quickly to either side to make certain there were no witnesses, she grabbed Joel roughly and appeared to be trying to lift him over the barrier. Joel's startled and terrified wail rang out as he clung desperately to the rail. If Sandra succeeded in breaking his grip, in a moment he would be unconscious prey for the predators waiting on the rocks.

A horrified Ellie tore through the shrubbery that had concealed her, crying an outraged, "No! Joel, hold on tight!"

Joel's head whirled around. Sandra, caught in the act, went rigid for a second. Then, surrendering to panic, she took off in the direction of the bird house.

A security guard, who had been approaching from the camel yard, was alerted by Ellie's call. "She tried to kill him!" she shouted, pointing toward Sandra.

The guard flew past her and went chasing after the redhead. Ellie, leaving the pursuit to him, was interested only in Joel. By the time she reached him, he had climbed down from the rail.

The first words out of his mouth were an angry, "She was gonna make tiger meat out of me!"

Half crying and half laughing in her relief, she caught him in a tight embrace. "I know, sweetheart, I know."

"Ellie?"

"What?"

"I lost Hobo."

"No, you didn't. He's right here."

They could hear the sound of police sirens nearing the zoo as she placed the puppet in his hands.

ELLIE STOOD IN THE BAY at the side of her parlor, studying the painting in progress on her easel. She decided it wasn't worth completing, and with good reason. It suffered from a lack of enthusiasm. She had tried to keep as busy as possible this past day and a half, but a perpetual state of anxiety kept interfering with her concentration.

She couldn't stop thinking about Noah. They hadn't permitted her to see him again, or Joel either. The child had been returned to the McCormicks after the episode at the zoo. But Noah's lawyer was working to win his release, which could occur at any hour. With Sandra O'Hara under arrest, having finally confessed to Howard Buchanan's murder, Noah Rhyder would be a free man again, able to legally recover his son.

What then? Ellie wondered. But she didn't dare to count on the future. All she could do was wait and hope.

Having decided to abandon the work on the easel, she was cleaning her brushes when the sound of a car pulling into her driveway made her catch her breath with anticipation. Was it possible?

The weather had turned again overnight, with the afternoon so warm and sunny that it was almost like summer. She'd left the inner door open to the porch. Now, trembling with eagerness, she went to the screen door and looked out.

Her excitement immediately subsided. The handsome figure emerging from the dark sedan wasn't the man she had been ready to welcome. What was Brett Buchanan doing here? He was the last person she expected to see arriving at her home.

He came up on the porch, smiling a confident greeting as he discovered her behind the screen door. "How are you, Ellie?"

"Hello, Brett." She realized he was alone. "No driver today?"

"Peaches and I have parted company." The tone of his voice suggested that he must have learned of Peaches's involvement with Lew Ferguson and hadn't been pleased about it. "Are you going to ask me in?"

She hesitated and then reluctantly opened the screen door. He came into the parlor and wandered toward the bay to regard the painting on the easel. "Nice," he commented.

But she knew he wasn't interested in her art. She followed him to the bay, asking a direct, "Why are you here, Brett?"

"To apologize." He turned to face her. "We got off track in North Carolina after Sandra arrived. I admit I was temporarily blinded by her."

She shook her head. "We were never *on* track."

"We could be."

There was a seductive quality in his voice that she didn't appreciate. "As sorry as I am about it now, how can you possibly be interested when I tried to implicate you in your father's murder?"

"I'm not complaining about it."

"Brett, this is—"

"Rhyder, huh?" he interrupted her. "You're telling me I don't stand a chance because of Rhyder."

She didn't answer him.

"Ellie," he told her gently, "you can't count on him. He only needed you because of one thing, and he has that now."

"That's not true."

"Then why isn't he here? He was released almost two hours ago. I checked before I drove over here."

"Joel...he would have wanted to get Joel first."

"He already has him. He went straight to the Mc-Cormicks and collected him. That couldn't have taken more than a few minutes. Face it, he isn't coming."

She struggled against a sudden despair that threatened to overwhelm her.

"Did he ever once tell you that he loved you? Did he, Ellie?"

"If he hasn't," came a sharp, deep voice from the direction of the screen door, "he plans to. Just as soon as you clear out of here, Buchanan. And I suggest you don't waste any time about doing just that."

Ellie and Brett had been so occupied they hadn't heard the arrival of another car out front. Her gaze flashed to the open door. A rush of joy made her light-headed at the sight of Noah standing there on her porch.

Ignoring his rival, Brett searched Ellie's face. The glow in her eyes told him all he needed to know. He had never stood a chance with her. With a little smile of resignation, he moved toward the porch. Noah held the screen door open for him.

"No hard feelings, I hope," Brett said as they passed each other on the threshold.

"None at all," Noah assured him, closing the door firmly behind him.

When Brett was gone, they faced each other across the parlor, both of them experiencing a moment of uncertainty. Noah cleared his throat.

"Aren't you going to ask me where I've been since I was released?"

She didn't care. He was here, and that was all that mattered. "Where?" she asked, trying to sound interested.

"You ever hear of Livermore's?"

Livermore's? Of course, she knew it. It was the finest art gallery in St. Louis. "What were you doing there?"

"I did some design work for Edgar Livermore once. An addition to his house. It got me a meeting with him today."

"You never mentioned you knew Edgar Livermore. Artists kill to get his attention."

"Yeah, well, you've got it, Ellie, and you didn't have to

strangle anyone. I showed him one of your pictures. He was impressed. He wants to see more of your work, and if he likes it, he's interested in mounting a show.''

She was astonished. "One of *my* pictures? Which one? How?"

"Uh, I sorta snitched it from your portfolio in the van on the road to North Carolina. The pastel you did of Joel when he was living with you. It's beautiful, Ellie.''

"But—"

"Look, I didn't want to come to you today empty-handed. Not this time. You gave me back both my life and my son, and I wanted to bring you the most valuable thing I could. That's why I went to Livermore's.''

"It's wonderful, but don't you realize *you're* the most valuable thing you could bring me?''

He grinned happily. "Yeah?"

"Yeah."

In three quick strides he was across the parlor, his arms closing around her in an eager embrace.

"You willing to work the same magic on me, Rembrandt, as you did with my kid in that portrait?''

"Absolutely." And then she remembered. "Where is Joel?"

"Playing on the swing set out back. I told him his old man needed a few minutes alone with you. I explained to him I'm one of those guys who can't propose with anyone looking on but the woman he loves. He's thrilled.''

"Propose?"

"Yeah, as in marriage. You and me. See, I plan to spend the rest of my life telling my wife how glad I am I abducted her that night. That is, when I'm not designing high-rises and you're not painting masterpieces. Okay?''

"Okay. I do love you, you know.''

"Good. Then we're in agreement. Now we can get to the essential part.''

"I thought we just had.''

"Uh-uh, *this* is the essential part."

His mouth angled across hers in a long, deep kiss that was a commitment beyond words. Savoring the moment, she reached up to stroke his angular jaw as his mouth finally parted from hers. She could feel the throbbing there that was familiar to her by now. That curious pulsing that always signaled his arousal.

"What?" he asked, noticing the gleam in her eyes.

"That muscle is twitching again."

"Oh, yeah? Then we're gonna have to do something about that," he promised, his voice husky and rich with meaning. "Real soon."

She had no argument with that. None whatever.

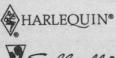

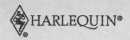

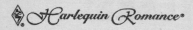 
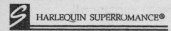

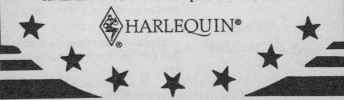

Presents
Extravaganza
25 YEARS!
It's our birthday
and we're celebrating....

Twenty-five years of romance fiction
featuring men of the world and captivating women—
Seduction and passion guaranteed!

Not only are we promising you three months of terrific
books, authors and romance, but as an added **bonus**
with the retail purchase of two Presents® titles,
you can receive a special one-of-a-kind keepsake.
It's our gift to you!

Look in the back pages of any Harlequin Presents® title,
from May to July 1998, for more details.

Available wherever Harlequin books are sold.

HARLEQUIN®

MEN at WORK

All work and no play?
Not these men!

July 1998
MACKENZIE'S LADY by Dallas Schulze

Undercover agent Mackenzie Donahue's
lazy smile and deep blue eyes were his best
weapons. But after rescuing—and kissing!—
damsel in distress Holly Reynolds, how could
he betray her by spying on her brother?

August 1998
MISS LIZ'S PASSION by Sherryl Woods

Todd Lewis could put up a building with ease,
but quailed at the sight of a classroom! Still,
Liz Gentry, his son's teacher, was no battle-ax,
and soon Todd started planning some
extracurricular activities of his own....

September 1998
A CLASSIC ENCOUNTER
by Emilie Richards

Doctor Chris Matthews was intelligent, sexy
and *very* good with his hands—which made
him all the more dangerous to single mom
Lizette St. Hilaire. So how long could she
resist Chris's special brand of TLC?

Available at your favorite retail outlet!

MEN AT WORK™

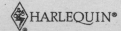 

FREE BOOK OFFER!

Dear Reader,

Thank you for reading this *Harlequin Intrigue*® title! Please take a few moments to tell us about the role that mystery plays in your fiction reading. When you have finished answering the survey, please mail it to the appropriate address listed below and we'll send you a free mystery novel as a token of our appreciation! Thank you for sharing your opinions!

1. How important is the mystery/suspense element in a series romance paperback?

   1.1 ❑ Very important   .3 ❑ Not very important
    .2 ❑ Somewhat important   .4 ❑ Not at all important

2. Which of the following types of paperback books have you read in the past 12 months? (check all that apply)

   2 ❑ Espionage/Spy (e.g. Tom Clancy, Robert Ludlum)
   3 ❑ Mainstream Contemporary Fiction (e.g. Patricia Cornwell)
   4 ❑ Occult/Horror (e.g. Stephen King, Anne Rice)
   5 ❑ Popular Women's Fiction (e.g. Danielle Steel, Nora Roberts)
   6 ❑ Fantasy (e.g. Terry Brooks)
   7 ❑ Mystery
   8 ❑ Science Fiction (e.g. Isaac Asimov)
   9 ❑ Series Romance Fiction (e.g. Harlequin Romance)
   10 ❑ Action Adventure paperbacks (e.g. Mack Bolan)
   11 ❑ Paperback Biographies
   12 ❑ Paperback Humor
   13 ❑ Self-help paperbacks

3. How many mystery novels, if any, have you read in the past 6 months?

   Paperback _____ (14, 15)   Hardcover _____ (16, 17)

4. If you indicated above that you read mystery paperbacks, what are the most important elements of a mystery book to you?

   _____ (18, 23)

5. If you enjoy reading mystery paperbacks, which of the following types of mystery fiction do you enjoy reading? (check all that apply)

24 ❑ American Cozy (e.g. Joan Hess)

25 ❑ British Cozy (e.g. Jill Paton Walsh)

26 ❑ Noire (e.g. James Ellroy, Loren D. Estleman)

27 ❑ Hard-boiled (male or female private eye) (e.g. Robert Parker)

28 ❑ American Police Procedural (e.g. Ed McBain)

29 ❑ British Police Procedural (e.g. Ian Rankin, P. D. James)

6. How do you usually obtain your fiction paperbacks? (check all that apply)

30 ❑ National chain bookstore (e.g. Waldenbooks, Borders)

31 ❑ Supermarket

32 ❑ General or discount merchandise store (e.g. Kmart, Target)

33 ❑ Borrow or trade with family members or friends

34 ❑ By mail

35 ❑ Secondhand bookstore

36 ❑ Library

37 ❑ Other _____ (38, 43)

7. Into which of the following age groups do you fall?

44.1 ❑ Under 18 years

.2 ❑ 18 to 24 years

.3 ❑ 25 to 34 years

.4 ❑ 35 to 49 years

.5 ❑ 50 to 64 years

.6 ❑ 65 years or older

Thank you very much for your cooperation! To receive your free mystery novel, please print your name and address clearly and return the survey to the appropriate address listed below.

Name: _____

Address: _____ City: _____

State/Province: _____ Zip/Postal Code: _____

In U.S.: Worldwide Mystery Survey, 3010 Walden Avenue, P.O. Box 9057, Buffalo, NY 14269-9057
In Canada: Worldwide Mystery Survey, P.O. Box 622, Fort Erie, Ontario L2A 5X3